PRAISE FOR SATAN'S GAMBIT

"Must read for all especially in government, elected or bureaucracy. An eye-opener for most of the country for what is/can be happening to our country, our everyday way of life, our American survival."

– Fred M.

"Eye opening and stirring. What they should be teaching in our school systems and colleges. Anxiously awaiting for Book Three to arrive at the house this week! I thoroughly enjoyed it and have had a few conversations with my son about it. I look for him to read it soon. Thank you!"

- Reid J.

"A very compelling read. 'TRUTH AT LAST' about how our government and elected officials are going to make America dense.

– Ray R.

"This book and the truth about Satan's scheme to destroy freedom needs to be made available to all young people who are being brainwashed in our schools. Our churches need to get this vital truth to their people before America is destroyed."

– Randy C.

"Thank you so much for writing the Satan's Gambit books. I read both books in two days. I have not stopped talking about them since I opened the first book. My nineteen-year-old son is reading them now and has explained that he is using them interactively. As Dr. Lucci suggests student 'look up' a supporting article or YouTube video, my son does it and follows along with the students! Ingenious of you. Kids today, computer generation, need to verify everything. By including those supporting documents they can feel fully informed. I truly believe you have been divinely inspired to warn and inform. Thank you, again. I look forward to Book Three."

— *Dottie M.*

SATAN'S GAMBIT

SATAN'S GAMBIT

BOOK TWO
The Forces of Darkness Unleashed

A Novel By
GENE CONTI, MD

SATAN'S GAMBIT

Copyright © 2018 by Gene Conti

DISCLAIMER

Many of the characters and individuals whom I have included in the novel are real; and in some cases, famous celebrities. In reality I do not know if they are in agreement or in support of any of the ideas, tenets or propositions I have put forth in my novel. I have included them only in the hope of making the novel more interesting.

Cover Design by Perceptions Design Studio

Library of Congress Catalog in Publication Data available upon request.

Paperback ISBN: 978-1-949021-11-0
eBook ISBN: 978-1-949021-12-7

Printed in the United States of America
16 17 18 19 20 21 LSI 9 8 7 6 5 4 3 2 1

CONTENTS

PREFACE

After having escaped the clutches of Erik and his Blueshirts, Dr. Lucci's class is beginning to realize the impact of the Matrix and Dietrich's designs for control. The students' knowledge and thought processes start to mature from information gathered at the museums. Radical Islamic terrorists have now coordinated attacks on several large American cities; and the governmental Matrix, in response, decides to crack down on American citizens' First and Second Amendment rights. The World Ecology Flag now flies above the Stars and Stripes, and the RFID chip is being forced upon more people. Also a new law, the Personal Rights Protection Act, to go into effect on November 28th, will totally negate any outward religious expression whatsoever—under penalty of extreme punishment! Father Flanagan boldly confronts Erik when he attempts to execute this law, with untold consequences.

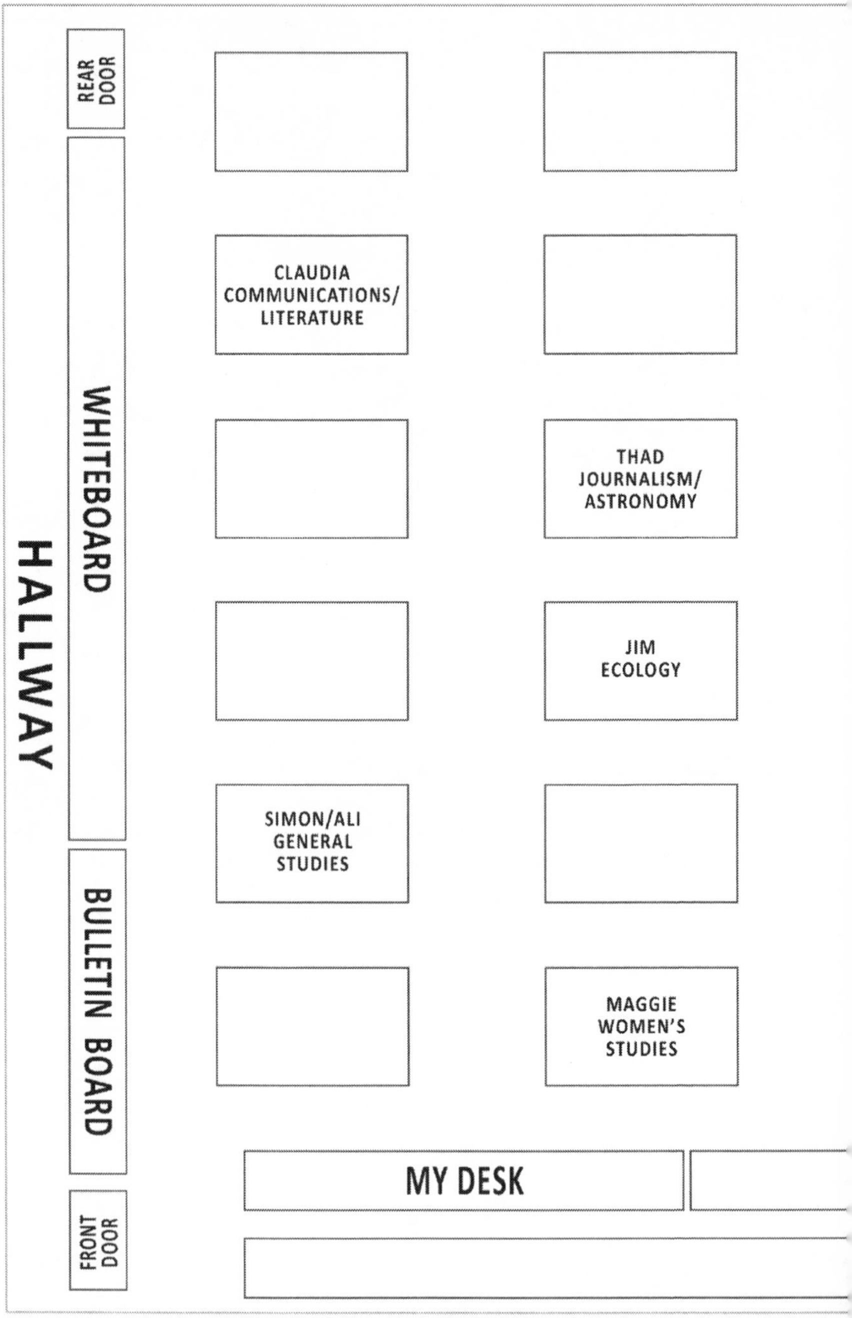

HALLWAY

REAR DOOR

WHITEBOARD

BULLETIN BOARD

FRONT DOOR

CLAUDIA
COMMUNICATIONS/
LITERATURE

THAD
JOURNALISM/
ASTRONOMY

JIM
ECOLOGY

SIMON/ALI
GENERAL
STUDIES

MAGGIE
WOMEN'S
STUDIES

MY DESK

PHILIP PHYSICS/MATH/ BIOCHEMISTRY		JUDE POLITICAL SCIENCE
	NATE BUSINESS/ COMPUTER SCIENCE	
ANDY ENGINEERING/ ARCHITECTURE	PETE GEOLOGY/ MARINE SCIENCE	MATT FINANCE/ MARKETING
	TOM HISTORY/ PRE-LAW	JUAN TEACHING/ PSYCHOLOGY
MARIA NURSING		SANTI SOCIAL SCIENCE

WINDOWS AND WINDOW LEDGES

LAB TABLE

WHITEBOARD

CHAPTER SEVENTY-SEVEN

A LESSON
ABOUT RIGHT AND WRONG

Having escaped the clutches of Erik and his Blueshirts, the Prevost, with Brother Francis at the helm, was effortlessly cruising down I-81. We were now comfortable, on our bus, on the way to the geologic sites and museums. The sun was up and had burned away all remnants of the fog. The students were also up and had been chattering nonstop with one another since the incident at the college with Erik and his troops. Cindy somehow had managed to fall asleep. She must have been absolutely exhausted.

The kids wanted to talk about what happened, so Fred and I moved up to the front, in order not to disturb Cindy. Tom, our history major and legal mind, took over as spokesperson - initially anyway.

"Doc, we have all been discussing what took place back at Immaculate Conception College (ICC). What has happened to our First Amendment rights: free speech and assembly? We weren't going to be able to leave. Why?"

"Tom's right," Thad added. "All of us have been on numerous school bus trips to museums over the years. Nothing like this has ever happened."

I scanned the students sitting in their comfortable recliners, and my eyes came to rest on Thad. As I leaned on the partition behind Brother Francis, I said, "I'm sure you are aware, through all your newspaper journal writing and research, of the incalculable instances around the country of students being 'asked' to remove or turn inside out a T-shirt that has an American flag or a Christian symbol on it in order to wear it on school grounds."

Thad and others nodded.

Juan spoke up. "A guy in one of my classes at our mostly Hispanic high school was beat up for that. First, his teacher and principal told him he was racist, intolerant, and bigoted, as well as insensitive of others' feelings. At lunchtime, one of the Latino gangs jumped him."

"He probably deserved it," I answered Juan, as I surveyed the others in their seats.

I got the response I was looking for. Matt almost jumped out of his seat.

"For wearing a USA or Christian T-shirt? Give me a break, Doc."

"But Matt, weren't you the one that early on, when the class first started, emphatically stated that there is no right or wrong? You explained that according to your courses in situation ethics and relative morality each of us determines what is right or wrong. Or am I misquoting you? And the school administration, having the power, determined it was wrong."

"Yeah, but ... a ... what about God?" Matt stammered, seeming stumped somewhat.

"What about morals and ethics?" Tom questioned, trying to help Matt.

"God? What God?" I probed. "I thought that fifteen plus years of schooling - as well as TV, the movies, and the media had drummed God out of your head and replaced Him with atheistic Darwinism married to Mother Gaia?"

Pete leaned over and whispered something to his brother, Andy. Maria and Maggie were sitting together silently chuckling. I gave them a wink.

"So Andy, tell us—whose morals and whose ethics?"

Andy leaned into the bus aisle and offered his analysis. "Can't you see that Doc is setting us up again, and we fall right into his trap, as usual?" Pete patted Andy on the shoulder, smiling knowingly at him.

Fred was standing just below me on the top stair, leaning on the rail of the first row of seats. "Hey, Doc, tell them about the golden rule of dictators."

"Do you mean, 'he who has the gold, makes the rules?'"

"That's the one," quipped Fred. Looking at the kids, he then added, "And what does the gold or money lead to?"

"Power and control," Nate instantaneously responded.

Maria was now out of her seat. "And so why would the governmental Matrix want us to learn the truth?" She proceeded to answer her own question. "They want absolute *power* over us. They want no God before them to challenge their *control* over us."

"Do you think Dietrich, who is really the power behind Erik—as we all know—would have given a rat's patootie," Maggie added piggybacking on Maria's comment, "if we were going to some atheistic museums that support the Matrix's brainwashing agenda?"

"Thank you, guys," I offered as I smiled at Andy, Maria, and Maggie for their insightful input.

Thad waved, wanting to be back in the conversation. I acknowledged him, and he provided some valuable insight. "I'm already getting pressure from Dietrich's Office of Social Justice for what I have been writing in my articles. So far, Dean Avery has been backing me up."

Jim was getting his keister in a knot and shaking Santi's seat in front of him. Santi turned around and stuck his eyes and nose over the seat back. "Oye, hombre, I'm not on a circus rollercoaster."

"Sorry, Santi," Jim genuinely apologized before forcefully expressing his sentiments. "We are back to basic right and wrong. And without God there is no right or wrong. Are you just supposed to do your own thing, until the Matrix and their jesters in the media, tell us what is right and wrong? Where is truth in all of this?"

"Bravo, amigo," Santi answered. "The government's got the oro . . . the dinero, so they make the rules for us, not God."

"And the government lets us *do our thing*," added Juan, who was sitting next to his cousin, "until, and or unless, it interferes with their power and control over us."

"Yeah," Maggie jumped in. "Abort your baby, smoke dope, accept alternative lifestyles as normal, marry a pig…a…be tolerant and accepting of the illegal terrorists…excuse me, refugees in your midst; just don't interfere with our goals, and our control over you." Maria gave her a high five while the rest of the class was still laughing at the 'marry a pig' comment.

Ali was sitting quietly by himself, playing his violent video games.

Claudia, who was seated behind Maria and Maggie, finally spoke up after taking it all in. "The government lets us have an illusion of freedom. They have us living in the Matrix they have constructed for us. But we dare not even poke at the façade because it is electrified and will strike back at us—mortally if they deem it necessary—as we have just personally experienced."

"Excellent analysis, Claudia. What you will see and learn on this trip frightens the Matrix; which brings us back to what is truth and who determines it."

"Amen to that," Brother Francis responded from his driver's seat.

I studied the students' faces. I believed I struck a chord.

CHAPTER SEVENTY-EIGHT

THE HYDROPLATE THEORY

We continued down I-81 for a while until we were in the Lexington area of Virginia. We were in big horse country and home of VMI, Virginia Military Institute, the oldest state military college in the United States. It was called the West Point of the South. Distinguished alumni include General George S. Patton and Mel Brooks. But there was no time for sightseeing on this trip, as we were on a tight schedule. Brother Francis turned right onto I-64 westbound, which meant we would be arriving at our first stop soon.

"Look at the screens in the seatback in front of you," I directed. "I'm queuing up a short YouTube video titled "*The Hydroplate Theory – The Flood (Newer version)*." This will help to explain in better detail what we are about to see on our first few stops."

"Doc, you're putting us on, right?" Matt queried as he stood in the aisle. "*The* Mel Brooks attended VMI? The guy made the best comic sci-fi movie in the world."

"Which one was that?" Brother Francis half turned in his seat to ask Matt.

"*Spaceballs*, of course! I mean it was brilliant. You had Lord Dark Helmet and the Schwartz, and Pizza the Hutt. Oh, oh and John Candy as Barfolomew. He was a rip."

"Nope, never saw it," Francis hollered back. "Sounds funny though."

Some of the other students poured on with their positive testimonials regarding the flick.

"Tell you what, guys. If you all settle down and watch this video now, tonight we'll show *Spaceballs* at the hotel, and I'll spring for the ice cream, okay?

"And whose room is gonna git trashed?" Cindy asked, wide awake now.

"Cindy is precisely right," Claudia imperatively voiced.

"We girls don't want you slobs messing up our living quarters," Maggie injected.

"Okay, okay. We'll use the larger suite where Matt, Tom, Pete, Andy, and I are sleeping."

There seemed to be wholesale approval of the upcoming evening's activities, and the kids immediately settled down to watch *"The Hydroplate Theory – The Flood."*

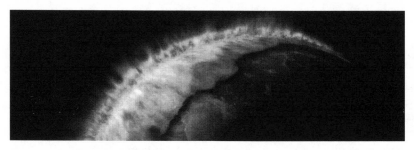

Rupture of the Fountains. Illustration Credit: Dr. Walter Brown

Brother Francis swung the mammoth Prevost off I-64 onto US 220 south going down through Clifton Forge. No sooner had we exited the small town when I asked the students to look out the windows on their left. Francis found a place to dock the monster bus. The timing for watching the video couldn't have been better.

It's as if I called for a fire drill. Brother Francis couldn't open the door fast enough, as the kids were almost falling over one another trying to get off the bus. The girls were trying to be ladylike, but I could sense their excitement as well.

Fred and I screamed at them to watch the traffic as they crossed route 220 to view the massive geologic sight. You would think we had a bunch of first graders that needed hand holding to cross over the thoroughfare.

But there it was across the small James River gorge and about three-quarters of the way up the mountain on the far side.

"Holy Toledo," Nate's arms were fully extended like he was telling how he caught a huge grouper or tuna. "That arch must span at least a quarter of a mile; it's multiple strata thick at that. It's . . . it's unreal."

James River Arch. Personal Photo

Tom observed, "Yeah, but see how the left end of the arch buckled when it slammed into that one section of strata and pushed it straight upright ninety degrees; someone climbed up there and put our flag on the top, like they had scaled Everest or something."

Vertical Arch with Flag. Personal Photo

Everyone was taking photos and selfies with the massive arch and upright strata section as backdrop.

"Look around you," I directed them. "What type of topography or landscape are we currently situated in?"

Santi, who had been inspecting the surrounding, commented first. "We are in a small cañón with a río below."

"And what does this remind you of?"

Juan stated matter-of-factly, "It's just like that canyon that was carved out by the Mount St. Helens mudslides, which left a small river at the bottom."

"Or even the Grand Canyon," Pete tagged on.

Nate was trying to get my attention, as he turned in all directions looking at the scene. He looked like a drunk ballerina.

"Nate, do you have something to add?" I asked.

"Man, I see it, I really get it now. The Flood deposited layer upon layer of sediment, pancake style. The layers hardened, but just a bit, like Juan's grandmother's moldable potter's clay. The tectonic action occurred, which then made the mountains rise and the water ran off into the oceans and valleys, which carved this small canyon out in the process. This canyon and the James river are all that's left."

"Excellent, Nate. This portion of the James is a branch called the Jackson, which is irrelevant. The key is, where did the flood waters that gouged out this canyon carry and deposit the massive quantity of rock and dirt? Hint: Where does the James flow?"

No sooner than I asked the question, Jim answered.

"The Chesapeake Bay, which goes into the Atlantic Ocean. And I just realized something really important." He stopped and was preparing what he was about to say.

Tom, who was impatient, commanded, "Would you mind sharing this 'really important' thing with the rest of us?"

"Man, cool it. I got this thing," Jim retorted. "The James River system empties into the Atlantic as do many other river systems like the Hudson, Penobscot, Savannah, etcetera. All the rock, dirt, and sediment washed into the Atlantic. That's why we have gentle sloping underwater coastal plains bordering the coastlines; mostly as a result of post Noah's Flood runoff, and not because of these river systems sloooowly depositing their sediment over millions of years."

"Hey, Doc," Jim continued. "I'd like to bring up something else I think I figured out, that I'd like to share."

"Sure, Jim, I'm all ears," I said, hoping the others would listen as well.

"After watching that Hydroplate Theory video, I started to read Chapter 7 and 8 in Genesis and . . ."

"You were actually reading the Bible?" Thad broke in, somewhat taken aback.

"Yeah," Jim stated forcefully. "But check this out. I did some basic math. After five months, the waters stopped rising and the Ark landed on the mountains of Ararat, which is in Turkey for those of you who are interested. Anyway, God made sure Noah and family didn't exit the Ark for another seven plus months."

"And what's so important about that?" reporter Thad queried.

"Think man. How did that psalmist put it? 'The mountains rose and the valleys sank.' Massive amounts of water were flowing off the continents hewing out canyons like this one and the Grand Canyon. Tectonic activity was still going on. It was dangerous out there. Someone writing just a fable probably would not have taken that safety timeframe buffer into account."

The students were mute. They looked at one another and then down into the James River and then up at the massive tectonic uplifts in the mountain across the gorge. Brother Francis had an extremely intense look on his face as he took in the topography and stroked his goatee. Fred and I knowingly smiled at each other.

"Good stuff, Jim. Anyone with any other observations before we leave?"

As Philip stared across the gorge and to the vertical tilt of the strata with the arch layers buttressing it, I could almost hear the gears turning in his head. He turned to the group. "Those layers," he said, pointing to the vertical strata behind him with the flag atop it, "had to be somewhat plastic and pliant before being pushed to their upright position by the arch strata. Had they been hardened in the horizontal over millions of years and then pushed up by the arch, they would have cracked and fallen apart. This had to have occurred while they were still somewhat tractable."

"Which means *each* of those strata couldn't represent tens or hundreds of thousands of years for *each* sedimentary layer," Andy clarified.

"Good going, bro," Pete congratulated, slapping his brother on the back. "It would be like building a brick wall on its side and only after it had dried and hardened for a million years, then raising it into a vertical position. Good luck with that!"

"Correcto," Santi confirmed. "It would have wound up like Juan's abuela's brittle and broken pottery."

CHAPTER SEVENTY-NINE

NORTH STAR RESTAURANT

We continued down 220 South a few miles to Eagle Rock. I had Brother Francis make a left turn onto James Street which crosses over the James River, where there should be some ample parking for the bus.

Before having Brother Francis open the door, I directed the students to walk back over the James Street Bridge to route 220. And after they crossed over the road, they carefully analyzed the sedimentary rock formation directly in front of them.

James Street Bridge Rock Formation. Personal Photo

"Watch out for the metal drainage grating at the base of that rock formation. We don't need any of you twisting an ankle. Otherwise you'll be hobbling on crutches for the remainder of the trip."

Pete and Thad climbed up several feet onto the bent rock strata and literally put their noses up against it.

"Man, I wish I had a magnifying glass," Thad complained.

"There are multiple upon multiple tiny layers, mere millimeters thick, all squashed and pancaked together; then bent and curved from forty-five up to ninety degrees." Pete observes.

"Any cracking through the layers?" I ask.

"No." Both Thad and Pete reply in unison.

Water Bottle at James Street Bridge Rock Formation. Personal Photo

"So, what's your conclusion?" I asked loudly enough so the rest of the students could hear me.

Pete answered. "It's obvious to me that this basement section of the mountain above us met with tremendous pressure and resistance when the tectonic forces hit it."

Thad continued, "Yeah, all these pancaked layers had to be malleable in order to be bent without fracturing. This had to occur shortly after the Flood runoff, as Jim mentioned back at Clifton Forge."

"Excellent, fellas! But now I'm going to play the devil's advocate; perhaps I'll be one of your professors, Pete." I scanned the group to make sure they caught my point. "As you know, intense pressure from the massive tonnage of rock above this site may have softened these layers throughout the supposed millions of years, and then afterwards, some tectonic activity occurred which then bent this formation without breaking it. Sedimentary rock can be changed."

The entire group looked at Pete. His pupils widen a bit as he strained to come up with the correct response. Francis especially seemed to be laser-focused on Pete. Cindy turned to her husband, and Fred smiled. She knew he had the answer.

Pete hesitated a bit. But I knew he could come up with the answer. "Pete, what type of rock can be formed from sedimentary rock under massive pressure?"

"Conglomerate." He quickly replied.

"Good. Now turn back and look at those thin pancaked layers and tell us—"

"Those are *still* sedimentary rock layers, originally laid down by water," he responded swiftly, with a triumphant smile on his face, after taking another brief look at the stone.

"Okay, good stuff. Now you two get off there and let some of the others get their faces up close and personal with the stone." Maggie climbed up to take a closer look. *That girl is fearless*, I thought.

Tom, who was still waiting to climb up, made a general announcement. "With all this talk about pancakes, I'm getting hungry. When are we going to stop and eat?"

***

The Prevost pulled into the limited parking area in front of the North Star Restaurant on Route 11, just south of Buchanan. "This restaurant has the best breakfast for miles around, and is a great favorite with the locals."

"This place is a hole in the wall," a few students grumbled. "Are you sure they serve good food here?"

"This ain't no chain restaurant, for sure."

"I'm not going to get ptomaine poisoning, am I?" Claudia stiffly remarked. Her snobby New York attitude showed.

"Don't judge a book by its cover," I countered. "Check out the parking lot; it's packed. What should that tell you?"

We all entered and Vickie the waitress greeted us. I reserved the back room for all of us, knowing that we would be arriving at the peak of the breakfast rush. The kids were getting a kick out of the quaint and funny in-your-face signs that adorned the walls.

"Be careful how much you order," I warned them. "The servings are very generous."

Some heeded my advice, others didn't. Pete, who was use to the modest portions served by most restaurants, was absolutely caught off guard. Brother Francis, Fred, and I were almost in stitches watching as Pete tried, but failed, to finish the large stack of pancakes with a side order of eggs and country ham. Andy just about had to carry Pete out at the end of the meal. Tom, the hungry one, didn't fare well either.

Once back on the bus, we hopped onto I-81 South again, which was just a half mile down the road from the North Star Restaurant. The food must have been satisfying, as almost the entire group was ready for a nap, including myself.

CHAPTER EIGHTY

CAPTAIN PLANET

About an hour later, I woke everyone up who was still sleeping. "Okay, gang, we have almost reached the first of the Christiansburg/Blacksburg exits; look out your windows on the right side."

"Fred, these are your old stomping grounds, why don't you explain what's going on with these rock formations we'll be driving by."

"I think the students know enough now to figure these out for themselves," he said, addressing the whole group.

"Hey, Mister Matt," Fred began, picking on Matt as he had the day of Dietrich's carnival. "As we do this *drive-by* of the rock formations, tell us what happened. Just talk, no shooting."

"Huh?" Matt replied.

Tom was sitting next to Matt and rapped him in his side with his elbow. Several of the group laughed and hooted. The kids really enjoyed Fred's quick wit.

"Oh, drive-by. Yeah, okay. Well, what we have here are multiple sedimentary layers that have been uplifted by tectonic forces," he stated in a monotone voice.

"Could you make your presentation a little drier, please?" Fred complained, rolling his eyes for all the students to see. The group was in hysterics.

"Mister Bombardier Beetle," Fred said, addressing Jim. "Did you ever find the missus?" he asked, mimicking Jim's antics with the binoculars. Before Jim could respond, Fred continued, "Notice anything different about the top tilted layers we just saw out the windows?"

"As a matter of fact, I did," Jim calmly responded.

"Weeeellll? Do you want us to wait a million years for your answer?" Fred razzed Jim a bit.

"When water slowly cascades down a window, it does so unevenly, looping and stretching downward with gravity in different lengths." Jim stopped for a moment.

"Go on," Fred encouraged.

"It looks like the muddy watery sediment 'froze' in place, then shortly afterwards the layers of strata were uplifted." He looked at Fred.

"It's analogous to a stream or river creating ripples in the sand or sediment as the water passes over it," Fred footnoted, and then scanned the group with a raised eyebrow.

Christiansburg/Blacksburg Rock Formation. Personal Photo

A light bulb went on in all the students' brains.

Jim eyes widened momentarily. "Yeah, the waters running off the land at the end of the Flood. Once there was no more water, or very little, the ripples partially hardened claylike somewhat; then the tectonic action of lifting forces occurred." Jim paused, contemplating further. "Yeah, the top layers, now stone, still exhibit the ripple effect formed post Flood. Of course, I see some erosion."

"Excellent, Jim!" Fred started to applaud, and others joined in as well.

"Thanks, Fred, that was good info," I complimented Fred for adding to the discussion.

Nate's hand went up, and I nodded for him to speak.

"We have always been led to believe that it takes millions of years for rock to form, including sedimentary rock laid down by water. You're doing a good job destroying that idea with Noah's Flood from only forty-five hundred years ago."

"Nate," I said, scanning the group, most of who were seated, "psychologists have understood for years that humans have a tendency to pigeonhole ideas. And we have an innate ability to keep concepts separated, in individual pigeonholes. Even when some of them totally contradict each other, we accept both as true."

"Could you translate that into English for us," Tom popped in.

"Sure, I'll give you an example of pigeonholing. All of you *already know* that it doesn't take millions of years for rocklike composites to form."

"We do?" Both Tom and Nate responded together. Others were looking around intrigued but confused.

"I'll present two concepts you have in your minds, each in its own pigeonhole. I promise you, you will break down the wall between those two concepts, immediately make the link, and determine that one is false and form a new conclusion."

"You're saying, Doc, that knowing rocklike structures don't take millions of years to form, is already in our brain? That once the wall between the two pigeonholes is opened, we'll arrive at the correct answer?" Nate was really trying to get it.

"Okay, here goes. Pigeonhole number one in your mind: Rocks take millions of years to form. Pigeonhole number two in your mind: Cement hardens to stone-like concrete quickly."

Jim smacked himself on the forehead. "I should've had that V-8!" he proclaimed. The rest of the group immediately put it together in their minds, and there was some erratic laughs and joshing, both at Jim and themselves.

"Notice pigeonhole one was a brainwashing concept that was placed in your minds, which you blindly accepted without evidence. Pigeonhole two you know to be fact. By breaking down the wall between the two, you have come to the realization that pigeonhole one is Barbra Streisand, to use Jude's expression."

Everyone nodded or shook their heads in disbelief as to what just mentally happened.

"Too bad Jude didn't come with us," Nate uttered. "This is awesome stuff. Do you have any other examples of things we have been brainwashed with, Doc?"

"As a matter of fact, I do. Have any of you, when you were little kids, watched a cartoon on TV called *Captain Planet*?"

Virtually all the hands went up.

"Good. And what was the show about?"

Matt put his right hand up so fast he accidently slammed it into the overhead storage bin. He dropped it down into his lap and rubbed it for a couple of seconds. Still wanting to be the one to answer the question, he shot his uninjured left hand up and hit the overhead unit again with an even louder thud. The group roared with laughter at his clumsy enthusiasm.

"Okay, Matt," I managed to get out between chuckles. "Why don't you explain the theme of the show for us?"

"Well," he started while massaging both sets of knuckles, "*Captain Planet* was a kinda blue-green eco-Superman flying around to save the planet."

"Save the planet from whom?" I inquired.

"The bad guys of course."

"And who were the bad guys, Matt?"

"The large evil corporations with their cigar chomping *fat* CEOs."

"Matt, did the cartoon *ever* portray the big corporations as good?"

"Huh? Come to think of it, I don't think so."

"So, if I understand the theme of the cartoon correctly, Mother Gaia good and *big* corporation bad."

"Yeah, I guess so. I was only four or five at the time, maybe younger."

"Can anyone on this bus give me the name of one, just one TV show and/or one movie that has portrayed big corporations in a positive light? I know of only two."

The entire group was abuzz as the students consulted with each other. Even Brother Francis leaned over from his driver's chair and admitted to me he couldn't think of one.

"Okay, give up?"

Several dejected responses from those in the bus admit defeat; they wanted to know the two shows that were positive regarding big business.

"The TV show *Bonanza,* from the early '60s, and more recently from several years ago, the movie *Atlas Shrugged. Bonanza* was about an honest family who owned large tracts of land and a cattle operation. *Atlas Shrugged* was Ayn Rand's definitive and final work about CEO John Galt who was a hard-working business magnate of integrity in the railroad industry."

The kids looked at me somewhat dumbfounded and amused at the same time.

"Now, I'm definitely not saying *all* large corporations are fair, honest, and trustworthy, but the reverse is *not* true, yet that is *all* that is portrayed in every TV show and movie I've ever seen, as well as in the media. Ever heard them use the term *Little Oil?* Or is it always *Big Oil*? And you yourselves admit you can't think of *one* exception to that."

"So, Matt," I continued, really addressing all the students, "what you are telling me is that, from the time you could barely walk until adulthood, you have been getting force-fed the idea that all big corporations are evil. And none of you ever realized that you were being brainwashed."

"Gosh, Doc," Matt replied, acting as a nonofficial spokesman for the group. "You're absolutely correct. All these years of barraging our minds with the same message, and none of us thought to question it."

Andy shot his hand up, and addressed the group, while looking at his brother. "Remember when we were kids Pete, the Lego Movie and a number of other movies and TV shows for us kids, promoting homosexuals and the LGBT community as just a normal alternative lifestyle," as I saw Pete nodding his head.

Immediately the students were conversing amongst one another about other children's movies and shows where they were brainwashed as kids.

"Lavado cerebral...uh brainwashing in Spanish," Santi remarked.

"Oh, by the way," Juan added, "wasn't Ted Turner the creator of *Captain Planet*? Last I heard, his estate had some pretty extensive corporate assets."

Almost like programmed robots, the entire group turned and stared back at Juan with slacked jaws and surprised expressions.

CHAPTER EIGHTY-ONE

MID-ATLANTIC RIDGE

"**A**s some of you may have noticed we made a slight detour down I-77; the views will be impressive. In the meantime look up the North American tectonic plate on your tablets, and also where the Appalachian mountain chain starts and ends."

Ali raised his hand, and I am so happy to see it go up. "Yes, Ali?"

"I'm having trouble taking pictures with my phone, and that last stop at Eagle Rock with all the bent and twisted rock formations *was* impressive."

"I'm sure your classmates will forward their pics to you at the end of the trip. You can also get a really good view of it on Google Maps right at the intersection of 220 South and James Street, which is just south of Clifton Forge. Just place the little Street View guy on the road at that intersection."

That seemed to satisfy Ali; he appeared happy with my solution.

"Brother Francis has informed me that we are passing through Fancy Gap. Keep your eyes peeled both at the mountain structures on your right and the vistas on the left. Since we are traveling southbound, the Appalachian Mountain chain will continue to be along the right side of the bus; you are about to see a massive rough plain to the east, which is on your left."

"Doc?"

"Yes, Thad."

"I've been taking photos like crazy with my camera. Some of these are absolutely going to be part of my upcoming articles for the *Veritas Beacon*. And I believe I speak for all of us when I say that we are seeing sedimentary layers all over the place now. Some small, almost insignificant, are projecting from the roadsides for only ten or twenty feet, while others are fairly massive, like the ones back at Christiansburg and Clifton Forge and Eagle Rock."

"Nate," I called, noting he wished to add his thoughts.

"Doc, my family lives in Boston as you know. The Green Mountains of Vermont is where we go skiing, and that's all still part of the Appalachian chain. There's this one cool cliff jump that my brother likes to take. He's an X-Games contender. The entire cliff face is all sedimentary rock, but I never paid much heed of it until today."

Fred added his two cents. "Have any of you or your family thought about buying a particular make and model car? From then on, that's the only one you see on the road, whereas the day before you never even noticed it existed."

"Fred's absolutely right," Andy quipped. "Remember the first car I was going to buy, Pete?"

"How can I forget? Every time we passed one on the road you talked my ears off for twenty minutes. Drove me crazy."

"I did?"

Pete turned and gave Andy a quirky "are you kidding me" look.

"Juan," I acknowledged.

"Doc, I looked it up, the Appalachian Mountains, that is. They extend from Alabama all the way up into Canada, specifically Labrador and Newfoundland."

"Thanks, Juan. I hope you all caught that."

Suddenly a small female voice from the back of the bus called out. It was Cindy. "Y'all better stop your jaw flapping and look out the left side windows."

Everyone moved to the left side squeezing against each other to take in the massive rugged plain and valley below.

"It goes as far as the eye can see," Thad enthusiastically stated.

Appalachian Plain. Personal Photo

"That plain comes in straight at us, and hits the base of the mountains which must be a thousand feet below us, maybe even fifteen hundred feet or more," Maria exclaimed, her face pressed up against her eastern window.

"And the mountains on our right . . . we . . . well, I can't even see the tops of them above us," Maggie added, as she is careening her neck trying to look up with her face against the opposite western window.

Appalachian Uplift with truck in distance. Personal Photo

Philip put his hand up, and I wave for him to address the class, but first I asked the group to settle down a bit, as they were all chit-chatting among themselves, and going back and forth from one side of the bus to the other alternately looking at the acutely inclined sedimentary formations on the mountain side and the plain-valley on the other.

"Okay, Philip, I think you have the floor now."

"From what I have been researching, the North American Tectonic Plate extends from Canada and Greenland into eastern Siberia down the east coast and around Florida toward Mexico."

"And which direction does it appear to be moving, Philip?"

"Away from the Mid-Atlantic Ridge . . . toward us."

"Seems it met with a slight bit of resistance about where we are now," I mentioned slowly, deliberately, and rather sarcastically to the group.

"Holy cow!" Jim shouted, practically launching himself. Good thing he was already standing. "Those two videos we watched. The whole thing started with the rupture of the 'fountains of the great deep' which formed the Mid-Atlantic Ridge."

"That plate," Nate continued, "was doing okay as it moved away from the Mid-Atlantic Ridge, until it met with resistance and warped upward forming the Appalachian Mountain chain. And we can see it right here on this bus. Incredible!"

Claudia was nervously looking out the eastern window of her bus seat and appeared very shaky as she looked down the thousand or more feet to the plain-valley floor below. "But what if that tectonic plate decides to move more in our direction?" she asked, becoming very pasty-faced.

"As I said, Claudia, it *is* moving," Philip stated nonchalantly, to her dismay and consternation.

CHAPTER EIGHTY-TWO

INSECT-FREE

"**B**ut only about two inches per year on average," Philip said, smiling compassionately at Claudia, which seemed to relieve her anxiety somewhat.

"That's right," Pete added, joining the discussion. "My professors have told me the same, stating that they have always moved at that rate. Now I know better. Current rates can be measured fairly accurately, but, and it's a big but, they are *assuming* it's always been that way in the unobserved past."

"And the unobserved past means conclusions are speculation, not repeatable, testable science," Jim, still standing, proclaimed. "At the time of the rupture of the fountains of the deep, these heated plates, "greased" from the hot water and magma beneath them, were moving possibly at highway speeds, which makes more sense given the evidence before us."

"Could we stop for a restroom break soon?" Cindy pleaded while squirming a little in her seat.

"Can't you girls use the well-appointed bathroom on the bus?" I inquired.

"Not now we can't!" Maggie adamantly rebutted. "Have you been back there yet? The guys made a mess trying to maintain control at seventy miles an hour."

I looked over at Brother Francis. "There's a Love's Truck Stop ahead," he told me, "where I was planning on pulling into so we could all stretch our legs, anyway."

"Okay, ladies," I announced. "Brother Francis will be getting off a few miles up the road for you."

"At a rest stop, I hope?" Cindy caustically remarked.

"Yes, at a rest stop." Fred stated with a slightly sarcastic tone. "We won't have you use the bushes . . . at least this time." The guys howled with laughter, but the women clearly were not amused.

Brother Francis was actually the first one off the bus and made a beeline to the restrooms. A few of the guys decided to take a jog around the truck stop complex a few times to loosen up.

Once back aboard, the girls moved to occupy the rear portion of the bus; Fred and myself, with the rest of the fellas, congregated at the front, allowing Brother Francis to easily join in.

"Oh, ladies," I shouted back toward the rear. "Brother Francis was kind enough to completely clean and disinfect the bathroom for you."

"Tell him, he's the only gentleman on board," Cindy cried back.

"Well, you heard her Brother Francis - looks like you're the only one in their good graces."

"Guess I'm still in the dog house," Fred, half jokingly lamented.

Most everyone had picked up some soft drinks and snacks at the truck stop. The candy bar of choice, for most, appeared to be a Butterfinger bar - the crew wanting to get sugared up for the final leg of our trip today.

"Doc - Jim, Andy, and I had been discussing, during our jog, ways we could combat the false information being bottle-fed to us by our professors. Any ideas?" Pete asked in all seriousness.

I nodded my head. "I'm sure you are aware of fossilized marine life atop many mountains, including Everest."

Pete looked at Jim, and they both nodded.

"Are you aware that the majority of the marine clams are found fossilized with their bivalves closed? What should all this be telling you?"

"Que es un bivalve?" Santi asked.

"Pete, that should be an easy one for you - given your studies in geology, marine biology, and your experiences at sea."

"Santi, bivalves are mollusks with two hinged shells like oysters, mussels, clams, and scallops. When they die, their shells automatically open up. However, those that have been found fossilized on mountaintops like Everest, are found closed."

"Claro, like Shell gasolina."

"You got it, man," I said, watching both Pete and Jim straining their brains to figure this one out.

"That means that the bivalves had to have been quickly covered by an underwater muddy catastrophe," Pete added thinking out loud.

"Yeah," Jim interjected animatedly. "Just like those fossil fish Doc showed us. The one giving birth takes the cake. The bivalves had to be smothered quickly under the sea and suffocated with their shells still closed. Then '*the mountains rose and the valleys sank.*'"

"Right on, Jim," Pete congratulated him, giving a thumbs-up. "The tectonic activity, with the heated plates moving rapidly from the hot fountain waters, folded up in some places like the Appalachian chain here; as well as in Nepal where the Himalayas and Everest are located."

"Excellent analysis, guys. Good thinking."

"Is there any other evidence for the sedimentary layers being laid down quickly during the year of Noah's Flood?" Jim asked, really wanting to be able to counter his professors.

"Okay, Jim, this is going to be your baby, given your background in ecology."

"Sock it to me, Doc."

"When you look at all these sedimentary layers, even as we drive along, they are primarily all flat one on top of the other, with barely a knife edge between them. And each thin layer supposedly represents thousands of years at a minimum. Doesn't that strike you as odd?"

Jim had his hand on his chin, eyebrows narrowed; he was stumped.

"Okay, I'll help you a bit. The top layer of the earth that we are on right now, will be covered with another mini local flood somehow in ten thousand years or so, according to the evolutionary geologists. Right?"

"Right." Jim replied, but still unsure.

"Look around you, is any of this flat, I mean really razor blade flat? Think about the Grand Canyon layers, or those at Mount St. Helen's Canyon."

"Okay," Jim hesitated. "We are standing on soil/dirt . . . I've got it! I got it! If I was to get off the bus and take a cross section of any of these layers, or even those at the Grand Canyon, there is no dirt between the layers."

"And ecologically, what are the most prolific organisms on the planet?" I posed my question to Jim.

"Insects!" Jim exclaimed. "I bet there is no evidence for any burrowing of any insect holes, nor tunneling, nor worm tubes, between any of these layers because they were laid down so quickly." He was literally jumping up and down in the aisle as all of us are laughing along.

Pete and the others gave Jim high fives. The mood was definitely over- the- top as the guys were hooting and hollering like they struck gold or something.

"What are you guys clamoring about up front?" Cindy inquired, as the girls were all glaring at us.

"Insects! There are no insects or worms." Jim practically screamed back at them.

"We are very happy for you. Now can we call 9-1-1 and have the lot of you hauled off to the loony bin?" Cindy abrasively panned us.

CHAPTER EIGHTY-THREE

TERRORIST ATTACK

We were finishing up our dinner at a restaurant near the hotel in Tennessee in the late afternoon; after having taken the tour of the Gray Fossil Site and Museum. "What a bunch of dumb bunnies," Matt declared, unable to finish a death-by-chocolate sundae topped with whipped cream and a cherry.

"Que es un dumb bunny? Santi asked Matt who had some spaghetti sauce on the side of his mouth.

Nate picked up the ball. "Look, you've got to cut these guys at the museum some slack. They don't know what we now know. A few months back, we were those 'dumb bunnies,' Matt."

Matt was not willing to concede. "But c'mon, common sense would dictate that you can't have one pig at a time fall into the same supposed sinkhole/pond over . . . what . . . two and a half million years, until you've got over one hundred and fifty pigs—to date—stacked up on one another. Pigs generally run in packs. Give me a break!"

"Matt's got a point," Jim added. "From an ecological point of view, they're assuming no change to the sinkhole/pond for two and a half million years, as the tapirs, properly called, fell in one by one. And then, only after that time frame, does the ecology change and the pit fills in!?"

Pete having polished off his gargantuan twenty-four-ounce steak, decided to contribute his observations. "They even admitted that this area is all sedimentary clay with some dolomite, which is also a sedimentary rock. Heck, just a few miles away is Limestone, Tennessee. Noah's Flood is right in their faces."

"Jim," Maria spoke up. "From the sixty different types of animals and plants they have found so far, many are tropical, such as the camels, rhinos, alligators, and elephants, not to mention the tapirs - which are still found in South America. Sure sounds like some global warming was going on *big* time prior to Noah's Flood."

"Yeah, Maria, you're right. I overlooked the info they gave us on the animal types they have dug up."

"And, Pete," Maria turned her focus, "haven't they found tropical plants and animals in Arctic latitudes, and palm trees and animals and coal at the South Pole? Now that's some serious global warming going on at the poles, no less."

Pete just stared at Maria, nodding his head in affirmation. He then looked over at me, with the entire table following suit.

"Yes, Juan," I said as his hand, still with a fork in it, went up.

"Before you get into the global warming thing, the tour guide mentioned that many of the bones they found were busted up—dis . . . something."

"*Disarticulated*, Juan. I probably did not make it clear, that many times archeologists find fossilized specimens of bones, literally jumbled up - and not found as one neat complete skeleton. Anyone what to take a shot as to why?"

Claudia, who was sipping on her after-dinner *eaux de vie* brandy with a raised pinky, added, "Like any catastrophic flood, some items are ripped apart and others are carried on the flood waters till they sink and are covered, still intact, by mud deposits. I'm sure Pete and Andy can verify this, having been through Katrina."

Andy and Pete both nodded their heads. Andy was swilling down a Miller Lite.

"Thanks, Claudia. How's that brandy by the way?" I asked her.

"It's tolerable. Definitely not in d'Armagnac class, but good enough."

"I believe we left off with some kind of global warming in the years prior to the Flood." I noticed Fred wanted to elaborate on this topic. "Take it away Fred!"

Fred cleared his throat as he brushed some breadcrumbs off the sleeve of his blue blazer. "Yes, the global warming was due to the massive number of gas guzzling SUVs driving around at that time, which caused instability in the earth's crust, which ruptured, releasing the waters of the fountains of the great deep in order to cool the earth." He then took a final sip of his wine.

Cindy slowly turned to him. "Suuurrre, and where did the SUVs come from?"

Without missing a beat, Fred bounded back, "From Noah's nasty CO_2-polluting factories, of course." He said this while picking at some crumbs, still lodged in the buttons on the sleeve of his sports coat.

Cindy rolled her eyes, and everyone started gagging and laughing quite loudly.

"They're going to throw us out of this place," Maggie commented, still chuckling.

"Fred! Now why don't you give us the *correct* explanation, since you are on such a roll!?" Stated Cindy energetically, lampooning her husband.

"Okay, honey. Just having some fun with all the global warming stupidity out there." He turned to Brother Francis. "Francis, when does the Bible first mention cold weather?"

"Let me double check, but I believe it's not until after the Flood." He fumbled with his pocket Bible a moment. "Here it is. Genesis 8:22: 'cold and heat, summer and winter.' Which means that the earth pre-Flood was a temperate climate, and probably tropical in areas, given the current discoveries at both poles."

Jim grabbed the Bible from Brother Francis and at the same time stated, "What about when God formed the earth, something about signs and seasons." He thumbed through the opening of Genesis. "Ah, here, Genesis 1:14: 'Let there be lights in the expanse of the heavens . . . and let them be for signs and for seasons.' Doesn't that mean that there were the normal four seasons *prior* to the Flood?"

Francis gave Jim a big warm smile as he addressed the table. "Most people think that is what it means. But the Old Testament was written in Hebrew. The Israelites term for *season* means 'appointed feast or festival,' which brings us back to the first time cold weather is mentioned in the Bible, which is in Genesis 8:22, *after* the Flood."

"Brother Francis is right," Matt confirmed. "I just Googled the Hebrew definition. Boy, wait until I tell my dad about all this. It's going to blow his mind."

Francis then turned to Fred. "Ball's back in your park. What made the weather change from mild to mean after the Flood?"

There seemed to be a commotion of sorts going on from the bar where the patrons were half attentive to some ESPN sporting event on multiple large-screen TVs. It appeared there had been an interruption for a special news announcement of a terrorist attack on our soil.

"Turn it up! Turn it up!" Several of the people at the bar were practically yelling at the bartender to turn the volume louder to hear what was going on.

Our entire table stopped talking and turned toward the TVs.

As the volume was turned up, we could hear the newscaster: ". . . a number of bombs have exploded, and several RPGs were fired at the massive electronic billboards in Times Square. There are bodies lying all over the street and sidewalks, people bleeding and running at the same time; shards of glass and metal rained down from the billboards cutting them to ribbons. What you are viewing is unedited amateur cell phone videos coming into our studios from some of the uninjured bystanders."

I looked over and saw Brother Francis bless himself and Maria squeezed her cross. I looked at my watch. *Rush hour. It figures*, I said to myself.

"Wait . . . wait . . . I'm getting another report now," the newscaster said while holding his earpiece to get a better reception. "Yes, Washington . . . what . . . oh, no . . . oh, my God. I'm sorry we are now getting multiple communiqués, none of which have been verified yet. Apparently, there have been similar coordinated attacks on Washington, Chicago, and Los Angeles. We are trying to confirm this information; there are a great number of calls and reports coming in. Two of our servers have already crashed. . . ."

CHAPTER EIGHTY-FOUR

WHO'S ON FIRST

We drove back to the hotel and everyone was wired, wanting to watch the news reports on the attacks as they came in. I stayed up with the kids until about 11:30 p.m. and then I was ready to hit the hay. I really needed to get some sleep. Luckily I had the attached suite to myself; Andy, Pete, Tom, and Matt were still watching the news in their room.

Unable to call Emily on my cell phone, I texted her. After the umpteenth time, I was able to get through. She was safe at home, watching the news reports as they came in. Emily and I loved watching sci-fi movies. Of course, I poked fun of them for all the holes in the plots of the Category 10.5 "end of the world" scenarios. Somehow the cell phones, even at ground zero, always seemed to function, when in reality, the first communications to fail are cell phones.

The low level hum and murmuring of the TV voices in the background helped me drift off to sleep. As I did, my mind went back to the restaurant and Ali. I remembered as we were all leaving the restaurant, Ali walked toward the bar fixated on the bank of TV screens with what appeared, from my poor vantage point, to be a miscreant unnatural smile.

***

I walked into the breakfast lounge of the hotel about 7:30 AM and saw Cindy and her girls sitting together. I asked if I could join them. I wanted to meet Cindy and the girls in more of a social setting. They all were gracious and agreed.

"I'm going to grab some breakfast, and I'll be with you momentarily."

I then sat down at their table with some oatmeal, a yogurt cup, a banana, a hard-boiled egg, and some coffee. "How are you ladies this morning? Did you get any sleep last night?"

"We are still a little tired from watching the news reports last night," Cindy spoke for all of them.

"Why is all of this happening?" Claudia nervously asked. I could see the deep concern for her parents who resided in New York City. "I haven't been able to contact either my father or my mother." She had barely touched any of the food on her plate.

"Cindy, you would remember several years ago—and you girls were probably youngsters, totally oblivious to events that took place in the world—when the U.S. was importing illegals and 'refugees' into the states in large numbers." Everyone nodded their heads. "The chickens have come home to roost, as they say. There is a term used by intelligence agencies called *disinformation*. It is when a government or organization gets their opponent's news media, government officials, and citizens to think in a particular way by giving out false news reports."

"I don't unerstan," Cindy remarked, the other women smiled in accord.

"I'll give you an example of one which was eventually exposed and failed. During the Cold War, the Russian KGB funneled disinformation to some of their European press contacts, that during World War II, Pope Pius XII was collaborating with the Nazis. This disinformation eventually made its way to the U.S. news media."

"Why would Russia want to do that?" Maria soberly asked.

"Israel was one of our closest allies during the Cold War, and so was Pope John Paul II. It was President Reagan, Prime Minister Thatcher, and Pope John Paul who made possible the collapse of the Soviet Union. The KGB wanted to drive a wedge between the United States and the Vatican using disinformation. Remember there are many U.S. citizens of Jewish heritage."

"What does that have to do with what happened yesterday?" Claudia, still confused, asked.

"Does anything prevent one's own government from using disinformation on its own people—i.e., fake news?"

The women looked at one another. Maggie especially, was reflecting heavily on this. "That's right," she exclaimed boldly. "The governmental Matrix—the FBI, DOJ and the DNC through its lackeys in the media, used this disinformation against former President Trump on a daily basis. I almost forgot!"

Heads were nodding all around. I continued, "The U.S. government convinced the people that bringing in all these illegals and so-called refugees was a good thing, knowing that a certain percentage of them would never want to assimilate into American culture and would actually resent us and want to attack the hand that feeds them. Hey, remember that during World War II only 7 percent of the German populace were Nazis."

Maggie seemed to be agreeing with me. "I think I've got it figured out, Doc," she said. "The government let these people immigrate under the guise of a humanitarian effort, but knowing full well, that statistically something like this would eventually occur."

Maria jumped right in. "And because it's always about money, power, and control—"

"I'll bet," interrupted Maggie, "the citizens of our country are ready for the government to propose just about anything to make them safe."

"Anyone want to take a stab as to what the citizenry would now agree to, in order to have more 'safety and security'?" I inquired.

Maggie's eyes lit up with a fire in them. "Two things: First will be unofficial martial law with impromptu road checks, personal pat downs, and bag inspections. Many citizens will be 'relieved' of their legally owned firearms. Pete and Andy told me this happened to their parents during Katrina."

"What's the second point, Maggie?" I asked, hoping she would simmer down a bit.

No such luck. She launched into the second half of her tirade. "An RFID chip with GPS capability – for everyone," she stated angrily. "It's so obvious now, it's blinding. The people will practically beg for it, just so nanny government can know who's on first, what's on second, and 'just because' is in center field."

Everyone at the table laughed, albeit somewhat nervously, at the Abbott and Costello reference to the Matrix's control over us.

CHAPTER EIGHTY-FIVE

TIMELINE

"**T**here's something else about these attacks," Maria offered.

"What's that?" I asked. The others were waiting for Maria's answer as well.

"Let me approach it this way," Maria said, putting her thoughts in order. "Over half of American society is secular, including those who are nominal Christians. Americans, with prompting from the media, are now demanding *more* secularization; it's a way for the government Matrix to finally rid itself of *all* religions."

"How so?" Claudia inquired.

"After decades of evolutionary brainwashing—Darwinism being the 'proof' that God doesn't exist—a majority of Americans look at religion as irrelevant at best, and downright detrimental and dangerous at worst. The usual liberal drivel then arises, which is, 'religion is the cause of all war and suffering'."

"Well, isn't it?" Cindy snidely commented somewhat exasperated and a bit irked.

As we are waiting for Maria's response, I was thinking that it's amazing how even strong Christians, such as Cindy, have been so taken in by the lamestream media and progressive atheistic schooling, which twists the historic truth of Christianity.

Maria squinted her dark brown eyes as though she had been provoked. "Oh, you mean like WWI or WWII or the Korean War or the Spanish-American War or the War of the Roses or the Russo-Japanese War or the Punic Wars or the Mongol Wars or—"

"Okay, okay, I got yor point, Maria," Cindy humbly responded.

"And please don't bring up that weak clichéd argument of the Christian Crusades versus the poor defenseless Muslims," Maria retorted as her eyes flashed at Cindy.

"I must confess that was gonna be ma next counterpoint," Cindy conceded.

I couldn't contain myself, and finally had to butt in. "I'd like to bring something up on my tablet for all of you," I said, wiping my greasy hands on a napkin before handling my tablet.

"Ah, here we go. Check this out. This is a website that gives you a timeline of the Crusades:

570: Muhammad born in Mecca.
610: Muhammad had a religious experience that changed his life.

627: A confederation was created between Muhammad's followers and eight Arab clans.

630: An army of thirty thousand Muslims march on Mecca, which surrendered with little resistance."

"During his ten years in Medina, he planned sixty-five military campaigns and raids, and personally led twenty-seven of them." I looked up at the girls; they seem to be taken aback a bit.

"Just a slightly bellicose guy," Claudia sarcastically remarked as the others chuckled.

"Let me read this from the Qur'an in Sura 66:9, 'O prophet! Strive against the disbelievers and hypocrites . . . Hell will be their home.'"

"I see your point, Dr. Lucci," Claudia remarked.

"At least Christianity tried, unsuccessfully, may I add, to preach peace," Maria shook her head and commented, "Islam came brazenly with the sword!"

"Let me continue," I implored as I looked down again at my tablet and the timeline.

"632: Muhammad dies."

"Then for the next hundred years, the Muslim armies conquered Spain, Portugal and parts of France, before finally being temporarily stopped, at the Battle of Tours, France in 732, by the grandfather of Charlemagne, Charles Martel, better known as 'the Hammer'."

"I don't know about hammers," Claudia interjected, "but in epicurean circles, that's when the French developed the croissant, which means crescent, in response to their victory over the Muslims and their crescent symbol." As she finished, she tempestuously broke a croissant in half.

"Oh, and El Cid of Spain," Maggie added, "I had such a crush on Charlton Heston who played El Cid. I imagined myself as Sophia Loren who became his wife."

"Yes, Maggie. Both fought against the Muslim onslaught of Europe. The First Crusade, however, wasn't until 1096. By then the Muslims had also conquered Egypt, the Middle East, Sicily, and parts of Italy and Venice, including Rome itself."

"Rome!? Muslims attacked Rome?" Maria remarked, her big beautiful brown eyes wide with surprise.

"Yes, Maria, in 846, Pope Leo IV promised to pay a yearly tribute of twenty-five thousand silver coins for the Muslims to cease their plunder of Rome."

"Eight forty-six?! That's . . . that's 250 years before Christian Europe *finally* decided to launch a coordinated all-out assault against the heart of the enemy." Maria had to do some quick mental calculations to arrive at her conclusion.

"Geez, it's even *worse* than that!" Maggie blurted out, getting animated and fired up. "It would be like the Muslims attacking us constantly, even before the Pilgrims landed at Plymouth Rock in 1620, and *only now* - today deciding to retaliate against them on their home turf."

"Amazing, huh?" I said, looking up again at the women with their mixed expressions of surprise, disgust, and frustration for the Christian slow and weak response against the Islamic hordes.

"The eighth, and final, Crusade ended in 1247," I said, finishing the brief summary of the timeline.

"And they have been slaughtering, raping, and beheading Jews, Christians, and anyone else who does not convert to Islam ever since. I'll be damned before they force me to wear one of those black potato sacks with eye slits," Maggie, still impassioned, remarked.

I glanced at Cindy who appeared to have been very contemplative during most of the timeline exposé.

"I remember a high school history teacher of mine, who commented that at the beginning of the First Crusade on the way to the Holy Land, the crusaders massacred German Jews, and then later Turkish Muslim prisoners were beheaded," Cindy politely commented, searching for a truthful answer.

"Your teacher was absolutely correct, Cindy," I admitted. She raised her eyebrows, surprised that I agreed with her historical information. The rest of the girls were waiting for more.

"Maria, I believe you can probably answer this one for Cindy."

Maria was reflective for only a moment. "The Muslim mandate, based on their Qur'an, is to convert or die, or be subjugated into slavery or prostitution. In contrast, those errant crusaders performing horrific acts goes *against* biblical principles – which is why you brought it up in the first place, Cindy. You already know that Christianity doesn't support such bestial behavior."

Everyone was quiet for a moment, reflecting on Maria's comments. I took the opportunity to swallow a spoonful of my oatmeal—it was cold.

Brother Francis signaled to all of us that we needed to get on the road. As I exited the breakfast lounge, I turned one more time to the TV as I heard the newscaster announce another terrorist had blown himself up, taking with him a tactical swat team that was closing in on him.

CHAPTER EIGHTY-SIX

THE SAUROPOD

The kids were still ruminating over the multiple terrorist attacks on America as we cruised up I-75 on our way to the Creation Science Museum on the Kentucky side of the I-275 loop around Cincinnati.

Fred and I had taken up our usual positions at the front of the bus. Leaning on the upright post beside Brother Francis in his captain's chair, I decided to provoke the students.

"I have been hearing most of you express definitive animosity towards these poor Muslim 'refugees' for their acts."

I was barraged with numerous replies in tones of anger, resentment, and frank hostility at these extremists. Matt seemed to be the most vociferous.

"So, Matt, aren't you being negatively prejudiced in your feelings against these attackers?"

"Have you lost your mind, Doc? Those animals killed hundreds of our citizens yesterday," he retorted, as several other students backed him up with their supportive chatter, even giving me some dirty looks in the process.

"Perhaps these Muslims see themselves instead as freedom fighters." I exclaimed, looking to get under Matt's skin.

Matt was practically out of his seat bombarding me with insults, and accusing me of being complicit with the terrorists. I gave Maria and Maggie one of my winks. They both chuckled a bit.

"Now that I have gotten you sufficiently riled up Matt, I believe it was you, who in the early days of this class, said that 'each of us could decide right or wrong for ourselves.' And that absolute truth did not exist." I cocked my head to the side while raising an eyebrow at him. "So who are you to say that they cannot call themselves freedom fighters? That is *their* truth. And the mainstream media commentators seem to concur with me on this point."

I happened to glance at Ali, who didn't appear to pick up on my sarcasm, and he was grinning like a Cheshire cat. He seemed to accede that the maniacs *were* freedom fighters. I don't think anyone else noticed, as they were focused on either Matt or I.

Pete, who was sitting behind Matt, smacked him on the back of the head. "You fell into one of Doc's traps . . . again."

"So, Doc," Matt asked, "what is truth? Where do I find it?" he asked while rubbing his scalp where Pete whacked him.

"That's partly what this trip is about: for all of you to find some of those answers. It will be up to each and every one of you to determine whether truth, and therefore right and wrong, is found in atheistic evolution/Mother Gaia, Buddhism, Shintoism, Confucianism, Avatar, the Force, Islam, Magic Crystals, or . . . Christianity."

"Hey, Doc," hollered Jim, "you could add Socialism, Communism, Fascism, and Nazism, but then all of those use evolution to prop themselves up anyway."

"Well put, Jim."

I directed my gaze at Ali and asked, "Anything you would like to add to what Jim and I just said, Ali?"

He just shook his head. Probably too busy with his violent gaming.

Brother Francis tugged on my jacket, and I twisted to see him give me one of his big broad smiles.

***

The Prevost passed through the entrance gate at the Creation Museum, and the guard directed us to the parking area for the buses. I reminded the kids to bring their cell phones, as I was sure they would want to take a lot of photos.

Walking toward the museum, the first thing they saw was a large metal sculpture of a sauropod dinosaur on the pavement in front of the entrance, which absolutely caught their attention.

"A dinosaur?" Matt loudly exclaimed. "What does a dinosaur have to do with the Creation? I thought we were going to learn about Adam and Eve or something."

"Yeah, Doc," Tom, feeling a bit cranky, stated. "Dinosaurs died out millions of years ago, way before Adam and Eve and the Garden of Eden . . . *if* those two ever existed at all."

"Do you know that as a fact, Tom?" I asked. "Could you *prove* that in a court of law, counselor? Remember, it did happen in the *unobserved* past."

"Okay, okay, you got me. But this museum is going to have to supply a hefty weight of evidence to counter the prevailing 'millions of years' position."

"Guess we'll have to go in and find out . . .the truth," I said, giving Maggie and Maria one more wink. A few of the students rushed to take pictures of and with the dinosaur before entering the building.

Dinosaur in front of Creation Museum. Photo Credit: nwcreation.net

CHAPTER EIGHTY-SEVEN

MARCO POLO

The line in the lobby hallway was long, indicating we would have a bit of a wait before getting our tickets. I decided to turn lemons into lemonade.

"Why don't you guys start studying the display cases on the walls, I believe you'll find them more than interesting."

"Brother Francis, would you take the class through these?"

"Thanks, Doc, after that talk we had back on campus, I started to do some online research; besides I wanted to be prepared for this trip."

Brother Francis carefully explained to the kids that dinosaurs in ancient times were called dragons. That the word dinosaur wasn't coined until two hundred years after the Bible was first written in English. Those dinosaurs that were not on the ark perished and some were fossilized. The dinosaurs that came off the ark after the flood, multiplied and spread throughout the world, like the other animals onboard.

"Brother Francis," Thad inquired. "Are you saying that humans have seen dinosaurs, which is one reason why they were written about in the Bible?"

"Yes, Thad."

"Are there any non-biblical references of observations of dinosaurs post-Flood?"

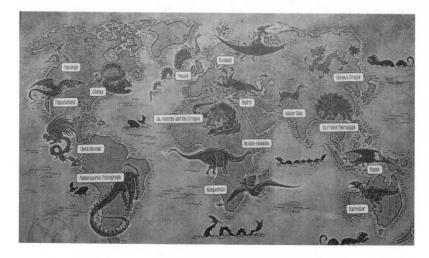

Map of Dinosaurs around the World. Personal Photo

"Check out this display case. I'm sure you are familiar with Marco Polo."

Thad was fervently reading the poster inside the display case.

"I remember a literature teacher of mine in high school berating Marco Polo's description of dinosaur-like creatures in China as fanciful imagination. She said that he was probably smoking opium. Even then I asked myself why would Marco Polo give such detailed descriptions of people, places, and events and then make up animal stories."

"That's good, Thad."

"One more point, Brother Francis. Marco Polo also talked about seeing Noah's Ark on Ararat. Needless to say, my teacher trashed that part of his travels also, but she praised his relationship as a confidant of the great Kublai Khan, the grandson of Genghis Khan."

"Oh, wow, check this out," Juan joined in. "I brought up Marco Polo on my tablet, and in his book he said that the royal chariot was pulled by dragons. And that even as late as 1611, the emperor appointed the post of 'Royal Dragon Feeder'."

"Oye, hombre," Santi exclaimed. "Why have a position of a Royal Dragon Feeder if there were no such things as dragons or dinosaurs to feed?"

Some of the visitors around us, who had been listening in, laughed.

"It is said," Brother Francis added, "that on his deathbed at seventy years old, Marco Polo declared, 'I did not tell half of what I saw.'"

Claudia's hand went up, and Francis recognized her. "Every Chinese restaurant I've ever been in has the twelve animals of the Chinese Zodiac on a placemat. Why illustrate eleven real animals and one imaginary animal—the dragon—unless of course Marco Polo was right all along."

"Philip," I cried out over the crowd at him, "what is the symbol of the Emperor of China?"

"The dragon!" He responded quickly, and with assurance.

"Just checking," I said as my eyes focused firmly on him, causing him to deliberately reflect on the whole exchange.

Tom had moved on to another wall case display. "Herodotus! My history professor was just giving a lecture about him. He is known as the 'Father of History,' and lived around 450 BC."

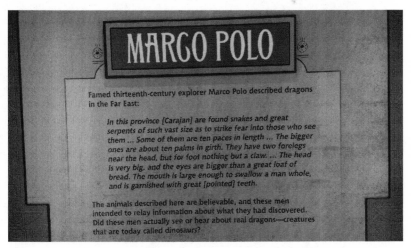

Marco Polo. Personal Photo

Tom was talking and reading from the display at the same time. "Man, my professor never mentioned any of these observations to us. Listen to this. Herodotus described a bone yard of winged serpents in Arabia."

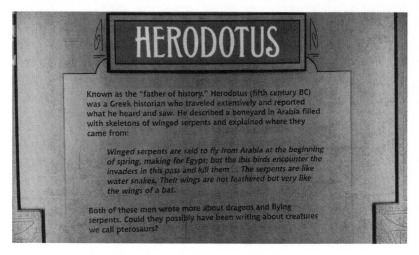

HERODOTUS

Known as the "father of history," Herodotus (fifth century BC) was a Greek historian who traveled extensively and reported what he heard and saw. He described a boneyard in Arabia filled with skeletons of winged serpents and explained where they came from:

> Winged serpents are said to fly from Arabia at the beginning of spring, making for Egypt; but the ibis birds encounter the invaders in this pass and kill them ... The serpents are like water snakes. Their wings are not feathered but very like the wings of a bat.

Both of these men wrote more about dragons and flying serpents. Could they possibly have been writing about creatures we call pterosaurs?

Herodotus. Personal Photo

"Sure sounds like a pterosaur to me," Tom surmised.

"A real Jurassic Park! With dead bones all over the place." Matt was wild with excitement as he slammed his arm onto Tom's shoulder while looking at Claudia.

Claudia snubbed Matt. Her eyes and nose immediately went up in the air. She moved quickly to the next display. Suddenly she pressed both her hands up against the glass and moved her face to just inches away as her jaw dropped. For a moment she was speechless. Then she stammered, "My . . . my dad saw this at the very same ancient temple in Cambodia on a business trip a few years ago. He told me his guide asked him what he thought was carved into the temple stone."

"Looks like a stegosaurus to me," Maggie off-handedly commented.

Stegosaurus engraving. Courtesy: Creation Museum

"That's exactly what my dad told the guide and me when he returned from his trip with essentially the same photo that's in this display case; he didn't know what to make of it."

"Guess he couldn't wrap his head around it, having been brainwashed for millions of years in school," Maggie said smiling at Claudia as they both laughed.

"What did the guide tell your dad?" I inquired. "And oh, have you been able to reach your parents yet?"

"Yes, thank you for asking, Dr. Lucci. They're okay," Claudia said before returning to her story. "The guide told him that these creatures lived in the jungles, but were eventually killed or driven off by the locals, hundreds of years ago."

I passed my cell phone to Claudia and asked her to look at the photo.

"It's a carving in the rock of a sauropod like the metal one outside the museum."

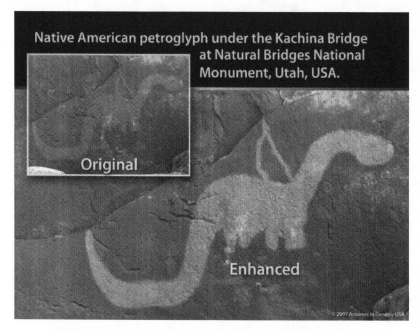

Native American petroglyph under the Kachina Bridge at Natural Bridges National Monument, Utah, USA.

Original

Enhanced

© 2007 Answers in Genesis-USA

Petroglyph (carving in stone) of Dinosaur at Kachina Bridge
Photo Credit: Answers in Genesis

"Move your finger to the next pic, Claudia."

"It's a photo of you standing next to the rock pointing up at the carving, and also one of, your wife, Emily, I guess."

"Yes, please pass my phone around, Claudia. These were taken in Utah, at Kachina Bridge, at the Natural Bridges National Monument Park. When we climbed back up to the ranger station tourist building, I asked the ranger what he thought was carved into the rock. He looked around first to make sure no one was in earshot and said 'a dinosaur, but you didn't hear that from me.'"

"That would mean," Nate analyzed, "that the American Indians who lived there at the time, perhaps a thousand years ago, carved it. That signifies they would have had to see one to carve one."

"Excellent, Nate! Good analysis. And Nate, remind me when we get to the hotel tonight to show you guys something I brought with me."

"Awe c'mon, Doc, tell us about it now," Jim insisted. "We're still twiddling our thumbs in this line." The rest of the group chimed in, wishing for me to reveal what I brought.

"Okay, I'll tell you about it now."

CHAPTER EIGHTY-EIGHT

ICA STONES

"**A**nyone familiar with the Ica stone carvings from Peru?"

"Yeah," Pete replied. "Someone in one of my geology classes mentioned it a while back. Our professor said they are nothing but a bunch of fake carvings on stones showing man and dinosaur together—a hoax to sell to tourists. There are hundreds of these things floating around."

"Well, I have brought some *replicas* with me. But did your professor mention when they were first discovered by European explorers to Peru?"

"No, nothing of discoveries," Pete replied, somewhat confused.

"I didn't think so." Turning to Tom, I asked, "Hey Tom, who conquered Peru?"

"Pizarro, in the early 1500s, looking for Inca gold. He wanted to accomplish what his distant cousin Hernán Cortés did when he conquered the Aztecs and Montezuma in Mexico."

"Shameful," Maria added.

"Tom, you know your history as well as your legal material," I praised. A brief note of sadness passed across Maria's face, as she clutched her cross.

"Thanks, Doc," he said standing a bit straighter and puffing his chest out a bit.

"Actually, the first mention of the Ica stones comes from a Jesuit priest, Father Simon, who accompanied Pizarro; some of these stones were sent back to Spain."

"Holy cow, five hundred years ago," Pete remarked with surprise.

"Tonight, when I show you my Ica stones you will see carvings of men fighting and even being devoured, Jurassic Park style, by dinosaurs; however—"

"Way cool!" Matt interrupted. "Dinosaurs chomping on people. Can't wait to see those stones tonight."

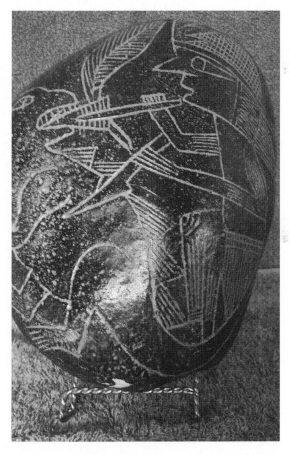

Ica Stone Dinosaur eating man. Personal Photo

"If you don't shut your piehole and listen, you'll be wearing one of Doc's stones on your noggin," Pete threatened, showing his annoyance at Matt's infantile behavior. Matt turned to Pete with a sulking pout on his face.

"However," I continued, "the engravings show circular markings on the sides of some of the dinosaurs. Until very recently even archeologists had no idea what they meant."

"I do." Andy piped up. "I've always been fascinated with dinosaurs since I was a kid. In some recent publication of *Science* or *Smithsonian* or somewhere, they had pictured fossilized dinosaur skin, which had those circular markings on it. Of course, the article said the fossilized stone imprint was millions of years old."

"And what does that tell you?" I directed the question to the class.

"That the Incas had to have seen one to carve one," Nate repeated his previous statement.

Ica Stones with circular markings on skin.

"I'm taking photos like crazy," Thad very exuberantly stated, "and I've got my mini digital voice recorder with me. I've got more material than I can handle already on this trip, and we haven't even officially entered the museum yet. Stephen, my editor-in-chief at the *Veritas Beacon*, is going to have a conniption fit with all the columns I'm planning on writing in the upcoming edition."

"Doc, why haven't we been told about any of this stuff?" Juan bemoaned. "It's always 'scientists know,' or 'it's a proven fact,' or 'what is shown to them is a fake, a hoax'; then they stoop to calling us names like flat-earthers, religious nuts, or anti-science."

"Oye hombre," Santi commiserated with his cousin. "It's miedo . . . ah . . . fear! They fear the truth, man."

Some of the other tourists and visitors in the line were listening to our conversation as we proceeded from wall display to wall display. "You are absolutely correct, young man," one gentleman addressed Santi. "Fear that their little fiefdoms, built on a pack of lies, will come crumbling down on them. Fear that they will lose their power and hold over the people. They want to be God."

"Hey Doc, this gentleman could sub for you," Fred commented as he shook the fellow's hand and patted his shoulder.

"I'm a retired chemical engineer," the fellow stated to our group. "I was an atheist for the longest time, and my wife kept bugging me to read a couple of books on creationism," he said nodding to his wife, who was standing next to him. "I told her she was just a Jesus freak and to leave me alone. Those two books collected dust, literally, on my night table."

"That's true," his wife added. "I never ever touched, nor dusted his nightstand."

"Martha prayed mightily to the Lord for me for years; right, Honey?" he asked, turning to her. Her gentle, old eyes smiled at him lovingly. "One day something came over me; I can't explain it. I walked into the bedroom and grabbed both those books; perhaps, I just wanted to get it over and done with."

"He read both of those books in two days, cover to cover," Martha affirmatively stated. "And he hasn't been the same since."

"I then proceeded to gobble up every book, technical journal, and DVD I could find on the creation-evolution controversy. Evolution doesn't have some minor flaws or shortcomings as some 'experts' have stated - it has more holes than Swiss cheese. And the holes are large enough to drive a tank through."

"You young people keep listening to your professor there," Martha gently advised the class.

"Sir, what were the names of those two books?" Thad asked, with his voice recorder pointed at the gentleman.

"*The Genesis Flood* by Morris and Whitcomb and *That Their Words May Be Used Against Them,* also by Morris."

"Hey, that's the book that was recommended to me," Fred announced loudly. "That's the one that also turned me around." Fred again shook the gentleman's hand.

"Next!" came a voice from the ticket counter.

"That's us gang." I proclaimed. We all wished the old couple well and advanced to pick up our tickets.

CHAPTER EIGHTY-NINE

ST. GEORGE AND THE DRAGON

We collected our tickets and started to walk down the passage to the main hall. Some of the kids had peeled off to have their pictures taken against a green screen with a T. rex about ready to attack. Matt was the first in line.

"We'll wait for all of you in the main hall by the mastodon skeleton," I cried out over the din of the crowd.

Pete turned to Brother Francis and me. "This millions of years deal is crumbling fast, and we haven't even officially started the tour. I have one question—"

"Now, you're only allowed one question, Pete," I jokingly interrupted him. Both Pete and Brother Francis chuckled.

"Okay . . . anyway . . . my geology professors are going to rag me about the K-T boundary. And how that Asteroid that crashed in Chicky-something Mexico is what caused the extinction event of the dinosaurs 65 million years ago."

"What's Pete talking about?" asked Brother Francis.

"Chicxulub, Mexico, where there appears to be the remnants of a very large impact crater."

"So?" Francis responded.

"Okay, both of you, this is where you really need to put your thinking caps on and parse out what is observed, provable fact, and what is assumption. So, Pete, what can we prove?"

"That a large object hit that area of Mexico and—"

"Stop! That's about all we can say with absolute certainty. Whether it was an asteroid or meteorite or comet is at least partial speculation, correct?"

"Asteroids do have iridium, which has also been proved." Pete reminded me.

"What's with this K-T boundary thing and iridium?" Brother Francis asked, still confused.

"Pete, explain about the K-T boundary for Brother Francis."

"The geologic column has numerous divisions. Two of those are the Cretaceous and Tertiary. Iridium is found between those two layers at that impact crater in Chicky . . . , Mexico." Pete said, still unable to pronounce the Aztec name.

"I thought Cretaceous was spelled with a 'C'? Why use a 'K'?" Francis asked, still confused.

"So as not to cloud the issue with the Cambrian layer, which already uses the 'C'."

"Gottcha." Francis replied. "So, when the asteroid, or whatever, impacted in Mexico, the geologists believe this is what caused the demise of the dinosaurs!?"

"You got it, Brother Francis." Then turning to me, Pete inquired, "But what about the iridium between those two layers? It is there; that is a fact!"

"You can double check with Thad, who's minoring in astronomy, but I'm almost certain that the iridium from the asteroid remained fairly local on impact. However, there is iridium between K-T layers around the world, even in areas where there are no impact craters from heavenly bodies. Want to take a guess what the source of that iridium could be, Pete?"

Pete smacked himself on the forehead, Jim style. "Matt's volcanoes, hundreds of them."

"Matt's volcanoes? What are you two talking about?" Francis asked looking at both of us as if we had screws loose.

"Matt, our real estate mogul, is going to buy waterfront property in Nevada before a series of undersea volcanic eruptions trigger the tectonic plates to cause the big one to hit California, and . . . you had to be in the class at the time," I said. Francis just shook his head. "It was funnier then, trust me," I added.

Pete, half ignoring Francis, was still thinking. "That's it! Volcanoes release iridium, and the fact that iridium is found worldwide, at the K-T boundary, more than likely coincides with the rupture of the fountains of the deep, which also triggered massive volcanic eruptions around the globe."

"Excellent, Pete! You nailed it." Pete then turned toward Brother Francis, who gave him a high five.

"I always felt that asteroid theory didn't make much sense. How could it have eliminated *just* the dinosaurs? And if it did happen, then the birds couldn't have evolved—using evolutionary logic," Pete stated, now with a strut to his step.

"To be fair, it's not the only evolutionary theory for the extinction of the dinosaurs. Some evolutionists think other animals ate their eggs or they developed cataract blindness or even died from constipation." Pete and Francis gave me weird looks. "Really, guys, those are some of the loony, unsupported theories from the evolutionists themselves."

"So how *did* the dinosaurs eventually die off? They were obviously around for hundreds of years after the Flood, and were able to populate well enough to migrate to different parts of the world from Mount Ararat—as distant as China and the Americas." Brother Francis asked.

Jim, our ecology major, walked up beside us. "Good timing, Jim. Why don't you tell Pete and Brother Francis what causes species extinction."

"Well first off, about one to two hundred species a day currently go extinct. There are multiple rationales for this. Among which is a radical change in climate where their habitats are, decrease of food supply, diseases, and, of course, predation—many times by man."

"And if an animal, like a fox raiding the chicken coop, becomes a pest or a nuisance, Jim?"

"Man, generally will exterminate that animal. Or if the animal is very large, like a bear, someone will want to be the hero and kill it."

"Like St. George and the Dragon to save the fair maiden?" Francis immediately added.

"Huh?" Jim quizzically asked.

"Thank you, Jim. You just explained to Pete and Brother Francis how the dinosaurs became extinct."

"I did?" Jim was totally befuddled, looking awkwardly at us, as we broke up laughing.

CHAPTER NINETY

THE RELATIVES

Finally, the rest of the troupe arrived in the main hall, all having had their pictures taken with the T. Rex; Tom was last as usual.

"Wow! That's one huge mammoth," stated Juan looking up at the impressive skeleton of the beast. "Where did they dig that up?"

"Oh, from a golf course in Ohio," I mentioned nonchalantly.

"Seriously? You're putting us on, right, Doc?" Tom asked with skepticism.

"Seriously!" I answered. "It was discovered in 1989 while the golf course was being excavated to put in a pond. It's a mastodon replica not a mammoth, by the way."

"How can you tell?" Nate inquired. "They both look the same to me."

"One way is by the teeth," I said while bringing up both sets of teeth on my tablet.

"Any of you, ever had any orthodontic work done?" I asked emphasizing the syllable '*don.*'.

"I had to have my teeth straightened," Claudia admitted, raising her hand. "Those braces made me feel very self-conscious as a teen."

"I'm sure they would at that age, Claudia," I empathized. Then I addressed all the ladies. "I'm sure you gals are familiar with a condition in women called mastitis." They all acknowledged me by nodding their heads.

The entire group was silent for a few seconds. Then Maggie started to giggle. "I can't put it properly . . . but I get it - 'mast' for mastitis in women and 'don' for teeth. Please let me see the teeth pics you have on your tablet, Doc."

I hand the tablet to her. "Oh yeah, it's a no-brainer to see which are the mast-odon teeth," she said, giggling again as she passed the tablet around to the others.

Mastodon Teeth. Photo Credit: Shutterstock

Mammoth Teeth. Photo Credit: Shutterstock

Everyone is having their chuckles as they see the obvious difference between the mastodon teeth and the mammoth teeth; Brother Francis turned red.

With the tablet in his hand, a confused Santi turned to his cousin, Juan, and admitted, "Yo no lo entiendo."

"Santi! Dios mio!" Juan said, cupping his hands at the sides of his chest, and then pointing to the mastodon teeth picture on the tablet.

"Oh, lo siento, I get it now: chichis . . . ah . . . breasts," he said hanging his head down.

Brother Francis approached Santi and put an arm around his shoulder. "It took me by surprise also, Santi. No te preocupes . . . don't you worry." Francis spoke to Santi in his native tongue and translated for the rest of us. Brother Francis has a heart as big as his smile.

"I guess we're all ready now to start the basic tour. This will give you a good overview of Earth history. And if we have any time left today before the museum closes, we can visit the Dragon Hall Bookstore and/or Noah's Café before we get back on the bus," I explained pointing toward where the entrances are to the bookstore and the café off the main hall.

Thad and others were taking some final shots of the mastodon skeleton as we started the tour. Matt was marveling at the animatronic dinosaurs in the main hall.

Mastodon Skeleton. Photo Credit: Creation Museum.org

As we reached the Garden of Eden displays, which also had animatronic dinosaurs in them, the questions and confusion started again.

"Dinosaurs in the Garden of Eden? That's not in the Bible."

"They would have attacked and eaten Adam and Eve. I don't get it!"

"How do we know if they were even real people?"

"And neither did I realize dinosaurs were in Eden." I responded firmly. "I was over forty years old before I became aware that something didn't jive properly with evolution and the millions of years. And what about that retired chemical engineer we met. He was probably in his late sixties before catching on. And Fred here was older that all of you—and Cindy also, perhaps." I didn't want to get into a tussle regarding a woman's age.

"And what about me?" Francis inserted himself. "I'm just getting rolling on this, but already I see how farcical and damnable the whole concept is to society. The small amount of research I was able to do prior to this trip has opened my eyes. The church, as a whole, has in essence abandoned Genesis and willingly handed it over to the secular, atheistic community, which is leading Christianity down the path to its own destruction."

"Looks as if you've got a mini-mutiny on your hands, Doc." Fred remarked as he heard the objections from the students.

"You're right, Fred. I'm taking them too fast through this. They are not mentally prepared yet. Those comparisons I made using myself, you, and others was stupid. Brother Francis made the only intelligent statement."

Maria and Maggie, who had been doing much extracurricular research, came up to me knowing the quandary I was in. "Why don't you show the students their 'ancestors'; of whom our government schools have indoctrinated them," Maria calmly and quietly suggested, flashing her soft doe-like brown eyes.

"Yeah, Doc," Maggie added, displaying passion in her fierce blue-gray eyes. "You need to stick it in their faces to wake them up to the truth."

"You both are right about this. I totally agree. Thanks."

"Okay, so what are you planning on?" Fred asked, still not in sync.

"Just watch and follow my lead, Fred." The two girls smiled at us.

"Okay everyone, we'll come back to this display later. I'm going to take you to meet your relatives."

"I know my relatives, Doc. Who are you talking about?" Tom asked.

"Yeah, I also know my in-laws; bunch of outlaws is what they are." Matt commented.

CHAPTER NINETY-ONE

LUCY IN THE SKY
WITH DIAMONDS

We approached a large freestanding glass case. Inside was an excellent designed model of a three-foot ape.

"*This* is your most primitive hominid ancestor from 2.5 million years ago, dug up in Ethiopia in 1974," I forcefully proclaimed, pointing at the encased figure.

Matt and Tom were hovering about the glass case, oohing and aahing.

Nate and Jim were looking at each other after curiously watching Matt and Tom. Nate disdainfully remarked to Matt and Tom, "Maybe you guy's relatives were apes, but mine weren't."

"Yeah," Jim tagged onto Nate, "my relatives didn't marry no ape."

Juan was jumping around Matt and Tom like a chimpanzee, arms stretched out with his hands under his armpits, making monkey sounds. The rest of the class was laughing, hooting, and hollering along with Juan. I couldn't help but chuckle some myself.

"Listen, you guys are on security cameras in this museum. You wouldn't want a copy of this leaked to your friends now, would you?" I inquired as some other museum patrons passed by, amused by my students antics as well.

A few moments later the group quieted down.

"Donald Johanson discovered the skeleton. It's hanging on the back wall of the case, behind the ape. At best, only 40 percent of the bones were found. It was named 'Lucy.' Does anyone know how they arrived at that name?"

"Wasn't the Beatles song, 'Lucy in the Sky with Diamonds' playing at the time his team discovered the skeletal remains?" Pete injected.

"That's correct, Pete," I acknowledged as a confident smile appeared on his face.

"Now Pete, this is a very good replica of the original skeleton. All of you, on your tablets, why don't you bring up model re-creations of Lucy from some of the museums around the world?"

Several of the students punched up my request.

"Notice anything model to model, museum to museum?"

"No two models are alike," Pete replied. "However, all the museums, except the one we are in, portray Lucy as some half-human–half-ape transition."

"Good. Anyone notice anything else from the other museums' Lucy models?"

Some of the students compared notes of the various photos with one another.

"All their models have human hands and feet, which means she was a human," Matt observed, giving us that big used-car salesman smile of his.

"Would you all mind looking at the skeletal remains on the back wall of the case?"

"There are no hand or feet bones," Nate practically hollered out. "What a rip-off!"

"The model in this glass case," Philip commented, "is presented as a fully designed ape with curved fingers and toes. So, how does *this* museum come to that conclusion, since the original skeleton didn't have any hand or feet bones, as Nate detected?"

Lucy ape exhibit in plastic case. Photo Credit: Creation Museum

"Good thinking, Philip. Subsequent discoveries of skeletal remains of this animal *have* possessed curved finger and toe bones and locking wrist joints consistent with apes," I commented. "This supposed hominid has been given the Latin name of *Australopithecus afarensis*, which means southern ape by the way."

"Was she a Confederate?" Fred asked, evoking some sparse chuckles; Cindy gave him a friendly elbow to the ribs.

Jim was waving his hand, and I could tell his temper was starting to flare. "I'm looking at the St. Louis Museum depiction of this creature and she is in contemplation, with her hand under her chin, thinking of . . . of . . . Einstein or somebody. Her brown eyes are staring pensively into space. What a crock of—" Jim stopped mid-sentence, his lips pursed into angered frustration.

"Speaking of eyes, why don't we move around to the rear of the glass case and take a look at several facial illustrations that have been drawn of Lucy."

"Again, no two faces are alike," noted Thad somewhat bewildered.

"Okay, who are the CSI experts in the group?" Most hands go up, confirming the popularity of the former TV series.

Lucy St. Louis Museum standing model. Photo Credit: slideshare.net

"For the moment, forget the millions of years thing. Suppose a hiker in the woods comes upon a modern human skeleton under some brush. There are no organic remains other than the perfectly clean complete skeleton itself, which appears to be in several pieces with animal bite marks on a number of the bones and some extremely deteriorated clothing remnants, as well as a rusty knife still embedded in the remains. It's probably been many years since the murder. Who is the victim?"

Tom immediately responds. "CSI would obtain bone samples for DNA testing to determine the identification of the John Doe."

"Fine, Tom. The DNA confirms the identity of the person to be . . . John Doe. What does John Doe look like? And let's assume the FBI has no facial recognition photos to match the DNA."

Tom just stared at me.

"C'mon, Tom, can't you just have a police artist hustle up a sketch of the victim, complete with eye shape and color, contour of the nose, hair texture and color, all based on just the skull? What was the shade and color of his skin? What about the ears? Bushy eyebrows perhaps? Maybe the victim had a beard or a dimple in his chin or a tattoo on his face."

I directed my gaze at Thad, who wished to answer. "Thad?"

"They can't produce *any* likeness whatsoever of the victim. Which means all these ape-men they draw, from decayed bones, must come solely from their imagination—to brainwash us into believing this rotgut." He proceeded to take pictures of the various versions of Lucy's face in the glass case.

"And Thad," I added, "you may want to take a few close ups of the cranial remains, what little there is of them."

"What a bunch of B.S." Thad mumbled.

Multiple Lucy facial images in case. Photo Credit: Creation Museum

"But it's even more sinister than that, Thad. Maggie, tell the group about the eyes." I knew she had the answer, as she had been giving me a knowing smile all along, ever since I first mentioned the eyes.

A number of museum visitors had been crowding around us, while I gave my little dissertation on Lucy. They were all listening with rapt attention, waiting for Maggie's explanation on the eyes.

"The whites of the eyes, the sclera as they're called, are found only in the human primate. If you want to draw an ape and really make it look human, you'll color the sclera white. Neat little psychological trick, huh?"

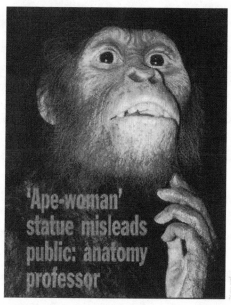

Lucy close up face. Photo Credit: yecheadquarters.org

"That's right!" exclaimed Matt. "Even those *Planet of the Apes* movies have all those chimps with white sclera, to make them appear more humanlike. Sucked us all right in, man."

"Doc, what about the FOXP2 gene that one of my professors has mentioned?" Jim asks. "They call it the 'language gene' and it's found in chimps and gorillas."

"And it's also found in mice and zebra fish, Jim. Language has been found to be much more complex than being relied upon by just one gene. After decades of working with apes such as Koko and

Kanzi, they still can't speak. If those same teams were to have worked with you for decades, you'd be speaking, writing, and singing in sixteen different languages. Think about it!"

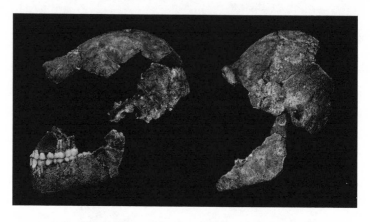

Homo Naledi Skull Fragments supposedly up to 2 million years old.
Photo Credit – Sciencenews.org

Artist's Conception of Homo Naledi
Image Credit – LosAndes.ar

With that, the entire crowd was abuzz, alarmed at the depth to which the evolutionists had stooped to convince the public that we evolved from apes.

"Young lady," one of the visitors, a bespectacled middle-aged woman, addressed Maggie, "how do we know for sure that Lucy was female?"

"We don't!" Maggie replied to the woman. "It's just another fabrication to give that extinct chimpanzee a more humanlike quality. Besides it was based on the Beatles song. What if Bobby Darin's 'Mack the Knife' was being played?"

CHAPTER NINETY-TWO

MARCH OF PROGRESS

A number of the museum visitors thanked Maggie and me for clarifying some of these ambiguous ape-man points that the media and the government school system had rammed down our throats.

"Where does Neanderthal fit into this picture?" Asked one very thin gentleman.

"The first of many Neanderthal fossil fragments was found in the Neander Valley in Germany, around 1860. The atheists were drooling with this find. Darwin's book *On the Origin of Species* had just recently been released."

"Why was that book so important to the Atheists," asked the gentleman.

"Well, it quickly became the atheists' bible. If it could be proven that humankind evolved from the lower animals, then God, the Bible, Adam and Eve, and creationism were dead. Without God, there is no supreme being to be answerable to. Truth, and right and wrong, become relative."

"Gosh, I never made that connection," he stated reflectively. "So what was discovered about Neanderthal? Wasn't he kinda stooped and hunched over like a gorilla?"

Many of these visitors were hungry for the truth. I could tell just by the look in their eyes.

"Dr. Rudolph Virchow, the famous pathologist and anatomist, was one of the first to discount the claim that Neanderthal was some sort of sub-human ancestor to man. He pointed out early on that the bones showed pathologic deformities, in many cases simply rickets, which is a lack of vitamin D. It wasn't until over a hundred years later that Virchow was vindicated."

The same pleasant woman who asked Maggie how they knew Lucy was a female, presented a question to me. "I always read, or hear on the radio or TV, of scientists finding some bones proving apes evolved to man. Do they ever find bones proving something evolved to the apes?"

I couldn't help but to laugh, and then I apologized to the poor woman. "Ma'am, I'm sorry. I'm not laughing at you. I'm going to ask one of my students to answer that one for you. Thad?"

Thad chuckled a bit also. "Ma'am, there ain't no research money for finding ape bones. That's why any scrap of bone they find, they claim it's on its way to becoming human."

"Well, my Lord, I see your point, young man. It's all about the money."

"Hey, Doc," Thad called out. "Has this lady been taking your course online?" The rest of my students chuckled at that.

Thad turned back to the woman. "Lady, it's even worse than that."

"How so, son?"

"The money leads to power and control. Destroy the concept of God, and what do you have left?"

"Nothing, I guess."

"Well, nature hates a vacuum, and without the Judeo-Christian God, anything goes."

"Yes, I see. Like all of this lawlessness and government corruption and Hollywood filth? I understand where this all leads now. No God means no heaven or hell, no reward or punishment. Therefore, when you die," she continued in a very stern almost angry fashion, "you go to nothing. So why *not* behave like a pagan, a liar and a thief."

"You got it, ma'am."

"Thank you, young man. I have never in all my years heard a young person speak as you just did. Where on God's green earth did you learn all this?"

"From him," almost my entire class answered in unison as they pointed at me.

"Hey, Professor," called a fellow with a large handlebar mustache who was standing in the back of the large crowd that had gathered. "What about the March of Progress line you see everywhere of an ape evolving to a human? You can't ignore that!"

"Jim, do me a favor and look up *Bernard Wood: Human Evolution Icon Illusion,* and then please read it aloud for everyone, including for that gentleman at the back."

"Sure, Doc. I'll let you know when I got it."

"While Jim is bringing up this statement from Professor Wood, let me give you a bit of his background. He is an M.D. and PhD. A paleoanthropologist who was teaching human origins at George Washington University, and had himself, studied under the famous Richard Leaky. Dr. Wood is an evolutionist, but an honest one. I see Jim is ready now."

Jim cleared his throat. "'There is a popular image of human evolution that you'll find all over the place. . . . On the left of the picture there's an ape . . . on the right, a man . . . between the two is a succession of figures that become ever more like humans. . . . Our progress from ape to human looks so tidy. It's such a beguiling image that even the experts are loath to let it go. But it is an illusion.'"

"And where did he make that statement, Jim?"

"In *New Scientist.* His article 'Who are we?' published October 26, 2002."

"Are you saying that this guy still continues to believe in and teach this stuff anyway?" the gentleman with the handlebar mustache queried.

"Believe it or not, yes." I said, as the fellow shook his head in profound disbelief.

Matt raised his hand. "Yes, Matt?"

"Here's one phony ape-man discovery I found that I think everyone will really enjoy."

"Okay, but it needs to be the last one. We are causing a bottleneck in this room, and we need to move on."

"In 1922, a discovery of a single tooth was made in Nebraska," Matt said, trying to sound very professorial like. "The tooth was shown to Dr. Henry Fairfield Osborn, professor at Columbia University—"

"Sounds like a real hoity-toity stuffed shirt to me." Some overweight visitor with colorful suspenders commented, cutting Matt off.

"As I was saying," Matt continued. "It was determined the creature was halfway between ape and human. Osborn and staff weren't sure if Hesperopithecus, as they named it, was an ape-like man or a man-like ape."

The crowd laughed at that one, although I believed Matt was trying to be serious.

"Anyway, in 1922, the *Illustrated London News* published a full-page layout of a drawing of Nebraska man, his wife, his kid, the tools he used, and a panorama of where they lived. It was complete with animals and a seething volcano—in Nebraska!"

The crowd howled with laughter. "All this from one tooth?" The guy with the suspenders screamed back at Matt.

"A few years later, they discovered other bones from the creature, and it turned out to be a pig. It was actually a pig's tooth," Matt said looking up from his iPad at the crowd.

"Oye, hombre," Santi said, tapping Matt on the shoulder. "It looks like the pig made a monkey out of the evolutionist."

With that, the crowd of visitors, as well as my group, doubled over in hysterics. The heavy-set fellow popped the snap on one of his suspenders, he was laughing so hard.

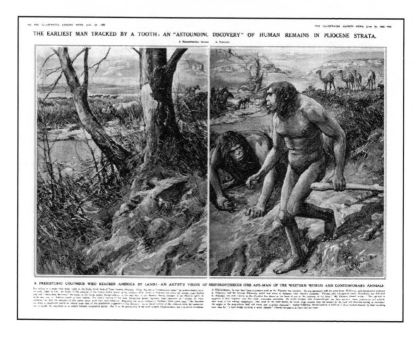

Illustrated London News Nebraska man. Photo Credit: Historic Images

CHAPTER NINETY-THREE

HALDANE'S DILEMMA

We moved on through a few other sections of the museum. The students were more self-motivated to study the displays and read the explanations on their own. They also seemed to be using their tablets more often to enhance what they were learning, sharing information with each other as they went.

Ready to take a break, our troupe found itself outside in the garden. The weather was spectacular and the colorful garden paths, lined with festive fall foliage, invited us to explore every nook and cranny. The students were very talkative as they compared notes.

The girls found a great spot where we could all sit by one of the idyllic ponds.

"Hey, Doc," Matt asked, squirming trying to get comfortable on the ground. "I need to be able to answer my friends who say that we must have evolved from chimps because our DNA is 98 percent the same."

Nate's hand went up in a flash. "From what I have been finding out in the museum and online, the whole thing is a bad joke. And I have the stats on this."

"Okay, Nate give us your findings," I responded.

"Many of the studies were carried out on *selected* genes only, like the cytochrome C protein," Nate said with a smirky smile.

"Whoa! Whoa!" Jim interjected, getting riled up. "Are you saying that these scientists didn't study and evaluate the *entire* genome?"

"That's right, Jim. They studied only a tiny fraction of our roughly 3 billion DNA base pairs that comprise our genetic blueprint. Slick, huh?"

"Hey, that's not fair," Matt added. "That's . . . it's . . . cheating!"

I got my chance now. "Matt, and who are you to say these scientists are wrong? It's the truth in their eyes."

"Besides," Thad joined in, "they don't get the research bucks if they don't *prove* humans came from monkeys. Isn't that what the Matrix wants?"

"In reality," Nate continued, "the latest studies show we are down to around 81 percent similarity, but the lapdog media isn't reporting those statistics."

"Why even 81 percent, Nate?" Juan asked.

"If everything evolved from blind chance, all life should be one big jumble of different organisms. But if you have a common designer, one would expect some continuity."

"Kind of like being able to spot a Renoir or Monet," Claudia piped up, excitedly. "A trained art expert, or forger even, knows what to look for in terms of brush stroke, use of color and shadow, composition, paint, etcetera."

"That's an excellent analogy, Claudia. What was the Grand Designer's signature or trademark? What is the common thread that weaves through all of life?"

"DNA, obviously," Maria decidedly rejoined.

"Now if Jude were here, I'm sure he'd say something to the effect of 'given enough time, monkey can become man,'" I said, looking at Nate, our statistician.

"I'm ready for you, Doc. I did some research while we were still in the museum."

"What did your calculations show, Nate?"

"To date, there are about 125 million DNA differences between man and monkey. The evolutionists claim that chimps have been around about 6 million years or so. That means that there would have to be 40 million separate mutation events—gene substitutions, insertions and deletions—that would have had to occur to have a chimp turn into a man."

"The bottom line, Nate?"

"It ain't gonna happen. Again, not enough time, even if there *were* millions of years. A staggering number of mutations versus a relatively small number of generations, and you have a problem known as Haldane's dilemma. Most of those stats came from one of the books in the museum. I can't take all the credit."

Andy raised his hand. "Doc, most of us are now convinced that we didn't evolve from apes. Okay, that leaves God who had to create us, which started with Adam and Eve . . . I guess." Andy was hesitant to ask what he wanted.

"Go ahead Andy, what exactly is your question?"

"Well . . . a . . . what color were Adam and Eve?" He asked somewhat embarrassed. "The movies always seem to portray them as white with blond hair and blue eyes."

"That's right!" Ali adamantly retorted. "It's all white racism to put down the black man. A white Jesus, white Santa Claus, white Easter Bunny."

Some started to laugh at the Easter Bunny comment, but they stifled it immediately when Ali's eyes, burning with hatred, stared them down.

"What do you believe, Ali?" I asked him as gently as I could.

Ali slowly stood up and took a threatening posture. "This white Adam and Eve thing is racist propaganda. Africa is supposed to be the cradle of civilization - the bones of prehistoric man are always found there. And all of you were taught that, too," he said, pointing directly at Claudia, and then swinging his arm around willfully casting an accusatory aim at each one of us.

The color drained from Claudia's face. She would have fainted if she hadn't already been seated. The rest of the group was visually unnerved and shaken.

CHAPTER NINETY-FOUR

THE HUMAN ZOO

"If Adam and Eve existed at all, they were *black* and came out of Africa," shouted Ali still agitated, pointing his finger at us.

"Actually, Ali, you are partly correct," I conceded, trying to get him to simmer down.

"What are you saying, that Adam was black?"

"No, Ali, Adam was not black; but I'm agreeing with you regarding the white racism."

"Explain this to me," he stated firmly, but still refusing to sit down.

"Yeah, me too."

"And me."

"I've got to hear this."

A number of the students expressed their curiosity with my comment.

"Ali, I'd like you to bring up a statement, by Doctor Stephen J. Gould of Harvard University, regarding racism."

After a few moments, Ali stated, "This guy was a heavy hitter. He was a paleontologist, evolutionary biologist, and won the Phi Beta Kappa Award in Science—twice!"

"And his statement, Ali?"

"Ah, yeah," he exclaimed, looking back again at his tablet. "'Biological arguments for racism may have been common before

1859, but they increased by orders of magnitude following the acceptance of evolutionary theory.'"

"What's so significant about 1859," Juan asked of no one in particular.

"That was the year Darwin published his book, the *Origin of Species*," Jim remarked.

"What does Gould's statement have to do with Darwin, racism, and Adam and Eve?" Ali demanded of me.

"Okay, Ali, and all of you for that matter, let's look at this, starting with Africa, the supposed 'cradle of civilization,' where racism became hyperbolic."

"Man, how can the fossil bones of hominid black men be racist? I've seen the pics on the cover of like *Time* and *Nat Geo* and such, showing that the first men had to be black," Ali said proudly and arrogantly.

Time Magazine how man became man. Photo Credit: Time Magazine

"Ali, seeing that you still believe in the evolution of man, and assuming you are correct that humankind first evolved out of Africa millions of years ago, what was the next color to evolve upward and onward?"

"Huh? What? Evolve upward? What are you trying to say to me?"

"If the black man was first to evolve from the apes, then what color was next to evolve? That should be simple enough. Was it brown, then yellow, then white?" Ali's eyes widened as he realized the predicament he had put himself in. "Then the top of the heap is the Aryan race!" I snapped my heels together and cracked a Nazi salute to Ali and the class, "Sieg Heil!"

"I . . . uh . . ." Ali stammered, looking at me with my arm still extended in the Nazi greeting, as he tried to come out with anything coherent.

"That puts the blacks at the bottom of the totem pole, just above the apes," Maria commented, "and the Aryans at the top."

A deflated Ali turned toward Maria. "I . . . I . . . had no idea. I never thought of evolution that way."

"The Scopes Monkey Trial of 1925, which really was a spectacle or carnival to put Christianity on trial, had John T. Scopes on the stand for teaching evolution. The biology textbook he used, *A Civic Biology* by George Hunter, presented the races of man in a very condescending fashion," I explained to the group.

"Yeah," Maggie joined the fray, "Maria and I had read about this a few days ago. Dr. Mercurio had given us some suggested reading to prepare ourselves for the Creation Museum trip. That Scopes biology text presented the five races of man. The Negro and the Australian Aborigine were the most primitive; then the brown race of the Pacific Islanders, the American Indian or Redman, and then the Mongoloid race of China, Japan, and the Eskimos were next; and finally, the Caucasians were the highest. Hitler took it one final step to the Aryan race. And by the way, Doctor Henry Fairfield Osborn was at that trial with his 'pig's' tooth."

AUSTRALOID

NEGROID

MONGOLOID

EVOLUTIONARY ANCESTOR

CAUCASOID

RACES

© 2006 Answers in Genesis

Evolutionary ancestor and races. Photo Illustration: Answers in Genesis

"I see," Ali exhaled totally dejected. He plopped down on the grass, his head hanging down on his chest.

"There is only one race – homo sapiens," Philip remarked from the back of the pack. "There are many varieties in color, shape, and size, from tall Watusi to short Pygmy to heavy Sumo Samoan wrestlers to beefy Neanderthals. We all can reproduce with one another. This has been proven by fruitful inter-marriage and genetic confirmation over and over again."

"Maggie," Jim called out looking at her. "The Bible speaks of giants like Goliath who fought David. Were they real?" he asked.

"My history professor," Tom interrupted, "told us that the Roman Emperor Maximinus Thrax was eight feet six inches tall. Obviously, some really tall genes were floating around."

"And for that matter," Maria added. "Goliath was not that much taller than that Roman Emperor. Goliath was over six cubits, which is almost ten feet in height."

"Hey, Philip," Nate called out. "Did you know that Neanderthal actually had a larger cranial capacity than so-called modern man?"

"Yes, I did, but cranial capacity does not necessarily equate with intelligence. If it did, the sperm whale with its eighteen-pound brain would be smarter than humans with our three-pound brains."

"Does brain size correlate with . . . a . . . certain organ size . . . you know?" asked Tom, as he threw a stone into the pond.

"I think we'll leave that discussion for another time," I said, to some mixed guffaws and chuckles.

Maria swiveled to face Ali who was sitting diagonally in front of her. Sweetly, she said to him, "Because of evolutionary racism, a pygmy by the name of Ota Benga, was purchased from African slave traders and placed in the monkey house at the Bronx Zoo, in 1904, as an example of human evolution."

poignant and wild recital of greed, exploitation and social Darwinism in turn-of-the-century America."
—Chicago Tribune

Ota Benga with chimp. Photo Credit: Historic Images

He immediately looked up at her with disbelief. "No . . . no . . . how could they? What happened to him?"

CHAPTER NINETY-FIVE

FRESCOES

"He eventually committed suicide," Maggie replied, holding back her anger. "That's what evolution did to him." She sat stewing for a moment then continued. "Ever hear of Jessie Owens, Ali?"

"Yeah, wasn't he an Olympic gold medalist?"

"How about four of them," Maggie exclaimed. "In the 1936 Munich Olympics, Herr Hitler was showboating with his Aryan Supermen. Owens cleaned their clocks, four times over."

"What did Hitler say about a black man *then*, after winning four golds?" Ali asked eagerly.

"It is reported that his excuse for his Aryans losing was that 'they were racing against an animal.' He then stormed out of the stadium." Maggie proclaimed, putting her hands on her hips.

"How about we start heading back to the bus," I noted. "We have all day tomorrow for you people to continue your museum exploration. And tomorrow will be an open day. You can check out whatever you want at your own pace, and with whomever you wish to tag along with."

As we walked away from the beautiful garden setting, Matt and Tom were really horsing around and both wound up in the pond. Both fellows got somewhat stuck in the mud and were having a difficult time extracting themselves from the water.

Maggie called out to the group, "Next on our guided tour we have an example of evolution gone awry. The pond scum seems to have evolved into a mutated human form," she exclaimed casually, using her arm to point at the two soggy, mud-covered, struggling guys. The group stopped, turned, and began laughing to beat the band at Tom and Matt.

The boys were slowly making their way behind us - totally wet, muck-soaked, and shivering a bit; the sun was low on the horizon. Thad had an idea. He quickly turned and took some photos of Tom and Matt.

"What's the meaning of that, Thad? Blackmail?" Matt interrogated resentfully.

"Just a few more pics; already have some of you two sloshing about in the pond. Our Matrix–approved Biology texts claim we evolved from our cousins the earthworms, and we're all equal to them; nothing special about humans. So, I figured maybe I could make a few bucks, and sell your pics to the textbook publisher to have them put you in their next edition."

"Great idea, Thad!" Nate agreed with him, slapping him on the shoulder. "How about on the front page of the school paper also?"

Matt and Tom gave both Nate and Thad some dirty looks— literally.

On the way back to the hotel, Brother Francis had our sludge-soaked rats sit on the floor in the aisle of the bus. "And after dinner, you two can help me clean up the mud on the steps and floor of the coach, which you tracked in," he firmly told them.

***

Dinner was uneventful with most everyone getting updated on the terrorist attacks by sporadically watching the news on the big screen TVs. Brother Francis took the two boys out afterward to clean the Prevost.

"We'll catch up with you guys in the hotel lounge when we're finished," Francis called out to us as they left the building.

The rest of our group retired to an intimate and very comfortable lounge, which had a gas fireplace lit at the far end. Bookshelves holding some knickknacks and unimpressive literature were along a couple of the walls. There was also a large wall-mounted TV above the fireplace with Insta-screen capability, that was off for the moment. We boldly rearranged the sofas, love seats, and lounge furniture to suit our needs.

It seemed there was much discussion on our way back to the hotel from the Creation Museum regarding Adam and Eve. Mostly everyone agreed that man didn't evolve from the lower animals and apes. But the main questions were - What color were Adam and Eve? And where did all the different people groups arise from if not from Africa, the 'cradle of civilization,' as we had been taught to believe? Even Santa Claus and the Easter Bunny were in the mix again, thanks to Ali.

"I guess we're all here now. Brother Francis, Tom, and Matt will be showing up shortly. Okay, let's address the burning question of why the Easter Bunny is white."

That got me a load of hisses and boos from the group.

"Actually, I think we'll leave that till later. Santa is easy. St. Nicholas was a bishop in Turkey who gave presents out at Christmastime. Being Middle Eastern he was probably mid-brown. The Germanic peoples, the Dutch, and the Brits seemed to co-opt the concept early on, and they dubbed him Caucasian since that was their primary shade of color. Easy enough?"

"What about the white Jesus thing?" Ali asked, still pushing the race card.

"There is absolutely no physical description of Christ in the Bible. Since he was born in what is now modern-day Israel, he too, was Middle Eastern and probably brown. But let me ask you, Ali, which location, shortly after Christ, became the center of Christianity?"

"Rome," he replied curtly, with an attitude.

"And again, what color are most Europeans?"

"White. But that's not fair, they are not being equal and tolerant."

"Well, Ali, I guess you'll just have to run around Europe and repaint and replaster all the paintings, murals, and frescoes in all the museums and churches. That's life, deal with it."

He sat down in a huff, half mumbling something about 'they're *all* coming down, if we have our way.' I dropped the debate as I saw Brother Francis, Matt, and Tom enter the room.

CHAPTER NINETY-SIX

PUNNETT SQUARE

Nate started the discussion. "Okay, now that we're all here, we want to know what color Adam and Eve were. There is no consensus, as I've taken a poll of everyone during dinner."

"Actually, it is quite easy," I addressed the group. "I'm sure most of you remember doing your Mendelian genetic crosses on the Punnett square in high school biology."

"Sorta."

"Kinda."

I got half-baked replies from all directions. "We'll give you a quick refresher." That seemed to allay their fears some.

"Genes come in pairs as you may recall. And you get half of each pair from each of your parents. Likewise, when you go to reproduce, you personally will contribute only *half* those genes to your offspring, which are present in *your* gametes, or sex cells of the egg or sperm."

"So, each sperm or egg contains only half that number?" Juan asked.

"That's correct, Juan. Therefore, when sperm meets egg, the new organism-to-be is back to its full paired complement."

"Using your Gregor Mendel's pea plant experiments," I continued, "if you recall from high school, let's cross mommy tall pea plant (TT) with daddy tall pea plant (TT)." I turned on the TV, and activated the Insta-Screen to coordinate with my tablet, on which I was drawing a Punnett square using my stylus.

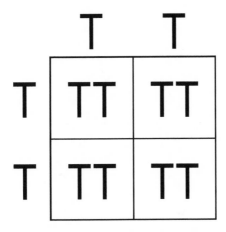

Punnett Square TT X TT

"All 100 percent of the offspring will be tall (TT). Or if both parent pea plants are short (SS), same result will be 100 percent of the offspring being short (SS)."

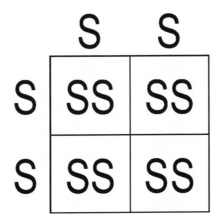

Punnett Square SS X SS

"What happens with medium-size pea parent plants?" Juan asked.

I drew on my tablet (TS), which transferred to the Insta-Screen. "This will represent medium height pea parent plants. Let's see what happens with the offspring."

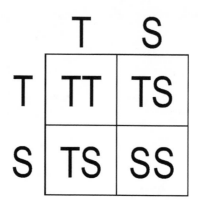

Punnett Square TS X TS

"Whoa! 25 percent tall (TT) offspring kids and 25 percent short (SS) offspring, but 50 percent medium height (TS) like their parents," stated Juan, pointing at the Punnett square boxes on the TV.

"Now in reality, one gene doesn't necessarily translate to one trait, and you can have many variations called alleles. There are several alleles in humans which control for color, but to keep things simple we'll just stick to just one, okay?"

"Fine by me," Juan stated, happy to keep it basic.

"Me, too," added Tom. "And me, three," Matt piggybacked immediately.

"Alright, based on what you just learned, what happens when a Caucasian male (WW) marries a Caucasian female (WW)?" I asked as I drew up the Punnett square which appeared on the TV.

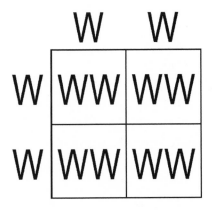

Punnett Square – WW X WW

"One hundred percent of the kids will be white." Juan pointed at the TV again.

"And if a black person (BB) marries a black person (BB)?" I asked.

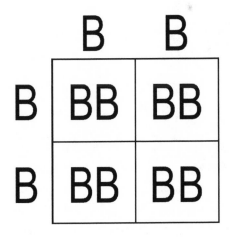

Punnett Square BB X BB

"One hundred percent of the children will be black," Ali now joined in. "That's obvious."

"So, tell me, could Adam and Eve have been either both white or both black?"

A resounding *no* echoed from everyone present, including Ali. Suddenly there were murmurs oscillating about the group. Finally, Maria boldly spoke up.

"Adam and Eve both had to be brown! May I have your pad and stylus, Dr. Lucci?"

I handed them to Maria, and she began drawing her conclusions as she spoke. "Brown will be represented by BW or WB, same thing. Adam was brown (BW) and so was Eve (BW)."

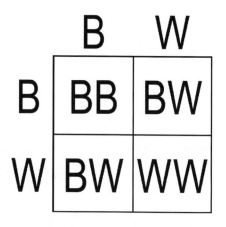

Punnett Square BW X BW

"Bingo!" screamed Juan. "Twenty-five percent of their offspring were white (WW), and 25 percent were black (BB), and 50 percent shades of brown (BW). All in one generation to boot."

"That's right!" exclaimed Tom. "Oh wow, take the nation of India. Most are brown, but then look at former South Carolina governor Nikki Haley (Nimrata Randhawa). Both her parents were Indian, and she's white. And the Tamil Hindu in India tend to be dark, similar to Bobby Jindal (Piyush Jindal), the former governor of Louisiana."

The entire group started cross-chattering about different ethnic and people groups around the world, having all descended from Adam and Eve.

Black and white twins
Born a minute apart, the two little sisters who strangers can't believe came from the same mum

Twin sisters Remee and Kian whose parents are both mid-brown
Photo Credit - dailymail.co.uk

"The Roman-Jewish historian Josephus claimed Adam and Eve had thirty-three sons and twenty-three daughters. Talk about a rainbow assortment of offspring," I mentioned offhandedly. "And does anyone happen to know what the predominant color of 50 percent of the world's population is even today?"

Santi raised his hand. "Mira, it is brown," he said smiling at us. "I can read and calculate percentages on the screen, and with those additional alleles that you mentioned, that puts that arrogant Aryan Erik very much in the minoría."

Most of the fellows in the room started laughing and making fun of Erik, mimicking Nazi salutes and Hitlerian mustaches, as he's probably the one individual everyone loved to hate on campus.

"Wait a minute. Wait a minute." Nate jumped up from his chair to address everyone. "Who did Adam and Eve's children marry? Brothers can't marry sisters. That's incest!"

CHAPTER NINETY-SEVEN

TRANSHUMANISM

"Well, if we evolved from the apes," Maria announced, standing to address the group, "would it have been okay, Nate, for brother ape to have married sister ape then? That occurs in the wild, anyway."

"I never thought of it that way," Nate replied, as he sat down.

"It shows, that even sub-consciously, we humans realize we didn't evolve from the apes, but were created Imago Dei—in God's image. But to put this idiocy to rest, I'd like to bring up the Soviet Communist dictator Stalin and his scientist Ilya Ivanov, if I may, Dr. Lucci?"

"Go ahead, Maria, be my guest." I knew the story would put the final nail in the coffin on the ape-to-man debate.

"Around 1926, Stalin ordered his top animal breeding scientist, Ilya Ivanov, to produce a super 'Planet of the Apes' army by crossing apes with humans."

"Really!?" Sci-Fi Matt was all ears.

Maria ignored Matt and continued. "Stalin is said to have told Ivanov, 'I want a new invincible human being, insensitive to pain, resistant and indifferent about the quality of food they eat.' He wanted to build a living war machine. Ivanov wanted to prove evolution true, and that God and religion were nonsense. The gorilla was considered closest to the black race, and the chimpanzee the nearest relative to the white race. Ivanov's plan was to impregnate, by artificial insemination, female 'volunteers.'"

"This is positively abhorrent and repugnant!" Claudia exclaimed, her face contorting with revulsion.

Maria nodded toward Claudia. "Needless to say, the experiments failed and Ivanov was exiled by Stalin to somewhere in Kazakhstan, where he died."

"Well, so much for the 98 percent genetic similarity between man and monkey," Jim stated in his, now usual, agitated demeanor.

"Gracias a Dios that foolery is behind us now," mentioned Santi, leaning against the stone which framed the fireplace.

"I wouldn't be too sure," I said, gazing around at the group with a mischievous smile on my face, which they all picked up on. "Anyone hear of the term 'transhumanism'?"

Andy and Pete looked at each other. "I remember," Andy broke in "showing Pete an article I read a couple of years ago in one of the scientific journals. It was about genetic scientists who are taking genes from hawks and eagles, and are splicing them with human genes to create super soldiers with eagle-like vision."

"Wow! Way cool," Matt blurted out.

Pete picked it up. "The article went on to say these scientists would like to use genes of major muscle groups from gorillas or some ape, and inject them into the human DNA, in the hopes of creating a bulked-up warrior for the military."

"Awesome!" Matt was getting more revved up.

Claudia had had it. She removed herself from her comfy lounge chair, stood up, and addressed the group - Matt in particular. "You are perverted," she said pointing at him. Then, speaking to the rest of the group, she shared, "This is the very same diabolical scheme of Stalin, just using modern genetic technology. The mind-set of today's scientists is the same: man is just an evolved animal and nothing more."

I decided to twist the knife a little. "Claudia, who made you judge, to decide what is good or bad, right or wrong?"

"Oh, Dr. Lucci, I believe I speak for most of us," she glanced at Matt with a distasteful expression, "when I say our parents and our grandparents have been so brainwashed . . . so . . . evolutionized, that they have rejected God and his laws of life to one degree or another. We are *so* selfish, *so* self-centered, 'it's all about me', and I'll admit I've been one of the worst."

Thad stood up. "Yeah, and besides the Matrix, which literally controls our lives, is injecting this . . . this . . . genetic crap into our brothers, sons, and daughters because they think they own us. We've given the Matrix our permission—no, our blessing—to inject even these RFID microchips into our bodies. What fools we've become turning the Matrix into our God to rule over us." Thad gave Claudia a conciliatory nod and took his seat again.

For a time, the lounge was silent, other than the hiss of the propane gas fire emanating from the hearth. Some stared at the flames lost in thought, others, like Matt, used their tablets to check out transhumanism.

Nate finally broke the silence. "I still want to know about Adam and Eve's kids. If they had married one another, wouldn't it have created all kinds of deformities like some of the European royalty who practiced much inbreeding, and wound up with offspring who were retarded and suffered from seizures, hemophilia, and stuff?"

"Maggie, you have been studying a lot of material from Dr. Mercurio. Do you feel you could handle this?"

"No problem. This was one area I personally had a lot of questions about, too."

"Okay, the floor is yours." I decided to grab a comfortable sofa chair near the fireplace.

Maggie stood and walked to the center of the group. She paused while she gathered her thoughts. She looked at Nate, who had persisted in asking about Adam and Eve's offspring. "Nate, even you will marry a relative," she said.

"No, I won't!" he replied resolutely.

"Nate, if you won't marry your relative, you won't marry a human."

"Huh? What the devil are you talking about?"

CHAPTER NINETY-EIGHT

THE FIRST FAMILY

"The problem with most of us who even believe in a creator, is that our creator is such a small and weak one. Don't you think the Creator of the universe knew what He was doing when He designed us? At the beginning, he had us marrying our relatives. I mean, Adam married his rib. Talk about a genetically close relative!" Maggie stopped and scanned the group.

"That means they were genetically identical, gene for gene!" Juan announced suddenly, realizing the implication. "But why no problems with the kids, like Cain and Able?"

Tom's hand shot up and Maggie acknowledged him. "I'm still confused. I thought that the Bible speaks of only Cain and Able; where did the rest of humanity come from?"

"Genesis 5:4 tells us that Adam and Eve had other sons and daughters."

"Oh, I didn't read that far." Tom said, which elicited a round of laughter from everyone, to Tom's embarrassment.

"Moving on." Maggie said, rolling her eyes. A few people chuckled as Maggie continued, "Adam and Eve were created perfect on Day 6, like the rest of creation. Perrr . . . fect! No errors. Not even a blemish. Adam would have made today's Olympians look like out-of-shape middle-age guys—no offense, Doc."

"None taken," I replied.

"And Eve would have put Miss Universe to shame. One look at her and the contestants would have packed up their bags and headed for home."

"A total fox. She was a 10 . . . make that a 20!" a bug-eyed Matt heartily concurred.

Tom jumped up, "Yeah, Adam took one look at her and his first words were, 'whoa-man!'"

"What's he saying?" Santi asked Juan.

"Wo-man. Woman," Tom explained to a confused looking Santi. "Female of the species," Tom elaborated, becoming frustrated.

"Tom, it went over like a lead balloon," Juan retorted, speaking for everyone. "Just sit down and let Maggie finish."

Maggie continued, "And intellect. They were both brainiacs. Think of Einstein, Beethoven, Newton, Galileo, Da Vinci, and Shakespeare all rolled into one. These two are your original ancestors, not some imaginary, knuckle-dragging, hairy troglodyte."

"May I, Maggie," I interrupted, wanting to augment her point. She yielded the floor to me. "Where do you think the complete gene complement came from that each of these famous people exhibited?" I asked pointing skyward. "And who was the original repository from where these gifts and genetic info were dispersed?"

"God placed them in Adam and Eve. But what happened to us?" Juan asked dejectedly.

"The Fall," Maggie, turning to Juan, replied.

"How do you know what happened in the fall? It could have been spring or summer; you don't know," Tom interjected, thinking he's getting back at Maggie for making him look foolish.

The group was silent for a moment. Fred leaned forward in his chair and whispered something to Tom. His face slowly turned red as we heard him say, "Oh."

Maggie continued. "God made *all* of creation perfect. The weather was perfect—even at the poles," Maggie said, recalling that findings at both poles show a prior history of tropical plants and animals. "It had to be, to be able to run around all day in your birthday suit." That comment brought on a number of laughs.

"Adam and Eve could speak, read, and write at an extremely high level. God programmed them that way, just as He programs some types of birds and butterflies to be able to fly back to their ancestral nests thousands of miles away, having been programmed to follow the sun and stars with an internal magnetic compass. Explain that from a slow piece-meal evolutionary assembly."

Santi's hand went up. "Mira, each new generation of birds and butterflies drowned in the sea, until one got it right. Although it's hard to reproduce and evolve when you're dead and drowned. ¿Me entiendes, hombres?" Santi said, adding some jocularity to Maggie's evolutionary illustration. Juan jokingly punched him on the shoulder.

"What language did God program Adam and Eve with?" Thad very curiously asked.

"No one knows for sure. It is speculated that it may have been ancient Hebrew," Maggie replied. "Since Genesis is clear that Adam was able to talk with God, it is logical that God Himself related to Adam how He created everything during those first six days of the creation week."

"And Adam wrote all this down, and passed it on to his kids, who gave it to Moses?" Juan asked, attempting to put it together.

"Adam may have given his personal chronicles and manuscripts *directly* to Methuselah, who was Noah's Grandfather," Maggie elaborated. "Noah, then may have carried these writings on the Ark with him."

"So, Moses, who compiled the Pentateuch . . . ah . . . the first five books of the Bible, which includes Genesis, probably had Adam's writings handed down for him to retell the historical events of the formation of the world and universe," Brother Francis surmised correctly.

"Wow! The true history of the universe," Jim, in reflection, stated aloud. "I never looked at the Bible that way before."

"Maggie, tell us about the Fall of man—and woman," Thad prodded, glancing over at Tom while chuckling. He placed his digital recording device on a cocktail table by Maggie. "If God programmed Adam and Eve so perfectly, how and why did they screw up?"

"God programmed man with instinct like the animals, but with man He also gave him free will—free to love or hate . . . or kill. He loved this creation of his so much that he wanted man to freely love Him in return, which meant man was also free to reject Him."

Jim was very energized and jumped up. "I get it now. Do any of you guys really want to give the girl you love and care for- Love Potion No. 9, so she will artificially love you; or do you want her to freely love you—no strings attached?" Jim looked over at Matt who seemed to be vacillating over his statement. "And Matt, we're talking about love, not lust!"

With that, the whole room who was now observing Matt, broke out in uproarious laughter. Matt gave a feeble version of his used-car salesman smile to everyone.

"Oye, Matt! And Dios made Adam and Eve, not Adam and Steve," Santi said, laughing at his own joke, which causes others to chuckle.

Maggie, trying to contain herself, continued to answer Thad and us. "The only command God gave to Adam and Eve was not to eat from the tree of the knowledge of good and evil, otherwise they would *die!* They could eat from any other tree in the garden. The serpent beguiled them, and they ate of the forbidden fruit."

"How did the serpent convince Eve to eat of the fruit?" Claudia, now very intrigued, asked Maggie.

"The devil made her doubt the word of God. He told her she would *not* die, and that by eating the fruit her eyes would be opened and she would be *like* God. Check out Genesis 3:4–5 on your tablets, if you'd like."

"Satan lied to them. Their free will was polluted by pride, and their desire to become gods prevailed. And that S.O.B. has been lying to all of us ever since," Claudia concluded, demonstrating her erudite thinking.

Jim looked like he's going to blow. "Absolutely! Satan has been trying to convince us from the beginning that we can be gods. It didn't start with Darwin's evolutionary theory that we would continue evolving to God-like status, nor with Hitler's Aryans, or Transhumanism, or even Vishnu avatars. Doubting God's Word has led to our death!" Jim stood there out of breath, angry and frustrated.

The group locked on Jim, thinking about what he just said. They then shifted their gaze to me.

"Thanks, Jim. You nailed it, man. Satan has been gambling with man, doubting and rejecting God and His Word, ever since the Garden of Eden. He just varies his gaming technique and approach."

"Maggie, I really appreciate all this good information," Thad stated. "Things are much clearer to me, but I still don't fully understand about the death and diseases thing. I lost a kid sister. How does a loving God fit into that picture?"

"And how could their children marry each other?" Nate asked, still not having his question answered sufficiently.

CHAPTER NINETY-NINE

GOING ZOMBIE

"**D**oc, I'm going to pass the baton back to you, if you don't mind."

"I'll take it from here Maggie; thanks, you did really well."

Looking around the lounge, I tried to formulate my thoughts on how to approach the topic on death for Thad. Loss of a loved one can be very difficult. It is one of the major reasons people either reject or lose faith in Christianity. It's the old question - How could a loving God permit this?

"Claudia, I understand that you are a vegan. And you told me you had attended a lecture by a vegan practitioner, who mentioned that even Adam and Eve were vegetarians."

"That's correct, Dr. Lucci. The Lecturer was an atheist, so I decided to check the Bible on this, and he was right. I even remember it was Genesis 1:29."

"So, what you are saying, Claudia, is that no animals were killed for food by them?"

"That's correct. God commanded them to eat only what grew from the seed-bearing plants and trees."

"What did the animals eat?" Thad asked. "Did they have fruit salads, too?" He had somewhat of a snarky tone in his voice.

"Thad, why don't you read Genesis 1:30 for us. And while Thad brings that up on his tablet, keep in mind that the world, before Adam sinned by eating the forbidden fruit, was perfect; there was neither death nor suffering."

"Got it. 'And to every beast of the earth and to every bird of the sky and to everything that moves on the earth which has life, I have given every green plant for food.'" Thad looked up at us. "They were all vegetarians. Animals not attacking each other, in harmony with Adam and Eve. Therefore, no death!" He sat down, still somewhat stumped.

"Mira!" Santi hollered out. "That would also incluyen the dinosaurios!", as the group all looked dumbfounded at Santi.

Philip spoke up. "Santi's absolutely correct…'*every* green plant for food'," he said, repeating the last part of the verse. "A perfect world." Philip relaxed in deep thought, reflecting on life in Eden. "Today, some green plants are poisonous," he sadly stated.

"And now we have this mess we live in," Tom interjected.

"Yeah, and all because our first parents screwed us," Matt added, appearing very annoyed.

"So, once they were thrown out of Eden on their keisters, is when everything started to degenerate to poisonous plants, ravenous animals, disease, and carnage," Nate discerned. He stopped, intently staring at the fireplace for a moment. Then he started jumping up and down. "Oh, oh, I figured it out! I figured it out!"

"Chill out man. Slow down." Juan grabbed Nate's arm. "What have you figured out?"

"The Fall. Adam and Eve. Being ejected from Eden caused everything to start to devolve. We're not evolving, we're *devolving*— the whole planet, the whole universe! God cursed the *whole* of His creation. I never did understand my pastor always quoting St. Paul in Romans 8:22 until today!"

"Oye, I think Nate's having a syllogism or something, hombre," Santi said quietly, while leaning over toward Juan.

"The second law of thermodynamics, everyone." Nate looked like a crazed Einstein pacing around the lounge in front of the fireplace, his arms flailing around. "Give me a second, I need to check on something," he pleaded, as his fingers were flying rapidly on the screen of his tablet.

"Where is Nate going with this?" Pete questioned aloud, while looking at Andy.

Andy turned to Philip, "Are you thinking what I'm thinking, Philip?"

"Yeah, Nate's onto something, and I believe I know what it is."

"Okay, okay," Nate started to decompress, more or less, "The second law of thermodynamics states that any isolated system tends to degenerate to a more disordered state or entropy. Correct?" He looked at all of us. "This applies to everything—from the microscopic to the macroscopic—right?"

"Hey hombre, could you translate that into English or even Español for me?" Santi asked, still sitting by the fireplace looking totally bewildered.

"Yeah, sure, Santi." Nate said, while framing his thoughts. "Everything, but everything, in the universe today tends to break down, going from order to disorder. A new shiny car gets old and breaks down. A new house gets old, and the paint chips and the roof decays. People get old, diseased, and die!"

"You can be young, and get a disease and die, like my sister." Thad countered Nate sharply.

"Disease is still a breakdown from the normal—from order to disorder. Take Ali's sickle cell disease. His red blood cells have gone from order to disorder—from the normal round to sickle shaped."

"As a matter of fact, Thad, since you're taking astronomy: Aren't the stars, including our sun, losing energy? Aren't they burning up? I mean the whole universe is headed for a heat death eventually. Is that not true?"

"Yes, your right."

"The rotational speed of the earth is slowing, and they have to re-adjust the universal time every few years—correct?"

Thad nodded his head.

"Stars explode and go supernova! And even we are breaking down and mutating rapidly."

"You mean we're going zombie?" Matt inquired with genuine concern.

CHAPTER ONE HUNDRED

THE ULTIMATE PRICE

N ate looked at the ceiling and extended his arms upward. "Oh, thank you, biology professor. I'm sending all of you two articles: *Genetics* 156 (1): 297-304; also, *Trends in Genetics* 29 (10): 575-584."

Andy was the first to bring it up. "During production of egg and sperm, DNA mutations can occur—and be passed onto the next generation," he read.

Pete picked it up from there. "'And scientists have actually measured this rate in humans in a number of studies.'" He stopped reading for a moment. "Holy crap, 'the mutation rate was found to be between 75 and 175 mutations per generation. And, they continue to accumulate over time in our genome.'"

Matt then spoke up in a very solemn tone. "It also says that, 'over 90 percent of the harmful mutations fail to be removed and are passed on to the next generation.' I knew we were going zombie."

Philip put the final touch on the articles. "Humans eventually will go extinct at a point called *error catastrophe*."

"Don't you see? It's obvious!" Nate, still wound up, exclaimed while pacing.

"I see . . . I see. We will go zombie, and then self-terminate," Matt predicted, still on his rant.

"No, reverse extrapolate the whole thing," directed Nate. "Something my Professor failed to do."

Maria got up and assisted Nate by sitting him in his chair and quieting him down. He mumbled some resistance while she brought some levity to the situation. "It's really quite simple. Nate, I understand your logic now. If we start with our supposed monkey ancestor Lucy from 2.5 million years ago, and average only 100 accumulated mutations per generation until today, and let's be generous and assume a generation to be 25 years—"

"That's 100,000 generations or 10,000,000 mutations in our genome," Philip suddenly broke in. "We would have *already* gone zombie." He looked at Matt and continued, "And reached *error catastrophe* or self-termination, using Matt's expression, a long, long time ago."

Maria ignored Philip's interruption and finished. "But if man has been around only 6000 years, there have been only 240 generations since the Fall of Adam, and therefore only 24,000 accumulated mutations."

"Oh, thank God!" Matt cried out, with obvious relief on his face.

"Sí," Santi responded to Matt. "It's like photocopying a document; and then continuing to make a copy from the previous copy – and so on – the quality degrada . . . a . . . degrades."

Nate jumped up again. "Therefore, since all of creation is devolving, all the other plants and animals are also accumulating mutations since the Fall, some faster than others."

"Yeah, like when you go to a carnival side show, and see the two-headed turtle and the five-legged cow. Weird!" Matt was at it again.

Jim jumped up mad as a wet hen. "I don't know how much more of this I can take. Lies upon lies, upon more lies. Even if some honest people want to tell the truth about creation, and Adam and Eve, they are gagged, muzzled, ridiculed, and marginalized. Anything to destroy God, so Big Brother or the Matrix can *play* God!"

"All this death, disease, and 'nature red in tooth and claw' to quote Tennyson, just for eating a piece of fruit?" Tom asked, agitated with the whole narrative. "And God takes it out on us, the offspring?"

"They had it made in the shade," Juan observed. "Their pride and arrogance in wanting to be gods made them blow it, believing that forked-tongue serpent."

"Yes, they had it made. A perfect life. The only thing God demanded of them was to believe in Him and His word, otherwise they would die if they ate from that one tree." I told the kids.

"But they didn't die immediately," Tom countered nastily.

"The original Hebrew translates to English as 'in dying you will die'. In other words, you both will get old and die. Remember they could have remained young and lived forever," I explained, trying to get Tom to understand.

"Let me give you an analogy," I continued. "You are married and have a wonderful life. You are warned that you should be faithful to each other. One of you cheats, and you both get AIDS. Who ultimately pays the price?"

"Mira, the niños . . . the children," Santi immediately answered.

"That's right. The children get the HIV virus passed down to them," I confirmed, nodding at Santi, and then looking to Tom.

"And so, this is what we have to experience and suffer, from now until eternity—all because our original parents screwed up? Bummer, man! Somebody ought to pay for this!" Tom responded bitterly.

"Someone *did* pay, so mankind would not suffer unto eternity, Tom."

With that, the hotel manager came into the lounge to inform us that it was after 11 PM and the lounge was closing for the night.

"Hey everyone, let's return the furniture to where we found it, please," I requested of the group. "The hotel was kind enough to let us use this room."

As we were leaving, Thad came up to me privately. "Thanks, Doc, a big weight is off my shoulders. I understand now that my little sister is with Him in Heaven. The Creator Himself paid the ultimate price for her . . . and us. She hasn't just turned into useless worm food." His eyes swelled and reddened as some tears rolled down his cheeks. "Punishment must always be paid for wrongdoing. He must love us a lot to personally pay for Adam and Eve's crime by sacrificing His own life."

My arm was around his shoulder. I nodded and gave Thad a smile. "He did it for His own Creations; wouldn't you do the same for *your* own flesh and blood - *your* children?"

As we entered the elevator, Nate half-jokingly complained, "And I still don't know yet how their kids were able to marry each other."

"Tomorrow, Nate, tomorrow."

CHAPTER ONE HUNDRED ONE

VIDEO VIGNETTE

We arrived early the next day at the Creation Museum and were first on line when the doors opened at 10 AM. Seemed everyone had already planned who they were going to break off with.

Maria, Maggie, and Claudia began with the Starting Points Tour. Pete, Andy, and Jim took off to the Dinosaur Dig Site. And Thad, Philip, and Nate decided on the Planetarium and the Special Effects Theater.

I noticed Tom and Matt making a beeline to Noah's Café. They said they were still hungry. I could hear Matt whining that he wanted to go see the Aliens—Fact or Fiction Presentation first, after they ate; but Tom wanted to go to the Dragon Theater.

When I asked Juan and Santi what they preferred to check out first, they told me Dr. Crawley's Insectorium. I had no idea bugs turned them on. Cindy wished them well, as I saw her shutter a bit and make a squishy face at the thought of viewing impaled dead insects through a glass case.

Ali said he was happy to just wander about the museum at his own pace.

Fred wanted to see the many fossil exhibits on the main floor. So, Brother Francis, Cindy, and I agreed to do that first.

The prospect for the day's weather was very promising. All of us agreed to meet for lunch on the outside patio of Noah's Café around 1:30 PM.

After about thirty minutes or so, Fred was totally engrossed in the exhibit, but Brother Francis and I could see Cindy was getting bored with looking at fossils. Brother Francis made the overture to Fred that perhaps we could return later to look at more fossils, since Cindy had expressed interest in taking the Seven Cs of History Tour. She had read that it was the heart of the Creation Museum's exhibit design.

Cindy had taken some design courses in college and was blown away at the level of detail and realism that each exhibit offered. We eventually found ourselves in the Cave of Sorrows where we caught up with the three girls.

Claudia was riveted by a three-dimensional video vignette of a teenage girl crying in her room over the prospect of deciding whether or not to have an abortion. She was pressed up against the display; her lips quivered as tears wet her cheeks and mixed with her makeup, creating a bizarre graffiti effect against the glass. Her knees started to buckle, and she slumped to the floor, softly sobbing and moaning. The very low-level light in the room only magnified the macabre spectacle. Understandably, mothers hurried their young children out, and away from that sector.

Brother Francis and I started to move toward Claudia, as Fred seemed frozen in place. Cindy immediately and correctly assessed the situation, and took charge.

"Y'all move on; we'll catch up with y'all later," her voice was firm, and her eyes steely. She bent over to embrace and comfort Claudia. Maggie and Maria also remained behind.

Brother Francis, Fred, and I quickly left that tableau of sorrows and exited into the hall for some air. Fred seemed to be the most flustered. A crying woman completely disorients some men.

"This museum has dinosaurs; let's look at 'em." Fred nervously directed the statement to me, but his eyes were aimlessly looking around as if those behemoths were going to pop out of nowhere.

"This way to the Dinosaur Den, guys; follow me." I led the way.

Somehow, walking among the life-size gargantuans seemed to calm Fred down. He must have read every plate beneath each one explaining about the creatures. Brother Francis was enjoying himself, taking selfies with all the dinosaurs, like they were rock stars signing autographs. "This will make the other monks jealous," he said, as he moved among them snapping his pics.

I looked at my watch. "Wow! It's already 1:45 PM. We were supposed to meet everyone on the Noah's Café patio for lunch fifteen minutes ago."

By the time we got up there, most of the class had already eaten, probably wolfing or inhaling their food. Cindy and the girls were still absent; however, there was another group present that my class seemed to be interacting with, and quite vocally!

CHAPTER ONE HUNDRED TWO

LGM CHURCH

A s we approached, I noticed that everyone in the other group had on tin foil hats. I looked over at Fred, and all he could do was shrug his shoulders in bemusement and disbelief. Brother Francis blessed himself; he wore a serious facial expression. *He must know something I don't*, I thought.

Both groups seemed almost faced off against each other, with most everyone sitting on a couple of the tabletops or their chairs. I stood behind Nate. "What gives?" I asked him softly in a low voice, as there seemed to be a debate going back and forth.

Nate turned slightly and leaned in close to my ear. "This is a group of atheists that have come to the museum. In my estimation, it's just to ridicule and trash the place. They're not serious about wanting to learn anything."

"What's with the tin hats?"

"That's just their gig. They call themselves the Church of LGM."

"The church of what?" I asked, giving Nate a very confounded and quizzical expression.

"The Church of Little Green Men," he answered me in all dead seriousness.

"Yeah, but they're not a legitimate church, are they?" I still had a puzzled look on my face.

"501c3 status from the IRS, they claim. Even though churches are no longer tax-exempt, the government still requires it of them.

Their 'church' even performs marriages. The fat chick over there, with the spiked red-orange hair, is married to a bridge."

"A bridge!? You mean like the kind that cars and trucks drive over?" My mind was spinning in circles.

"Yeah. She must like the strong silent type." Nate half chuckled in my ear. "Oh, and see the skinny anemic one over there, with the straggly purple-black hair, the Christmas ornaments dangling from her neon green braids?"

"I see her. How could one miss a purple-black Christmas tree? The tin foil hat must be the star."

"She's married to Satan. She said if a Catholic nun can be married to God, she demanded equal treatment under the law to be married to Satan; it's the non-discrimination, fairness, and tolerance tactic. And the funky bald fellow, with the black lipstick, arguing with Pete - he's trying to marry his pet goat, but so far Peta is blocking the marriage from taking place."

"Sounds like a case for the Supreme Court to me," I answered Nate, in as sarcastic a tone as I could.

The black lipstick guy was trying to make his point with Pete. "And besides, there is more than ample proof of extraterrestrials, such as Area 51 in Nevada."

"Really!?" exclaimed Pete with a doubtful, pained expression on his face. "Could you show it to me?"

"Well, the government is obfuscating the whole thing. The alien bodies have now been moved away from the Area 51 compound to another secret military facility."

"Oh, I see. And where did these Little Green Men come from?" Pete, still with a tinge of sarcasm to his deep voice, inquired of the funky bald fellow.

"More than likely from the Andromeda Galaxy," the fellow stated with arrogant assurance. "They are the super intelligent beings that seeded our planet with life, not that pie-in-the-sky imaginary God with a long white beard somewhere up in the clouds."

Matt looked ready to strike. "So, you are saying that these aliens are what started the evolutionary process here on earth?"

"Absolutely, that's correct. We'll help you see the truth and the light," lipstick man announced in an arrogant condescending tone to our class, and to Matt in particular.

Matt saw me and smiled. He remembered back to one of our first class sessions where he first learned the truth about E.T. "Let me ask you a question. I'm confused about something." Matt asked of Mr. Lipstick.

"Go ahead, I'll be happy to enlighten you," he responded with his chronically haughty demeanor.

"If these ancient astronauts from the Andromeda Galaxy helped us to evolve here, who helped them to evolve?" Matt stared him down.

"Well . . . a . . ." Lipstick blinked as Matt's salesman smile stretched across his face. "They were seeded from another galaxy—"

"Far, far, away?" Matt interrupted Lipstick's response.

"Uh . . . yes . . . a . . . from another faraway galaxy." A bead of sweat formed on Lipstick's forehead as he looked around for some support from his LGM followers.

There was a momentary pause of silence; then some laughter erupted from our students, followed by some nervous chuckling from the LGM group, including Lipstick himself. He knew he had been taken to task by Matt.

CHAPTER ONE HUNDRED THREE

DATING PROBLEMS

"Well, yeah but . . .what about the fact that scientists have discovered water in space, including on Mars?"

That's what I just loved about atheists. I thought. *Once cornered, having no answer, they quickly change the topic, always starting with a 'yeah, but.'*

"And so?" Matt asked, looking at him askance.

"Well, water is necessary for life. So, if you find water there must be life!" Lipstick smiled back at Matt.

"That's a poor syllogism, *sir,*" Tom answered, now animated by the debate. "You are making untenable assumptions that would not hold in a court of law. Isn't space considered sterile, *sir?*" Tom firmly augmented his voice with every 'sir.'

"Well, yes," Lipstick peered at Tom, perplexed as to where Tom was directing the conversation.

"So, if I take distilled water, which is in a sterile flask and is hermetically sealed, tell me - when will something grow?"

"A . . . when the water in space contacts space rocks and with lightning—"

"Lightning in space, *sir?*" Tom bored in on him.

"I mean . . . with the cosmic rays of the sun and millions of years, you can get life."

"Can you prove that? Or are you *assuming* that that happened?"

"Well, it happened on earth . . . a . . . that's why we're here." Some more beads of sweat formed on Lipstick's forehead.

"I thought you said that life was seeded onto our planet?"

"A . . . well, what about the Miller-Urey experiments, from the '50s, which produced life?"

"They never produced life. They produced an 85 percent toxic tarry mixture of amino acids which were 50 percent left handed and 50 percent right handed, that nullified and canceled each other out, *sir*! Would you care for me to show you on my tablet?"

"Yeah, well, what about the millions and billions of years? You've got to take that into account. I mean what about the millions of years of carbon radiometric dating? You Christians are anti-science and don't believe in that!"

"You mean the uranium-lead radiometric decay? Carbon decay doesn't show millions of years, *Bud*!" Pete put his arm across Tom's chest indicating that he's got this.

"Oh, yes, the uranium decay method, that's the one for sure."

"You do understand, *Bud*," Pete said, replicating the tone Tom took with his 'sir', "that rocks need to be of volcanic origin to radiometric test them; whether it's the uranium to lead decay, or potassium to argon, or rubidium to strontium, or if you prefer, samarium to neodymium decay."

"Ah, yes, any of those would be fine." Lipstick's mouth and lips appeared to be getting dry and his make-up was becoming smudged on his face. Guys wearing lipstick and trying to be cool just don't have the same finesse as a woman, and everyone had taken note of it. "Scientists can calculate decay rates to a very high level of exactness and certainty."

"Exactness, yes, *but* there are some severe limitations to the testing process." Pete nodded his head at Lipstick.

"What are you talking about?"

"Are you familiar with the eruption of Mount St. Helen's volcano?" Pete asked, accessing his tablet.

"Of course, it occurred in 1980."

"Therefore, what should the radiometric decay show for age, using, say, potassium-argon?"

"That's dumb. It'll show about forty years, give or take a couple of years for acceptable error range."

Pete handed Lipstick his tablet, and his eyes widened. "There is something wrong with these numbers. Probably contamination of the samples or something."

"Let me see," demanded Christmas-tree girl as she grabbed the tablet from Lipstick. "What? Impossible! These numbers range from 350,000 years old up to around 2.8 million years old. The devil . . . uh . . . God screwed with this and changed it!" She practically threw the tablet back at Pete.

	SAMPLE	AGE / MILLIONS OF YEARS
1	Whole rock	0.35 ± 0.05
2	Feldspar, etc.	0.34 ± 0.06
3	Amphibole, etc.	0.9 ± 0.2
4	Pyroxene, etc.	1.7 ± 0.3
5	Pyroxene	2.8 ± 0.6

Potassium-argon 'ages' for whole rock and mineral concentrate samples from the lava dome at Mount St Helens. Chart Courtesy of Institute for Creation Research

"Okay, how about a multi-strata comparison at the Grand Canyon using *all* of the above methods?" Pete quickly accessed the information, which he had seen earlier in the museum. He showed them a chart of four rock layers at the Grand Canyon. Each layer having been tested with *each* of the four radiometric dating methods. He handed the tablet again to Lipstick.

Rock Unit	Ages (million years)			
	Potassium-argon	Rubidium-strontium	Uranium-lead	S marium-neodymium
Cardenas Basalt	516 (±30)	1111 (±81)	—	1588 (±170)
Bass Rapids diabase sill	842 (±164)	1060 (±24)	1250 (±130)	1379 (±140)
Brahma Amphibolites	—	1240 (±84)	1883 (±53)	1655 (±40)
Elves Chasm Granodiorite	—	1512 (±140)	1933 (±220)	1664 (±200)

Table 1 - Radioactive ages yielded by four Grand Canyon rock units. (The error margins are shown in parentheses.)

Chart Radioactive Ages. Chart Courtesy of Institute for Creation Research

Lipstick studied it for a minute. "How can the Cardenas Basalt rock units give multiple different readings? 516 million years for the potassium-argon test all the way to 1,588 million years for the samarium-neodymium test. Man, this is all messed up."

Christmas-tree girl took the tablet from him again. "And the other rock units/layers and radiometric test dates are even worse. I mean . . . like man, the number of years for each is all over the map. Different dates for the *same* rocks?" She shook her head as the ornaments tinkled on her swaying neon braids.

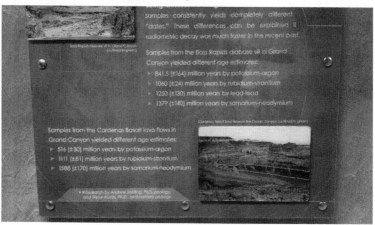

Personal Photo of Chart of Bass Rapids Diabase.
Research by Andrew Snelling, PhD. and Steve Austin, PhD.

"So, Bud, tell me how can we trust these methods to give us a correct reading of rock ages from eruptions which happened in the un-observed past, when we are given erroneous readings of the lava dome from Mount St. Helen's on an eruption which we know *precisely* - to the minute - when it happened in 1980."

"I . . . I . . . ," Lipstick stammered, turning to his little LGM church group. "Does anyone have anything to say about this? Were any of you aware of this problem?"

"Would you like to see the radiometric dating results from other very *recent* volcanic eruptions, which also give millions-of-year ages, such as Mt. Ngauruhoe in New Zealand and Mount Kilauea in Hawaii?" Pete asked, tempting him a bit.

"A . . . no . . . those Mount St. Helens results are sufficient enough," Lipstick said, backing off. "I always thought that scientists can measure *exactly* the decay rate."

"They can measure it exactly, but there are other problems that affect the *final* result." Pete was ready to zing him.

"Now I'm totally baffled," mumbled Lipstick, as his fellow churchgoers just remained mute watching Pete.

Pete took out a small hourglass egg timer he had purchased in the book shop and placed it on the table.

"Think of the sand in the top half of the hourglass as the parent isotope for uranium 238, for example. As it passes, or *decays*, through the narrow bottleneck, imagine the sand in the lower half as the daughter isotope, lead 206."

"Uranium, the parent, decays to lead, the daughter; got it," Lipstick confirmed, as his group nodded their heads.

"Now imagine you had a magnifying glass; you could count each individual sand grain as it passed through the narrow bottleneck of the hourglass. Or the scientists can 'count' the *exact* rate of decay as the uranium decays and passes through the narrow bottleneck turning into lead."

"Ah, I see now. They *can* measure exactly sand grain for sand grain or atom for atom; therefore, the speed, or *rate,* of radiometric decay can be measured exactly—no problem." Lipstick agreed with Pete. "But how does this affect the final result?"

"Was any geologist present in the unobserved past when the rocks were created at time zero—whether that time zero represents creation at 6000 years ago or evolution at 4.5 billion years ago?"

"Of course not; I'm still following you."

"Anything in that unobserved past *cannot* be proven. We can only make inferences. Are we in agreement?" Pete peered directly into Lipstick's eyes to make sure he understood.

"I see; I'm still with you."

"Since no scientists were present at time zero, is it *possible* the sand in the top half of the hourglass also could have contained some daughter lead atoms *in addition* to the parent uranium atoms? Is it *possible?*"

"I guess so," Lipstick admitted, shrugging his shoulders.

Christmas-tree gal leaned over and whispered to Lipstick, and his eyes widened.

"Therefore, when the scientists tested rocks from Mount St. Helens, their wrong assumptions yielded old ages," Lipstick stated.

"Hey, Bud, you're catching on," Pete said while looking at Christmas-tree girl, knowing she figured it out. "And we all know what happens when we *assume,* right?"

"Makes an *ass* out of *u* and *me?*" Lipstick said, scratching his head as Pete smiled back.

"Now, unlike the hourglass, which is sealed, rocks are exposed to rain and snow and heat and more; and therefore, are open to contamination by a gain or a loss of parent uranium or daughter lead isotopes; is that not *possible?*"

"Sure, that's obvious," Lipstick confidently stated.

"Wouldn't all this affect the *final* result, as in the Mount St. Helen's testing giving age ranges in the millions of years?"

"A . . . yeah . . . I guess so, sure. Man, like I never realized how many assumptions were involved in this process."

"I'd like you to read something by a qualified evolutionist, himself in this field of geochronology." Pete handed his tablet to Lipstick.

Lipstick was obviously nervous, but started to read out loud: "'It is obvious that radiometric techniques may not be the absolute dating methods that they are claimed to be. Age estimates on a given geological stratum by different radiometric methods are often quite different (sometimes by hundreds of millions of years). There is no absolutely reliable long-term radiological "clock."'"

"Who wrote that?" asked one of Lipstick's tattooed followers from the back of the group.

"William D. Stansfield, in his book *The Science of Evolution,* published by Macmillan in 1977," Lipstick read from the quote.

"Damn, I know of this guy," the tattooed follower replied. "He's a big gun. I believe he is, or was, professor emeritus at California Polytech."

"I don't know about all this atomic hourglass dating stuff," the corpulent female with the flaming red hair butted in. "All I know is that the dinosaurs lived millions of years ago. And Noah is supposed to have squeezed them on that floating zoo of his. Give me a freakin' break."

CHAPTER ONE HUNDRED FOUR

SMART METER

My cell phone started to ring. It was Emily's ring, and I silenced it immediately. I walked away from the group to call her back.

"Hi, Hon. What's up? I'm at the museum with the kids."

"The electricity in the whole house has been going on and off. I'm trying to clean, and wash and dry clothes, and it's impossible. At first I thought it was one of those rolling brownouts we've been having regularly over the past few years, ever since the rationing due to Mr. Pen and a Phone driving most of the coal-fired power plants out of business."

"What do you mean it's going on and off?"

"Starting at 9 AM, every other hour, the electricity has gone off for exactly one hour. It comes back on again exactly one hour later, for exactly one hour; then off again, exactly one hour after that."

"Basically, alternating on and off every other hour?"

"Yes, that's correct."

"How do you know it's exactly every hour on the hour if the clocks are messed up?"

"By our windup grandfather clock. And when it strikes on the hour now, I know what's going to happen."

"Are our neighbors affected?"

"No, I've called almost all of them, and they have had absolutely no problems with their electricity."

"Have you checked with the power company?"

"Yes, they said there have been no outages nor brownouts, and none have been reported. So, I gave them a piece of my mind and hung up."

I reflected on the information Emily gave me before giving her an answer.

"This is a warning from Dietrich," I told her. "He has government connections."

"Yeah, I eventually came to the same conclusion. What can we do about it?"

"Has it stopped yet?"

"I believe so. It should be off during this hour, but it's on."

"Thank God we don't have Alexa or Amazon Echo or that Google spybot."

"Yeah, Dietrich would really be having a field day. He was probably just rattling our chain a bit. I have a feeling you'll be okay from now on. If it starts to happen again later today or tomorrow, call Sheriff Mack to come over to our house to document it. He's a Constitutional Sheriff, and won't put up with the Federal government's harassment of the citizens of our county."

"How is it going with the group?" Emily asked. "Tell Cindy I miss her, and say hello to Fred for me. I wish I was with you. Feels creepy that the government can literally control us through that smart meter."

"If you need to, call me again. I miss you, Honey."

"Hugs and kisses from my end, too. I better get downstairs to the dryer; the clothes are all damp, and I need to run another wash cycle on the half-washed clothes. Oh, oh, the vacuum is running. I was wondering what that hum was."

"I gotta go, too. I hear a commotion brewing again with the atheists."

"Atheists? What are atheists doing at the Creation Museum?"

"Being converted . . . maybe? Bye, Hon."

CHAPTER ONE HUNDRED FIVE

RED PUFFER FISH

By the time I returned to the group, our spiked flame-haired obese dame, who smelled like an ashtray, was going off on a rant about dinosaurs living millions of years ago.

"And besides, you Christians are nuts to think that humans lived alongside dinosaurs. The last of the dinosaurs died out around 65 million years ago; modern humans didn't evolve until around 100,000 years ago, give or take. And you flat-earthers claim that Noah put giant dinosaurs on his boat around 4500 years ago. You people are idiots! How would they have fit on board anyway?! Retards."

Brother Francis attempted to answer her. "Don't you think God would have sent Noah juveniles of all the animal species—not only so they would be comfortable on the Ark, but for reproduction purposes at the end of the flood to repopulate the earth?"

"God? Jeezus, that's all I hear around this place. There is no god; there's only evolution, by blind chance processes—you fools! Time and death, that's all that exists in the cosmos, and that is from the great Carl Sagan himself. I am my own god! I decide what is right and wrong, good or bad. I'll do whatever I damn well please." She started to become short of breath.

Cindy and the girls had shown up in my brief absence. Maria stepped forward to try and calmly confront the red-haired atheist. "My name is Maria, and yours?"

"It's D-Rad," she bellowed in Maria's face.

"Can I just call you Dee?"

"Yeah, that would be okay," she said, as she started to simmer down a little.

"Are you familiar with dinosaur footprints which have been found in coal beds?"

"Yeah, and it's obvious to anyone with a brain in their head that that proves the dinosaurs are millions of years old. Coal is a fossil fuel . . . from the time of the *dinosaurs,*" she said, laying it on thick. "Haven't any of you Jesus freaks filled up with Sinclair gasoline, which has a sauropod dinosaur for its logo?"

"And coal comes from organic material, correct, Dee?"

"Of course, I'm not an idiot. What have we been talking about?" She rolled her eyes for her companions.

"Then you know, anything organic that was once alive, can be carbon-14 tested to determine how old it is."

"I *know* that," whined Dee with much rancor.

"Do you know the upper limit of age, by your evolutionary standards, which carbon-14 testing can reach?"

"Yeah, millions of years . . . goodie two-shoes." Dee had her hand on her hip as she was becoming impatient with Maria's questions.

Our tattooed friend from the back moved forward and whispered a while to Dee. He had long dreadlocks and tattoos on every exposed part of his skin. He also had a myriad of piercings, including nose rings and lip rings. Both ear lobes had very large rings imbedded in them.

Dee uttered "Oh" multiple times while our tattooed dreadlocked friend advised her.

She cleared her throat of the mucus buildup. "Well, okay, C14 testing is only accurate up to a maximum of one hundred thousand years. What's your point?"

Maria had been bringing up some info on her tablet. "Since coal is organic, we should be able to radiocarbon test it, correct, Dee?"

"Yeah, but you won't get any reading since coal was formed millions of years ago; there won't be any C14 left to measure—two shoes."

"Dee, before you scream foul, let me tell you that your own secular scientists did the testing with the newer accelerator mass spectrometry, or AMS method."

"So?"

"They found C14 not only in coal, but in oil, fossilized wood, and natural gas samples. Here's the reference on my tablet from Paul Giem in his article, 'Carbon-14 Content of Fossil Carbon'," Maria said, as she attempted to hand her tablet to Dee.

Dee held her hand up to stop her. "Don't bother."

"Be honest with yourself, Dee. Shouldn't you at least *consider* that all fossil fuels were formed because of plants, animals, and people, in sedimentary rock, being compressed, and then chemically altered, due to the geo-tectonic actions of Noah's Flood?"

Before Dee could answer, Matt chimed in. "Wow! I never thought that I was putting squished great-great-great-grandpa into my gas tank when I filled up." The thought of that seemed to relieve the pressure build up between the two groups, as everyone started to laugh—some with Matt, and some at Matt.

"I just don't understand how oil and gas can form in the few thousand years." Dee seemed confused about the whole process of fossil fuel production.

"But you already know that oil can be produced quickly." Jim entered the discussion.

"I do?" Dee responded more confused than ever.

"Yeah," Jim replied, "ever hear of Mobil 1 synthetic oil?"

Dee's face lit up with a very surprised look of realization.

"We've been doing this now for decades - using crude oil porphyrins and other oil by-products. Oil can now be produced in a lab in less than twelve hours, and harvested algae—a plant, converted into oil—in as little as one hour. Noah's deluge then, could very easily have produced fossil fuels." Jim smiled kindly at her.

"You're right. I have seen those commercials on TV that Big Oil has their labs working with algae to make oil."

Brother Francis got his courage up to engage in the discussion. "Miss Dee, you may not believe that preliminary evidence indicates C14 has been found in diamonds that are supposed to be between 1 to 3 billion years old. That's a *B* for billion."

"Why not? Diamonds are just carbon under pressure, so millions, billions, at this point I'm liable to believe anything—even grandpa in my gas tank." Her hands went up in the air with a sense of carefree abandon.

Everyone laughed at her retort.

I elbowed Brother Francis and whispered to him. "Tell her about the diamonds I told you about."

He looked at me, gave me that kindly broad smile of his, and with a twinkle in his eye said, "Yeaah."

"Miss Dee, if oil can be made in days, then why not diamonds?"

She whipped around quickly to face Brother Francis; she had been talking with our tattooed friend. She stared at him with a somewhat quizzical look. You could tell she was thinking. Suddenly her mouth dropped and her eyes got big, making her take on the appearance of a red puffer fish.

"My girlfriend just got one of those diamonds from her fiancé, and I can't tell the difference."

CHAPTER ONE HUNDRED SIX

X-BOX

The atheist group was arguing among themselves, questioning their beliefs. Suddenly, our Christmas-tree girl dropped her can of unopened soda.

Jim bent down to pick it up for her. "If you'd like, I'll open it for you," he said, grasping for the tab.

"No, no it'll spray all over the place," she cried out, attempting to grab the can from Jim.

He pulled the can away. "No, it won't. The soda in the can is millions of years old, and the carbonation has leaked out and escaped."

"Huh? What are you talking about?" She questioned still reaching for her soda can.

"Oil in wells is under pressure from the weight of the rocks above it. When an oil prospector drills down into the earth's crust, the oil is forcibly ejected to the tune of twenty thousand psi." Jim handed her unopened can back to her.

"Yeah, my brother is a roughneck and works in the oil fields. He told me they have to be very careful due to the pressure of the oil coming up from deep wells."

"According to geologists, that kind of pressure can't last for more than ten thousand years, at the most," Jim explained. "The oil would eventually seep into the surrounding sedimentary rock structure. So why is the pressure still there, if the oil formed millions of years ago?"

Christmas-tree gal had a nasty, perturbed look on her face. "So, are you telling me that only Noah's Flood, from a few thousand years ago, is the one thing that makes sense of this?"

"I didn't say it. You came to that conclusion on your own—unless you have a better explanation for me." Jim countered.

Her face was red with anger. She ripped the pull tab off the can, and the soda sprayed mostly on Jim. "Well, I guess the soda in the can is not millions of years old." Jim laughed, which got Christmas-tree gal to laugh as well, to her consternation. She then handed him a napkin to dry himself off.

"Radical, man, radical!" The tattooed, dreadlocked man walked to the front of his group and faced my students.

"What's radical?" Pete responded to Dreadlocks.

"Christians having answers that make sense. I'm not saying I totally agree yet, but you do have me thinking. Is there any hard evidence that you guys have that dinosaurs didn't live 100 million years ago?"

I raised my hand. "I think I can help you with that."

Dreadlocks looked around our group in the direction of my voice. "Who's the old grey-haired dude with you?" he asked, pointing at me.

Pete answered for me. "That's Doc. He's our professor." I nodded at Dreadlocks.

"Okay, Doc, shoot. What's the dope on the dinosaurs?"

"Well . . . a . . ."

"It's X-Box. Call me X-Box."

"Okay, X-Box, first we need to put millions of years into perspective. Let's assume each second represents one year. So, counting sixty seconds would be equivalent to sixty years. How long would it take to count forty-five hundred seconds, or equivalent to forty-five hundred years?"

Almost immediately he answered, "Seventy-five minutes, or one hour and fifteen minutes."

"Wow! That was fast." I told him, being legitimately impressed.

"That's why I'm called X-Box. I have this knack for being able to do math calculations very quickly in my head."

"And a million seconds or a million years?" I then asked.

"That would take . . . a . . . 11.57 days." Again, he produced a very rapid and correct response.

"And one hundred million seconds or one hundred million years, X-Box?"

He bent his head forward, placed his right hand on his forehead for a few seconds, and then popped up. "3.17 years to be exact," he exclaimed, giving everyone a big smile through his lip rings.

"Holy Toledo!" Matt interjected. "Counting a year every second, it would take you over three years to reach one hundred million seconds, or years. I would never have guessed!"

I gazed across both groups, "Kinda puts millions of years into perspective. And X-Box, file those numbers away for a moment; you'll be using them shortly."

"No problem, Doc. They are locked and sealed." He pointed to his brain.

"Now, let's take a live cow, throw it in a ditch, and cover it up with dirt. What will be left of the cow in, say, ten years?"

"Just bones, more than likely."

"And in one thousand years, X-Box?"

"Probably dust. Although bones have been found somewhat intact up to a few thousand years old, depending on the soil and climate they were buried in."

"How about Egyptian mummies from three thousand or so years ago, which were well preserved and then buried in a very dry climate?"

"Hell, they have been able to detect partial DNA fragments, and even grown some wheat that was buried in the tombs."

"The DNA has been verified; the growing of the wheat has been disproven and discounted, as a fraud and myth, just to set the record straight," I informed.

"Oh, okay . . .that's new info for me." X-Box admitted, seeming to be receptive to my explanation.

"And what would be left of the cow in 65 to 100 million years?"

"Man, are you serious? Unless it fossilized to stone - nothing!"

"Alright, X-Box, I'm going to make a slight change. Let's switch the name of cow - to dinosaur."

X-Box just gave me a dumb stare, like I hit him between the eyes.

"Do we have a problem, X-Box?" Maggie and Maria were aware of where I was going. They both gave me a wink.

Maggie moved forward and addressed him. "So, X-Box, are you going to change your position now that you have a dinosaur instead of a cow?"

Dee piped up. "What are you people talking about?"

I answered Dee, as well as the rest of the group, who may or may not have been aware of some discoveries. "Over the last thirty plus years, various still-flexible tissues from multiple dinosaurs, from various locations around the globe, have been found. The tissue has been discovered by secular scientists, in most cases, and verified by multiple repeat testing in many cases, and confirmed to be red blood cells, cartilage - still with elasticity, chitin, and other intact proteinaceous tissue, which has *not* fossilized."

Matt responded quickly. "Yeah, the movie *Jurassic World,* from several years ago, addressed this. Iron hydroxyls preserved the tissue from becoming fossilized." He gave everyone his big used-car salesman smile.

Philip added his two-cents to the discussion. "Matt, I'm sorry to burst your sci-fi bubble, but iron with hydroxyls, shreds protein and DNA; instead of preserving, iron destroys tissue, but it does make for good Hollywood movies." Matt's face turned sour.

X-Box was putting it together. "So, the 4500 seconds, or 4500 years, which took an hour and fifteen minutes to count, represents Noah's Flood; the dinosaurs which were not on the ark were buried in the watery catastrophe."

"So far, so good, X-Box."

"And if mummy DNA can be preserved, at least partially, for three thousand or more years, it's not a stretch to think that so could dino tissue."

"Very good, X-Box."

"I see your point, Doc. 100 million years - being three years - versus Noah's Flood, at 4500 years - being a little over an hour - puts things into perspective."

"It's kinda hard, X-Box," I said, "to reconcile the massive age and time range regarding tissue preservation." X-Box nodded in agreement.

"But why are the scientists so insistent on claiming that there must be a way, even after thirty years of searching and testing, to explain how these delicate tissues avoided total desiccation and decay for the . . . well now . . . supposed millions of years?"

"For the same reason your group is making fun of us. A recent real worldwide geo-tectonic hydraulic and volcanic cataclysmic event, which Christians call Noah's Flood, can lead to only one conclusion."

"So, you're claiming that the tissue preservation is due to a recent event, the Flood, and that there is a God who caused it?"

"Bingo, X-Box. Now the only thing you need to resolve in your minds, is can you humble yourselves before such power and majesty, *or* remain aloof and arrogant, thinking that you are gods unto yourselves, answerable to no one?"

"Wow! You just laid a heavy trip on us, Doc."

I nodded my head at X-Box, while my eyes scanned the atheist group slowly. "Perhaps we'll see you guys tomorrow at the Ark Encounter."

As our group left, we all noticed the Church of Little Green Men seriously conversing among one another.

CHAPTER ONE HUNDRED SEVEN

SECURITY THREAT

On board the Prevost on our way back to the hotel, Juan addressed me and the class. "As we were leaving that LGM group, one of their members asked me about tree rings."

"What about them, Juan?" I inquired.

"The guy said that there are trees that have been found with enough tree rings to verify that they are greater than five thousand years old, which would put them older than Noah's Flood, when supposedly everything was 'wiped from the face of the earth' according to the Bible. I didn't know what to tell him."

Jim was obviously excited and wanted to handle this. "Tree rings are not necessarily annual rings. Everyone thinks that each ring represents one year. That has been discredited time and again. Many times, a tree can form multiple rings in just one growing season alone—problem solved!"

***

We awoke the following day to a dreary overcast sky threatening rain. Once on the bus driving down I-75 to the Ark Encounter, it started to drizzle. The Ark Encounter was about a forty-five minute drive from the Creation Museum. We were on the road for no more than about five minutes when we saw police lights flashing behind us.

"State trooper," Brother Francis stated, glancing over at me. "I'm not speeding; maybe a tail light is out or something."

We pulled over to the side. Within short order, there were several trooper vehicles around the bus. The trooper, who had initially pulled us over, approached the driver's side window. Brother Francis gave him all the requisite documents—license, registration, and insurance—and he walked back to his cruiser.

Brother Francis looked at me and shrugged his shoulders. We sat and waited.

"I wonder what's going on." I said to Brother Francis and Fred, who was with me up at the front.

Fred queried Brother Francis, "When you were driving the big rigs, did it ever take this long for them to get their act together?"

"No," he responded. "Something else is going on out there. I've noticed three black Suburbans or Tahoes also pull up—weird." We all looked out the windows.

Nate, who was seated behind me and looking out the massive front windshield, said loud enough for everyone to hear, "Check it out! One of the suits from one of the black Tahoes is walking toward us." He approached the front door. Brother Francis opened it, and the suit walked up the steps into the bus.

"I would like everyone to exit the bus and bring your identification with you. If you're already chipped, that will be sufficient enough ID."

"May I ask who you are, and what is the reason for this?" I politely, but firmly inquired.

"I am Agent Claymore of Homeland Security." He showed me his badge. "We have reason to believe there is a security threat aboard this bus, which must be dealt with."

I looked at Fred and Brother Francis. We were all of the mindset that this agent was not going to give us any credible information, and we may as well do as he says.

"Okay, everyone, grab your raingear and let's go," I stated loudly, indicating I was a bit peeved at the same time.

As we exited the bus, Fred half whispered to me, "They could have checked ID while we were on the bus; there's no need to subject us to this nasty weather."

"I totally agree with you, Fred; something else is afoot."

Being fall, it was a cold drizzle, and we tried to huddle together outside. No one came to check our IDs right away. They just had us standing in the wet grass. Several of the agents had boarded the Prevost and were turning it upside down. A few more had Brother Francis open the luggage compartments, but they were empty, of course. Several of the troopers were handling the traffic, as the rubberneckers were slowing down, creating a long back up on the interstate.

After about fifteen minutes, Matt pointed to the sky and called out, "Look! Mini-drones with machine guns. Whoa, these guys mean business." We all gazed up at the cold grey sky. Three small quadcopter drones circled the area just above us.

"Anyone want to take bets," I predicted, "that a local news chopper from Cincinnati will show up anytime now?" At first the group was giving each other some dumb stares.

Pete was the first to put it together. "Dietrich! That son of a sea cook," he exclaimed, trying to hold his anger back. "He is behind all of this. I feel it in my bones!" No sooner had he finished his statement, when sure enough, high overhead a news chopper appeared.

"I've got a great idea," I proclaimed aloud to the group. "I agree with Pete, Dietrich is trying to pull a fast one, trying to make this seem like some kind of a drug bust to make us all look bad."

"Man, we should all flip the bird to that eggbeater," Tom staunchly announced.

"That's exactly what Dietrich would like us to do," I responded. "Instead, let's smile and wave at the camera on the chopper, like we're happy to be on TV."

"Yeah, that will totally confuse them. We don't need to look like a bunch of soggy busted dope dealers," Pete said, backing me up.

"Great idea!"

"Let's do it!"

A sense of solidarity united the class. We all started to wave and smile, and some hollered and hooted at the news chopper. The troopers and the agents turned and were watching us; they were totally confused at the scene we were making.

The copter made a few more passes and then left. Sensing a victory, we applauded and cheered even more. Finally, Agent Claymore approached us to let us know that we were free to go.

"And the 'security threat,' sir? I asked.

"We only found two bottles of unopened scotch in an overhead bin. Good label, expensive stuff."

"Keep it," Tom graciously offered to the agent. "It's my present to you for . . . a . . . keeping us safe."

"We're not allowed to accept gifts, but thank you anyway," he said as he walked off.

All eyes shifted to Tom as we looked at him with a "what's with the booze" look on our faces.

CHAPTER ONE HUNDRED EIGHT

HEADLINES

Once back on board the Prevost heading for the Ark Encounter, the class was ablaze with comments, questions, and opinions as to what just took place. Everyone was mad as hell that Dietrich wanted payback for making him look bad having outsmarted Erik when leaving ICC; and, of course, how I handled Dietrich in the free speech zone at the flagpole. He wanted his pound of flesh.

"It's more than that," I commented to the kids. "Thad has been getting hassled regarding his articles in the school paper." Thad nodded in agreement. "Dietrich, and the powers that be, simply do not want you learning about any of this creation stuff."

"My cousin, Santi, was right - these people fear the truth. They believe we are a threat to the power they wield over us."

"Sí, claro . . . they want to keep us estúpido and ignorante in their Matrix," Santi confirmed.

"Hey, how did Dietrich know exactly where to find us anyway?" Nate asked.

I chuckled a bit as I answered Nate's question for the class. "First, the bus has a built-in GPS, and second, the rest of you with your imbedded T-chips probably lit up every satellite around."

"The wonders of modern science," Pete responded very sarcastically to us all.

"I don't think we've heard the end of this episode today. I believe Dietrich will twist and spin this to his advantage using the compliant media."

"Doc, you're becoming too paranoid. They found nothing, other than two unopened bottles of liquor," Andy stated. "And, Tom, what were you thinking bringing booze on the bus trip, anyway?"

Tom, not in his usual braggadocious mood, was surprisingly very humble now. "I have . . . past tense, had a bit of a drinking problem. I admit I was planning on doing some partying on this trip. Notice I left the bottles on the bus unopened the entire time."

"What happened to make you change?" Andy asked.

"Erik, and the conflict when leaving the ICC campus. Something inside of me just clicked, and I immediately realized how important all of this is . . . and I knew I needed to get and stay sober, if I was going to make a difference."

"Just that one thing? C'mon give me a break, man!" Andy challenged.

"Yeah, one thing, but for me it was a *big* thing that happened back there at ICC. And this last deal with Dietrich and the Homeland Security Agents is the icing on the cake for me. To be honest, I still have some doubts about the ark, being I'm from Missouri and all."

"What are you going to have to do? See it, touch it, smell it or something?" Andy asked, still chiding Tom.

"Yeah, I'm a touchy-feely kind of guy," he admitted while looking at Maggie. His braggadocious style was coming through again. She looked over her glasses and gave him a "you are a sad sack" stare while shaking her head, which seemed to trigger quite a few chuckles.

"Oh, Doc, Doc!" Thad exclaimed, trying to get our attention. "The news on my tablet. It's already in the headlines: 'Immaculate Conception College in Front Royal, Virginia, has 'wild party bus bust.' They even have an aerial video clip from the news chopper. Of course, they've edited out our smiling and waving."

Almost immediately, all our phones and T-chips started going off.

TOP-DOG STATUS

"Thad, you had better contact Stephen, your editor, and give him the straight dope to be able to counter the critics."

"Doc, will you call Dean Avery?" Thad anxiously inquired.

"Yes, I will call both Father Flanagan and Dean Avery. They are going to be swamped by the media now."

As soon as Father Ed picked up, he immediately asked me, "I hope at least that it was good Irish Whisky that you had onboard, me lad," he said with a laugh. "Oh, and your girlfriend, Kathy Owens, has already been pestering Dean Avery and myself for an on-air interview." He chuckled again.

"'A tempest in a teapot' is what these liberal media types like to create. Ignore the fact that we have become, in effect, a police state, rousting law-abiding citizens. Make the conservative Christians look like the lawbreakers and loonies for the butt of their jokes on the evening news."

"Take it easy, Joe. Rich Avery and I will handle the home front; you just take care of the kids. Do you feel that everyone is getting something out of this trip?" he asked, trying to calm me down.

"I do. I've seen a definite positive change in almost all of them."

"Well, then . . . good. The Lord is working on their hearts . . . and minds. Why not call Emily, and set her at ease now?"

"Thanks, Father, I'll do just that. See you in a couple of days."
Click.

Everyone was either making or receiving calls, and seemed to be handling the media-created crisis with aplomb. I overheard some of the conversations and was actually very impressed with the way the kids handled themselves. As we reached our exit for the Ark Encounter, there appeared to be a big backup.

"Bummer, man!" Matt complained out loud, straining his neck to view the line of cars and buses along the exit ramp.

"Well, that's a good problem to have. It shows to the pagan world that people of all stripes are really interested in learning about Noah's Ark and the world that existed before the Deluge hit."

"Right!" Maria confirmed. "We should all be excited that there are more people out there like us searching for the truth."

Heads nodded in agreement all around the bus.

Nate's hand went up. "Since we will be on the bus for a while longer, Doc, we have time now for you to explain to me . . . a . . . to us, how Adam and Eve's children could marry each other and it not cause deformities in their offspring, and not be considered incest."

"Yeah, that's right," Andy said in agreement. "We'll have more than enough time for you to cover that."

"And how did they live so long?" Matt added to the inquisition, "That Methuselah dude lived to over nine hundred years old. Man, that's like outta some science fiction movie."

I saw the rest of the group wanted answers, as well. Maria appeared anxious, wanting to tackle the questions. She and Maggie had been logging the hours reading and researching in preparation for the trip.

"Go ahead Maria, give the class the low down on this."

Maria came to the front of the bus. "I'll need to transfer some info from my tablet to everyone's Insta-Screens on their seatbacks." She started her presentation, while looking up her information.

"I think we left off in the lounge last evening, agreeing that Adam and Eve - and all of creation for that matter - were originally created perfect when God completed His work at the end of the sixth day. All He had created 'was very good,' Genesis 1:31."

Thad raised his hand and asked, "So if I understand this correctly, Maria, based on what we have already learned, there was absolutely no death of dinosaurs or any creatures prior to Adam and Eve sinning; otherwise, God would have been the author of death, disease, and suffering from the very beginning?"

"That's right," Tom interjected. "We discovered at the museum, that even dinosaurs suffered from cancer, and had bite marks on their bones. This had to occur after the Fall." He looked at Maggie, smiling while raising both eyebrows in rapid succession. Everyone remembered his faux pas from last evening, and a wave of chuckling ensued.

"Very good, you guys," Maria responded. "This is where even some theologians make their fatal mistakes, and the atheists understand better than even those theologians do, that—"

"You can't have death, disease, and suffering prior to Adam's sin," Pete very excitedly interrupted her. "Otherwise, accepting of the existence of millions of years, is accepting of death, disease, and carnage prior to some ape evolving to human, or even accepting the creation of a *perfect* Adam *after* millions of years of death and destruction."

Andy slapped his brother Pete, on the shoulder. "Way to go, bro!" Andy then addressed the rest of us. "It's crystal clear to us now, Maria. All this disease and death started *after* Adam and Eve were thrown out of the Garden of Eden; and the first to die was Abel, at the hand of his brother, Cain."

"Sí, claro. And then when Dios got ticked off enough, the whole mess got buried, and some of the stuff fossilized in Noah's Flood," Santi chimed in.

"I've got an illustration to show you guys," Maria stated. "Check your Insta-screens now."

*Cartoon Illustration of Adam and Eve
in garden on top of mountain of bones.
Image Credit: Answers in Genesis*

Jim was hopped up as usual, shaking Santi's seat in front of him. "Are you going loco, hombre?"

"Sorry, Santi." Jim addressed everyone, "I need to apologize to an atheist friend of mine who I knocked out cold."

Maria looked surprised. "Jim, how could you?"

"I told him, as a Catholic and a Christian, we could believe in *both* millions of years and the Bible. He called me a dumb idiot, so I punched his lights out."

Most of us were taken aback that Jim would actually resort to unprovoked violence.

"I now fully understand that *I was* the dumb idiot. My friend truly understood Christian theology better than I did."

"So why did you beat him up," Maria asked, still flabbergasted.

"Well, he said, 'why would I want to become a Christian if your ogre of a God had already permitted millions of years of death, disease, and suffering before he made Adam, when your Christianity teaches that Adam started the whole death deal.' He said I was a fool, and that's when I clocked him."

"What are you going to do now?" Maria asked, still stunned.

"When we get back, I'm going to ask him to forgive me. The fossil record of those supposed 'millions of years' I believed in didn't occur before Adam. The fossils came after Adam, because of the Flood."

"Jim, think how I felt about the death of my kid sister," Thad added. "Because my pastor never understood nor could explain properly about Adam causing death and disease - I hated God, rejected my faith, and became a Buddhist."

Jim was still on a roll. "Yeah, the lie is 'death has been ongoing for millions of years' with more of the same to come in the future; and the only one to *save* you from this earthly fiasco is nanny government, Big Brother, the Matrix, the Illuminati, you name it! Here take another pill to keep yourself zombified, and leave the decision-making to us intellectuals."

"Maria, I think Patrick Henry is finished with his rant," I leaned over and half whispered to her. Fred and Brother Francis chuckled, having overheard me.

Matt stood up with such a serious and somber expression. "If God doesn't exist, we're back to the only other option, relative morality—there is no right or wrong." He paused momentarily to gather his thoughts.

"What about—" Tom started to ask.

"I'm not finished yet, Tom," Matt exclaimed, getting cross with him.

"Sorry, man, I thought you were done," Tom apologized.

"So why should I, as a head honcho of Big Brother or the Matrix, think that any decision I make is wrong? Everything I say and do is right in my eyes. And since I've evolved to become a god over others, I can do whatever the hell I damn well please. Pardon my bluntness, Doc."

"Evolution is survival of the fittest, Matt," I responded. "These guys have survived and made it to top-dog status, and they *will* crush you—think Robespierre, Hitler, Stalin . . . or Dietrich!"

At this, the students began to converse among themselves, having serious philosophical discussions on what Jim, Thad, and Matt had just said.

Nate raised his hand and addressed Maria. "And Adam's children intermarrying?" he asked with a hint of annoyance, mixed with jocularity in his voice.

CHAPTER ONE HUNDRED TEN

GOD AND SEX

"Okay, Nate. What is the dictionary definition of the term *incest*?" Maria queried.

Nate scurried to look it up on his tablet. "Well, according to Merriam-Webster, it means 'sexual intercourse between people who are closely related.'"

"And the legal definition . . . I've already checked out," Tom commented. It is 'the crime of sexual relations or marriage taking place between a male and female who are so closely linked by blood or affinity that such activity is prohibited by law.' Of course, it depends on each jurisdiction how they wish to handle the proscribed degrees of incest in their statutes."

"Hey, Tom," Juan called down the aisle, "does that mean that two guys, who are first cousins, can't get married. I mean, is that considered incest? Or can they protest under 'everything must be fair and equal' and . . . and the tolerance thing, since they love each other?"

"Oye, primo, I think the Adam and Steve thing no work so well," Santi replied to his cousin. "They no can have bebes."

Laughter rebounded up and down the aisles at Santi's correct gynecological observation.

"It seems to be a universal taboo, best I've been able to investigate," Tom stated, "except with the blue-bloods of royalty."

Maria regained control of the group. "Nate, c'mon man, you were the one that researched out the stats on genetic mutations. You said the number, on average per generation, was 75 to 175."

Nate pondered for only a moment. "Oh, it's obvious now—how did I not see it?" He turned around and smacked Jim on the forehead, as he said, "I could have used your V-8, Jim." This got the kids laughing again.

Nate continued. "Adam and Eve were created perfect—no genetic defects. The kids had only one or two genetic defects because of the Fall. Initially, there was no problem with brothers marrying sisters—like they had a choice, anyway."

"Very good, Nate," Maria complemented his analysis. "Even Abraham married his half-sister without problems."

"It would seem to me," Nate surmised, "that there would be two bottlenecks where the genetic load of defects *would* increase. The first would be the eight people getting off the ark at the end of the Flood—Noah and his three sons, and their wives; the other would be the splitting up of people groups at the tower of Babel."

Jim gave Nate a high five. "Way to go, man. That was super!"

"I still don't get it," Andy admitted. "How would they know when not to have any more close intermarriages? I mean did they wait until they began to have offspring that were deformed, retarded, and messed up?"

Maria turned her attention to Andy, and the whole bus was listening. "Don't you think our Designer would know at which point the genetic load would become too great, so He could advise the Israelites against close intermarriage?"

"Yeah, I guess so," Andy said, still unsure.

"Let me put an illustration up on your Insta-Screens," Maria said, and she engaged in activating the system again. "God told his chosen people, the Israelites, when to stop the practice of close intermarriage."

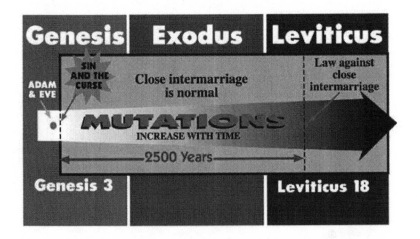

Illustration of mutations thru Genesis, Exodus and Leviticus.
Image Credit: Answers in Genesis

Immediately after viewing their screens, everyone looked up Leviticus 18.

"Holy crap," Andy exclaimed, speaking out to no one in particular. "Wow! God laid some pretty heavy laws on those Israelites. The whole chapter, I mean, like no same sex, no sex between father and daughter, no sex with animals. Geez, and Moses was given these commands directly on Mount Sinai?! No wonder he was up there for forty days."

Pete turned to Andy, "God and sex? I thought the Bible avoided that stuff."

Maria started to laugh, "Pete, God invented sex."

Everyone on the bus was now cracking up. I thought that Brother Francis was going to lose control of the wheel for a moment. Pete, after a brief hesitation, started laughing at himself, also.

CHAPTER ONE HUNDRED ELEVEN

RUNNING WATER

"Hey Matt, how old were you when you had your bris?" I asked.

"Eight days old. Why?"

"What's that?"

"Was it a kinda birthday party or something?"

"Matt, explain to everyone what a bris is."

"It's an ancient Judaic ceremony, which includes what you would call a circumcision. The cutting of the foreskin from the penis."

"How old is this ancient custom of yours, Matt?"

"Well Doc, it dates to the time of Abraham, around four thousand years ago. God said to Abraham, 'You shall keep my covenant, you and your offspring after you, throughout their generations . . . every male among you shall be circumcised.'"

"And how old was Abraham when he had to perform this on himself?"

"He was ninety years old," Matt stated.

Several of the guys squirmed in their seats, thinking about having this done as an adult male.

"Now Matt, why did God *specifically* state that the bris, or circumcision, was to be performed on the eighth day, as written in Genesis 17:12?"

"I . . . I really don't know why God wanted it performed only on the eighth day after birth," Matt conceded, appearing a bit dumbfounded, obviously having never thought about why the command was specifically for the eighth day.

"Because in neonates, the vitamin K and prothrombin levels peak on the eighth day, and then drop off again. These are factors that aid in blood coagulation. Perform the bris any earlier or later, and the baby could possibly bleed out."

"When did medical science discover that?" Matt asked with sincere interest.

"Scientists finally caught up with the Bible regarding neonatal eighth-day blood clotting only a few decades ago. Here is a graph you should be seeing now on your Insta-Screens."

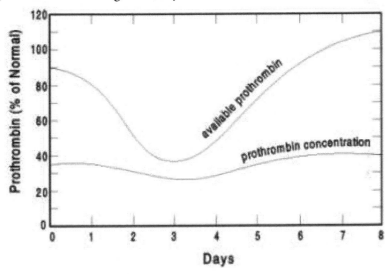

Chart of Available Prothrombin. Chart Credit: Apologeticspress.org

"Man, I'm going to text my dad about this right now. This will definitely blow his socks off," Matt pronounced full of excitement. "He has asked me to keep him up to snuff about crucial points I've been learning. I think he's actually becoming more open about the Torah, and the Bible in general."

The students were really talking, exchanging information they had just learned about the increasing genetic defects over time, and the blood clotting.

"Hey, Doc, do you have any more cool, scientific stuff that's in the Bible, that was later explained by modern science?" Andy asked, speaking for the group. Others nodded in accord with him.

"Okay, I have one for the ladies now," I said, perking them up. "I'm sure you have heard of post-partum infections after childbirth. It's called puerperal fever, which years ago carried with it a very high death rate of up to 35 percent."

Maria waved her hand wildly, and I acknowledged her. "We recently studied this a few months ago in one of my nursing classes. There was this Doctor Semmelweis, who worked in the Vienna General Hospitals First Obstetrical Clinic, where the death rate for the women who just gave birth was very high, like Doc said."

"When was this?" Andy asked.

"Around the 1840s, before Pasteur and Lister, and the acceptance of the germ theory of microbes. Anyway, the word on the street among the women was to try to get into the Second Obstetrical Clinic run by the midwives, as they had a mortality rate of only 4 percent."

"Well, yeaah! That was a no-brainer," Maggie announced. "If I had a choice between 35 or 4 percent, I'd take the 4 percent route. What were the midwives doing right?"

"It wasn't what the midwives were doing right, so much as what the doctors in the First Clinic were doing wrong. They started out the day doing autopsies, and then proceeded to deliver babies, and transferred the bacteria to those women. Remember they did this bare-handed back then, no gloves."

"Bunch of idiots!" Tom blurted out.

"Tom," I interjected, "they were only following the accepted science of the day," I continued, raising my eyebrows. "Like many of you who believed evolution and millions of years. Continue please, Maria."

"What Doctor Semmelweis discovered, and asked the doctors to do, was simply to wash their hands. As a result, the post-partum infection rates dropped to as low as 1 percent."

"Gracias a Dios!" Santi exclaimed.

"Well, not so fast. They expelled him from the hospital; he eventually went mad and was committed to an insane asylum, where he was beaten to death."

"Horrible, just horrible!" Claudia, who had been listening intently, expressed. "Why didn't the medical community abide by his studies and findings?"

"Because it took another thirty to forty years before the germ theory was fully accepted," Maria said, directing her answer to Claudia and the group.

"Or . . ." I paused and waited until I had everyone's attention, "they could just have read God's directive to Moses in Leviticus 15:13: 'and bathe his flesh in running water, and shall be clean.' And what do surgeons and doctors do today, Maria?"

"They wash their hands in *running* water," Maria quietly responded, to the group's amazement.

CHAPTER ONE HUNDRED TWELVE

BABYLONIAN CUBE

The entire bus chattered back and forth. Everyone voiced their opinions on the topics just covered. Eventually, Pete stood up.

"Everyone has asked that I give the consensus opinion of the group based on the facts we have just received. Our opinion is not upon unsubstantiated ideas . . . a . . . since we all know what a touchy-feely opinion is," Pete said, pointing to his backside. The bus roared with laughter and everyone clapped their approval.

"So, what have you arrived at?" Fred asked, standing next to me again on the bus step.

"Well, taking some good input from Matt, the creator of anything has to be greater than what he or she makes." Pete nodded at Matt indicating for him to take the reins.

"You know I like sci-fi movies and such. They always show the robots and machines taking over the world. A machine can go faster, like a car, than the person who built it; a computer can arrive at a result quicker than the person who programmed it; however, overall, the creators are *always* more intelligent than the objects they make."

"Your point, Mr. Matt?" Fred asked in a lighthearted way, triggering a few chuckles.

"Moses, or Abraham, or any of the old timey dudes who wrote the Old Testament, couldn't have been able to come to those medical/health conclusions on their own. Only the Creator who made man could tell man what He did."

As everyone was reflecting on what Matt posited, Brother Francis leaned over to me and, nodding his head, said, "That was actually very metaphysically profound."

With that, the Prevost started to pick up some speed, as we had been at a crawl since getting on the exit ramp. Finally, a tow truck passed us going in the opposite direction. It was hauling a car with mud halfway up the body and doors. "Probably tried to pass someone and got stuck in the mud," Thad declared.

We finally pulled into the Ark Encounter and were directed to the parking lot for the buses. We put on our rain gear before getting off the bus since it was now raining and a storm was approaching. We took the tram to the ticketing area and quickly passed through. The raindrops were getting bigger and falling faster, so we made a sprint to the shelter of the ark itself. We arrived just before the downpour started.

I looked around. "Where's Tom?" I asked as he always seemed to be last.

"He is standing outside marveling at the immensity of the structure," Matt remarked.

Finally, Tom came in. He had on a good, hooded rain jacket, but his pants were soaked.

"What were you doing out in the rain, Tom?" I questioned.

"It's . . . like awesome. I had no idea. All I remember seeing as a kid were those bath tub shaped arks with the giraffes sticking out the roof. Holy cow! Doc, what's a cubit?" he asked, as we all laughed at poor, drenched Tom. His sneakers made a squishy sound as he walked.

"Depends on which one. The Egyptian cubit, the Roman cubit, the Sumerian cubit, the Greek cubit, the—"

"Whoa, hold on," Tom interrupted. "Geez, I didn't realize how many different types there were. Which one did Noah use? And exactly what is a cubit, anyway?"

"A cubit is the length from the tip of your third finger to the elbow, which is eighteen to twenty inches. The Bible doesn't delineate which cubit Noah used for the ark. I believe the designer and builder for this Ark used the Egyptian cubit, which is about twenty-one inches in length."

"Dang, that makes this sucker . . . ah . . . five hundred and ten feet long," Nate said, quickly doing the calculation on his tablet. "It's more than seven stories high and about eighty-five feet wide, based on the dimensions given in Genesis 6:15."

"That would be the size of today's modern, mid-size cargo ship," Fred added.

Model of Noah's Ark. Image Credit: Creation Museum

Tom took off his jacket and nonchalantly stated, "It seems everyone in the world has heard of Noah and the Flood."

"Most everyone has," I replied. At that moment, we came upon the Flood Legends display.

"Wow!" Tom gasped. "There are over 270 accounts and folktales of the Flood from different civilizations and peoples, from around the world. Check out this one from China, Philip," Tom directed, as he started to read from the display. "'One ancient Chinese classic, called the *Hihking*, tells the story of Fuhi, whom the Chinese consider to be the father of their civilization. This history records that Fuhi, his wife, three sons, and three daughters, escaped a great flood. He and his family were the only people left alive on earth.'" Tom stared at Philip, waiting for him to respond.

Philip was entranced, reading some of the stories from other civilizations, from around the globe regarding the Flood: Hawaii, Mexico, Babylonia, Greece, Syria, and many more. He was noting the common thread to all the legends. "My mother read the *Hihking* classic to me as a child," Philip finally said. "I just passed it off as an ancient Chinese fairytale, and nothing more. At that time, even my mother had no knowledge of the biblical account."

Juan and Santi had been exchanging ideas. "Doc, how did the story of Noah and the Flood, get all the way to Mexico and the Toltec Indians?" Juan asked.

"Mira," Santi added, "I remember this really old Indio woman, who would tell us stories sometimes, including one of a worldwide flood. She said her ancestors had passed it down from generation to generation around the nighttime camp fires."

"Yeah, Santi and I figured they probably had heard it from some of the old Spanish missionaries, but Philip's *Hihking* classic preceded the coming of Christian missionaries to China by hundreds of years," Juan stated, having just checked his tablet.

"Have any of you heard of the Tower of Babel?" I asked the group.

"Of course," Jim responded confidently. "After the Flood, Noah's descendants began to multiply, and a hundred years or so later, all were still congregated in one place on the plain of Shinar, in what is now Iraq. With much pride, Noah's descendants decided to build a tower for themselves."

"Talk about being on a head trip," Tom added his psychological evaluation.

"And God confused their language into many tongues, which forced the family groups who then couldn't understand each other, to move to various parts of the world," Maria added. "They took the historical accounts of Adam and Eve, the Fall, and the Flood with them."

"I've been told," Claudia interjected herself, "in my literature classes, that the *Epic of Gilgamesh* predates the story in Genesis, and that the Israelites *stole* the story of the Flood from the Babylonians."

"That the Babylonians may have been the first to write down a version of the Flood event in the *Epic of Gilgamesh,* is problematical," I responded. "The *Epic of Gilgamesh* describes the ark as a cube."

"A cube!" Fred practically screamed before he started to laugh heartily, which got the others going as well. Fred used animated hand gestures, and comical facial expressions, to mime the folly of a square box tumbling end over end in the raging waters of the Flood.

CHAPTER ONE HUNDRED THIRTEEN

ACCORDING TO ITS KIND

As we moved on, I noticed Tom practically hugging one of the massive wood ribs, as he closely inspected it, while also admiring the colossal crossbeams of the vessel.

Everyone was taking note of the various methods Noah and his family used to provide for the animals. They used self-feeders, as is done with many birds today. For water, they used gravity-water systems made from leather troughs. The Chinese had used similar systems made of bamboo pipes for thousands of years. The animals could easily have been fed with stored grain, seeds, compressed hay, and even dried meats and plant material.

"But how *many* animals?" Tom asked, still having doubts. "There are over 8 million species of life on earth. There is no way Noah could have crammed two of each, even on this huge boat."

"How many animals did he really need, Tom? Surely, he didn't need any of the marine life which constitutes many species. Why not read exactly what the Bible itself states? Look up Genesis 7:14."

Tom took his tablet out and read the verse to our class: "'. . . and every beast after its kind and all the cattle after their kind . . . and every bird after its kind . . .'"

"Also, Tom, check out Genesis 7:22 for us."

He read again: "'all in whose nostrils was the breath of life, of all that was in the dry land, died.'"

"What conclusions have you arrived at, Tom?" He seemed a bit stumped.

"Jim, you're the ecology major, help him out," I urged.

"Well, insects don't have nostrils; they breathe through openings in their abdomen called spiracles, which eliminates around one million species that Noah didn't have to bring on board."

"Anything else we can eliminate, Jim?"

Jim pondered for only a moment. "Obviously, the fish, amphibians, invertebrates, crustaceans, and corals, and the plant kingdom. But that still leaves around twenty thousand or so species of birds, mammals, and some reptiles."

Tom was puzzled, and asked, "Jim, what is a *kind* that Genesis 7:14 talks about repeatedly?"

Jim was baffled and looked at Maria, who smiled and raised a finger knowingly.

"In the modern classification system, the biblical *kind* would probably have been the family level of taxonomic rank, which is a broader, more general level," Maria explained to our group.

"Yeah," Jim agreed with Maria. "It's biological classification from fourth or fifth grade science class. It starts with kingdom, then phylum, class, order, family, genus, and finally species."

"The point of all of this," I addressed the group, "is that Noah only needed to bring aboard probably two thousand, to the very most, sixteen thousand animals onto the Ark. There was more than enough room, with extra space to spare."

I brought up some info on my tablet as I continued talking. "Noah only needed to bring two of the dog kind on board. Originally, *before* they diversified, the dog kind probably started off as something akin to a wolf. Even the secular scientists believe this."

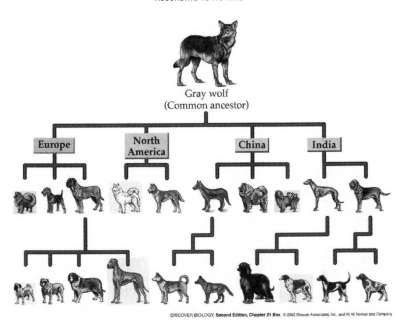

DISCOVER BIOLOGY, **Second Edition, Chapter 21 Box** © 2002 Sinauer Associates, Inc., and W. W. Norton and Company.

Evolution of Dogs.
Image Credit: Discover Biology W.W. Norton & Company

"Noah didn't need to bring a coyote, fox, collie, and jackal on board," I continued, "just two of the dog kind. Many of the specific species probably did not exist anyway, until after the flood."

"I got it, Doc," Tom exclaimed, now excited. "It was the same for elephants. He just needed two of the elephant kind. Noah didn't need to bring two Indian Elephants, two African elephants, two Mammoths, and two *Mast . . . odons*," Tom said, as he winked at Maggie, who ignored his flirting.

"As Doc said," Maggie fired back at Tom, "the . . . ah . . . other elephant species probably didn't develop and diversify until *after* the flood, anyway." Her eyes flashed displeasure at Tom.

"And after the animals exited the ark at the end of the Flood, they spread around the world. Different ecosystems, different climates, and different geographic pressures brought about the different species that we see today," Jim stated with confidence, very proud he was able to figure out post-flood species diversity.

"And don't forget, Jim," Maria said, complementing his correct analysis. "There was loss of information as the different species diversified." She had already brought up an illustration on her tablet that she passed around.

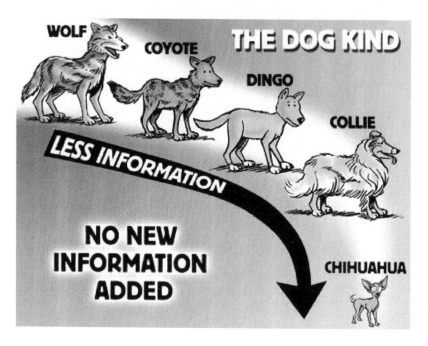

Cartoon Illustration of Dog Kind. Image Credit: Answers in Genesis

"And as we all know, the loss of genetic information also leads to health problems, especially with man-made selection, because genes are linked. It's not just one gene equals one trait," I reminded the students.

"Yeah," Andy broke in, "Pete and I had a mongrel dog for a pet as kids, and you couldn't kill it. Some rich kid friend of ours had some pure bred, specialty dog—ugly thing—which was always at the vet with some ailment."

"I can confirm that," Claudia added. "Our Afghan hounds were high maintenance, to say the least."

"So, when an animal loses info is when you could get a new species, but does the fact that it can still interbreed put it in with the same *kind* biblically? Like German Shepherds can breed with Great Danes, for example!?" Nate asked.

"I still can't visualize this loss of information thing," Tom stated, still confused.

"Tom, I think this illustration about length of hair in dogs will help you and anyone else," Maria explained, passing around her tablet once more.

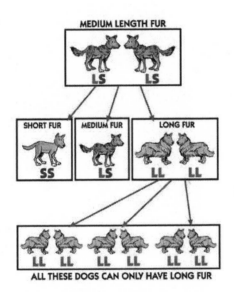

Cartoon Illustration of Dogs Fur Length.
Image Credit: Answers in Genesis

Tom, and some others studied Maria's illustration as the tablet was passed around.

"Okay, I understand how the genetics work, but why do you only find some dogs or other animals existing in certain areas and climates?" Tom asked Maria.

"I guessed you would ask me this," Maria stated. "I already have another illustration for you that explains why you won't find any hairless chihuahuas in Alaska. Somebody's going to crump and die out, taking their genes with them!"

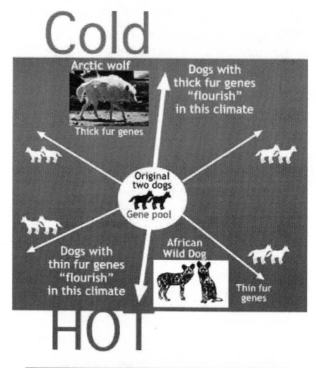

Cartoon Illustration of Cold/Hot Dogs Natural selection.
Image Credit: Answers in Genesis

"Okay, I get it now," Tom said, gleefully, "Geez, all this because of Noah's Flood. The pre-Flood earth had a semi-tropical to tropical climate, like palm trees at the poles—so Adam and Eve could run around in their birthday suits," he said, giving Maggie a wink. She just rolled her eyes, and that got everyone laughing.

"But afterwards," Jim added, "the fountains of the deep, which caused the breakup of the continents, also caused a major shift in weather patterns, creating many different ecological niches and species." Jim, still reflective, then commented. "I get it now! I get it now!"

"Would you mind letting us all in on it?" Matt half-mockingly complained.

"The other night at dinner, we learned that cold weather changes aren't mentioned in the bible until *after* the Deluge. I believe Brother Francis was quoting from Genesis 8:22."

A light bulb had gone off with everyone. You could see it in their eyes - the entire group nodded in agreement with Jim. Also, Tom seemed happy and content that his questions had been answered.

Maria addressed the group. "Natural—or even artificial— selection is a downward process. It involves a loss of genes from the pool, and *not* the gain of genetic information, which unfortunately they teach in evolution."

"Which is how we get a degenerated shit-tzu from the original brute of a wolf kind," Juan said, clarifying Maria's point and butchering the pronunciation, which elicited chuckles from the group.

Jim was getting animated once more. "Yeah, zebras from the horse kind, and pumas and pussycats from the feline kind. But there is a *limit* to the biological change of kinds. Fish are not going to become frogs or philosophers."

"Oye, this Noah thing goes way beyond just the Flood," Santi offered. "No wonder that lying Lyell friend of Darwin needed to destruir la inundación . . . ah . . . the Flood."

The group, as a whole, seemed to be putting the pieces of the puzzle together now, as they were vibrantly interacting with each other. Pete rubbed his thick black facial hair in serious contemplation.

"Doc," Pete's voice boomed. "I've got the sneaky suspicion that all this is going to dismantle a lot of the global warming . . . excuse me, climate change that our governmental Matrix has been ramming down our throats."

At that the entire group, almost in unison, turned toward me for my response.

I gave them all a sly smile. "I guess you'll all just have to wait and see," I said, nodding my head slightly.

Matt's hand went up. "I really would like to know how Noah got rid of all the . . . you know . . . ah . . . manure. The stench must have been awful."

With that the entire class cracked up, but I knew everyone, Claudia included, really wanted an answer.

CHAPTER ONE HUNDRED FOURTEEN

POOP CHUTE

From inside the safety of the ark museum, the storm raged outside, seeming to have centered itself directly overhead. Massive cracks of lightning and booming thunder vibrated the massive structure.

"That is why," I said, pointing upward, and loud enough to overcome the racquet from the wind and rain outside, "that the stench was probably kept to a minimum."

"I see," Tom said, pointing his finger upward toward the ceiling and directing it down the length of the ark. "That raised open window we saw on the top of the vessel let in fresh air. Boy, that was smart of God to tell Noah to install that natural A/C." Sporadic laughing ensued as Tom realized what he just said.

"And don't forget," Andy added, "the hatches above the windows also run the length of the ark. The windows could be flipped open at storm's end to let in light, as well as air."

"Oh yeah, that's right," Matt rejoined the conversation. "It was from one of those hatches on the roof that Noah released the dove to find land."

"And ol' Noah could also have kept select hatches open to collect rainwater that would have run into holding tanks, or cisterns, in the upper floors of the ark," Andy informed his fellow students. "There was no reason to haul water on board prior to the flood itself."

Light coming into Ark thru top hatches. Personal Photo

"That's good design thinking, Andy," Fred complimented him.

With that Andy quipped, "And unlike the solid floors in this model, the original one probably had slatted floors for air to circulate throughout the three levels."

"Yeah, I bet Mrs. Noah and Noah's daughters-in-law didn't have high heels that could get stuck between the floor planking," Tom said, pointing to Claudia's fashionable high heeled boots, which got everyone chuckling again. I was glad to see Claudia beginning to laugh at herself.

"Okay, okay, all this makes sense," Matt said. "But how did they get rid of . . . the stuff?"

"I think if you turn around now, Matt, you'll have your answer," I said, as we came upon several illustrations—as well as a full-scale mock up—of how easily it could be accomplished.

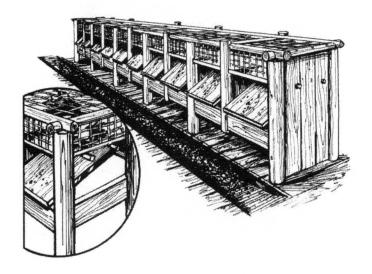

Illustration of cages/manure model. Image Credit: Answers in Genesis

"Oh, I see now," Matt acknowledged. "As the boat rocked and rolled, it sorta just carried it into troughs that fed into the bilge tanks."

"What about the larger animals, like pigs and horses?" Claudia asked.

"They used a larger version of a pooper scooper, Claudia," Thad answered, taking time out from his picture taking. "And then they proceeded to shovel it into the troughs."

"Then where does it go?" she asked.

"Where does it go on any ship or boat?" Matt asked. "It goes into a wastewater tank, or bilge, where it's released into the ocean," Thad answered, as he clicked off a few more shots.

A look of surprise and horror came across Claudia's face. "You mean boats contaminate the pristine emerald Neptunian world with their waste?"

Thad, without a thought, and while still shooting pictures with his camera, blurted out, "Claudia, where do you think the fish have been crapping for eons?"

Claudia bolted upright, blinking her eyes with a new realization. "I'm now starting to see how we have been brainwashed by academia and the media into this mind-set of a phony, pristine Lysol world."

Jim, his Patrick Henry oozing through, said, "So the Matrix Illuminati can tax our . . . butts to enrich themselves at our expense—fools that we are."

We passed by a group of college kids led by their professor. He was of average height with a casual surfer-dude appearance in baggy jeans, sneakers, and a large loose, linen pullover. His long, tangled sandy-blonde hair topped off his created image. He was trying desperately to grow the cool three-to four-day-old beard, but it was coming out in blond scraggly patches on his face, including the mustache. He was about Fred's age, late twenties, early thirties.

"As you can obviously see," the professor said, waving his hand in the air dismissively, stating with an air of superiority and arrogance to his following, "a vessel of this size would founder immediately upon impact from a large wave and capsize, or break in two. That's why no one was able to construct a wooden ship of this size ever! It's all been on Nova, the Discovery Channel, and others." he flippantly commented.

His students were lapping it all up, especially three girls who were almost encircling him and pawing him with their eyes, as he bathed in their adoration, listening to their oohs and aahs.

"The guy's a jerk!" Maggie leaned over to me speaking loudly, over the still raging storm.

"How's that?" I asked, not as astute as Maggie in picking up on the details.

"Check it out, Doc. The jerk's got his hand on one of those bimbo's ass - excuse my French."

Sure enough, Maggie was right. He did have his hand clasped onto the gluteus maximus of the most attractive of the three women.

CHAPTER ONE HUNDRED FIFTEEN

PROFESSOR RADISSON

Fred stopped in his tracks and turned to face the professor. "Excuse me, sir, but what you are teaching your students isn't quite correct."

"It's Professor Radisson, and who might you be, a marine engineer or something?" he asked with a chuckle, glancing at his students encouraging them to join him in the ridicule.

"As a matter of fact, I am currently majoring in marine engineering," Fred responded, giving a deadpan expression back to Radisson. "I'm sure your students would be interested to know how ol' Noah was able to perform such a feat in those *primitive* times."

Several of our group chuckled at Fred's mimed facial expression, and several of Professor Radisson's students were really curious about what Fred was going to say. Radisson was caught in a quandary. He was worried that this nobody would jeopardize his standing with his students.

"Sure . . . ah . . . go ahead, let's hear your *supposed* theory," he said, trying his best to discredit Fred before he even started.

"The ark, first of all, is a barge type of boat; it was built for safety and security, and not for speed."

"Wouldn't Noah have needed a fast boat to avoid the storm and heavy rains that were coming?" asked one of Radisson's students.

"The Deluge eventually covered the whole world, according to Genesis 7:20— 'the waters prevailed . . . and the mountains were covered,'—there was nowhere to go quickly, or slowly for that matter," Fred said, making one of his satirical faces and holding his hands palms up, which got everyone laughing. He was definitely breaking the ice with everyone—except Professor Radisson.

"How did Noah float over Mount Everest, which is over five miles high? With oxygen masks?" Radisson asked in a very snide condescending tone.

"I'm sure you are well aware of the fossilized marine clams which are found on the top of Everest. Right, *professor*?" Fred fired back.

"Oh, yeah . . . sure."

"Then, you also know that the clams are found with their bivalves all closed, which indicates they were first suffocated in an underwater cascade of mud."

"Yes, of course . . . that's . . . ah . . . obvious." Radisson responded, appearing a bit uncomfortable.

"And subsequently, at the flood's *end,* the Himalaya chain of mountains were pushed up by the Indian Tectonic plate, so no 0_2 was needed during the voyage, right?"

"Oh wow!" One of Radisson's students exclaimed.

"Cool beans!" Another, following through.

"Yeah, and then the ark landed at the end of the flood - wasn't it on Mount Ararat?" asked another of Radisson's students.

A number of positive responses emanated from Radisson's students; all the while our kids were chuckling, having been through the tectonic action of Noah's Flood before.

"Now, based on the ark's dimensions, we calculated that it weighed approximately a little over twenty-one tons. We analyzed three major safety parameters: structural safety, overturning stability, and seakeeping quality."

"On what footing, did you employ your study?" Radisson questioned Fred, probing for a weak point.

"We applied the ABS, the American Bureau of Shipping rules, and compared thirteen hull types against the ark. If you wish, I can go through the equations with you."

"No… no, a verbal explanation will be perfectly acceptable," Radisson replied, backing off a bit.

"The study showed that the ark had superior safety compared with other hull forms. We concluded that it had a reasonable beam-draft ratio for the safety of the hull, crew, and cargo in the high winds and waves imposed on it by the Genesis Flood. As a matter of fact, here is the diagram in the alcove on the wall behind us."

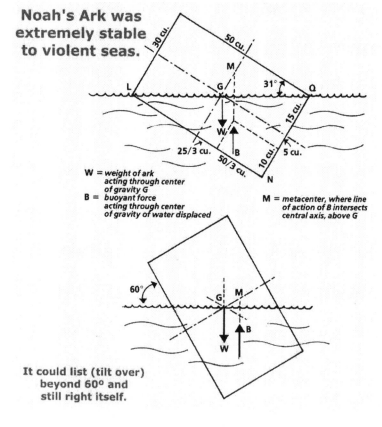

Diagram of ark stability high seas.
Image Credit: Answers in Genesis

Radisson's group was murmuring and nodding among one another.

"Not that I doubt your accuracy—or *integrity*—but can you offer any independent study that was done to analyze the ark?" Radisson asked, grabbing at straws now.

Fred shook his head, "Funny you should ask. As a matter of fact, Noah's Ark was the focus of a major 1993 scientific study headed by Dr. Seon Hong, at the world-class ship research center KRISO, in South Korea. And as for my *integrity*, my wife Cindy can vouch for me," he said, suddenly grabbing her about her waist, to her surprise. "My two little kids are also my best cheerleaders," he said, planting a big smooch on Cindy's lips, which caused both groups to start laughing—at Radisson's expense.

Radisson's eyes narrowed and his lips tightened, which was obvious to us all.

"Again, no hull was found to outperform the 4300 year-old biblical design, and none was found to be able to handle waves up to one hundred feet high," stated Fred performing his shenanigans, while moving his hands up and down mimicking wave action, and again bringing on some clapping and laughter. "Once again, there is an illustration of this on the same wall."

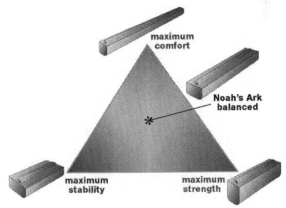

Illustration of Ark dimensions triangle.
Image Credit: Answers in Genesis

"I bet he was a biased *creationist!*" Radisson spitting out the last word as if it were a curse.

"Dr. Hong, who is now director general of the facility, claims that life came from the sea. Sounds like an *evolutionist* to me." Fred spit back the word *evolutionist* to Radisson, while making a funny face, which brought on another spasm of laughter from everyone.

"And *professor,*" Fred said, now zeroing in on him. "During the Hellenistic period, about 300 BC, Ptolemy IV built a trireme, a three-banked galley warship of four thousand oarsmen that was almost as large as Noah's Ark at around 390 feet long."

"Wow!"

"Holy crap!"

"Oh, I'm sorry," Fred continued. "That doesn't include the 400 sailors and 2,850 soldiers who were also on board—for a whopping total of 7,250 men!"

"Geez, and today's massive U.S. aircraft carriers only average five to six thousand men by comparison," one of Radisson's students piped up.

The comments from Radisson's group were coming fast and furious.

"These warships took time and labor to build," Fred said, capitalizing on the moment.

"How did they hold them together?" asked one of Radisson's students with great interest now. "The wooden ships of the 1600s and 1700s turned into leaky buckets, like the *Mayflower,* and its sister ship the *Speedwell,* which had to turn back."

"They didn't just slap the planks on the sides and caulk them with cotton or hemp. Here check this out on my tablet; we just passed a full-scale mock-up on this deck. They used mortise and tenon interlocking planks with wood dowels through them, which swelled with exposure to water and made the fittings even tighter and more secure. I wonder where that idea came from?" Fred asked while making more faces.

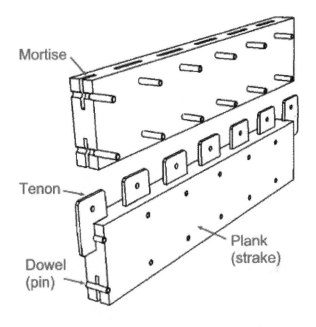

Diagram of mortise and tenon planking.
Image Credit: Answers in Genesis

"Hey, can we follow you guys around," one of Radisson's students hollered out.

"Yeah, this is some cool stuff we've never heard before," stated another.

"If you leave, you will get no credit for this excursion," Radisson threatened.

"It was an optional trip anyway, Radisson. C'mon who's going to come with me and follow these other guys?" questioned one of the dissenters, challenging Radisson's authority.

Three male students from Radisson's group walked over to us, along with the rebel.

"I'm warning you," Radisson screamed at them.

"Screw you, and your three favorite sluts with you," the same renegade shouted, while pointing his finger at the three girls hovering very close to Radisson now.

CHAPTER ONE HUNDRED SIXTEEN

RAINBOW PROMISE

The storm seemed to have passed over us fairly quickly, as I could finally hear myself think. We moved on through the Ark Encounter Museum, now with four new students in tow.

We found out that the leader's name of the insurrection against Professor Radisson was Jack. The others were Sonny, Spud, and Aaron, an African-American from Detroit. They were in Radisson's Philosophy class at the University of Wisconsin at Madison. From the beginning of the semester, the four of them had been unhappy with Radisson's obvious favoritism toward the women.

Fred went on to explain about the fixed rudder or skeg, at the back of the ark, which provided directional control.

"These stern extensions have been seen on the earliest of large ships in the Mediterranean," Fred noted, "and on the bow or front of the vessel, there is something to catch the wind; otherwise a drifting vessel could turn dangerously sideways to a wave, rather than approaching it directly head on. Same as for launching small craft at an ocean beach into the breakers."

"Yeah, definitely a hallmark of ancient ships," Andy chimed in. "Even the Viking ships had a high prow, usually with a dragon's head on them."

"I'm just a Tennessee farm boy," Jack stated, "but I can see how all these ship design technologies are within the realm of possibility for Noah to have incorporated."

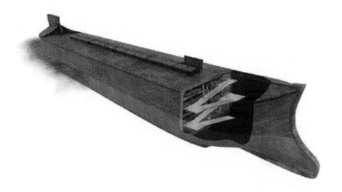

Illustration of ark with cut open section.
Image Credit: Answers in Genesis

"Man, why are they always portraying ancient people as primitive and dumb?" Aaron added, "I would never have thought of something like that."

"Hey, Aaron," Nate called. "Can you carve a flute, with properly spaced and sized holes, in order to play a melody?"

"Heck, the only thing I ever used a knife for in Detroit was for . . . well, you know."

"Neanderthals were able to carve properly designed musical flutes!" Nate commented.

"Whaa?" Aaron stopped and looked at Nate.

"You're kidding?" Spud questioned.

Nate then punched up on his tablet drawings of apes, showing how academia and the media color the sclera white to make them appear more human.

"You're saying that Neanderthals were really humans all along and were able to make a musical instrument with correct tonal qualities," Spud spoke, taken totally aback. "I play keyboard, but I don't have the ability to make a flute or any other instrument for that matter."

"So, there were only apes and humans—no transitional intermediates along the way. But what about the cavemen?" Sonny asked, getting in on the action.

"Hey, Sonny," Nate responded to his question. "Ever hear of the Anasazi Indian Cliff Dwellers, in the Southwestern U.S., who built houses inside huge open-air caves?"

Pete overheard the conversation and added, "My parents would take Andy and me to DeSoto Caverns in Talladega County, Alabama."

"Yeah," Andy joined in. "You liked to pan for gems, remember Pete?"

"The point is," Pete said, getting back on track, "the local Indians occupied the caverns there in the 16 and 1700s. During the Prohibition Era, the caverns were used as a speakeasy!"

"Those sure were some smashed and swinging cavemen during the Roaring Twenties," Andy commented.

"Hold the phone," Aaron said, looking very pensive. "If there were only apes and humans, and no in-between hominids, no evolution took place."

"Correct," Nate answered. "So, 'no evolution' only leaves you with one other option, Aaron."

Aaron couldn't bring himself to say it. He just stared at Nate.

"Okay, Aaron, you can persist in believing man evolved from the apes in Africa—the so-called cradle of civilization. What then, was man's skin color when he first evolved from the apes?"

Ali immediately pushed forward and inserted himself between Nate and Aaron. "Don't go there, man. Think about it before you answer. Or do you want *us* at the bottom of the evolutionary totem pole?"

Aaron seriously studied Ali for a moment. Then he exclaimed, "Oh, Ohhh, yeah . . . holy crap! I see now." He was pensive again, but for only an instant. "What color were Adam and Eve?"

Our whole group burst out laughing, a little to Aaron's embarrassment, while Jack, Sonny, and Spud looked on, a little confused.

"Ali, why don't you bring up the Punnett Square on your tablet and explain to our new inductees about Adam and Eve's skin color; we'll be at the next exhibit down the hall," I said, putting my arm on Ali's shoulder as a sign of confidence in him.

We finished the tour inside the Ark exiting to a clear blue sky. As I started to lead our new troupe over to the Tower of Babel exhibit, Juan hollered out, "Look at the sky behind the Ark." Everyone turned to see a beautiful complete rainbow arched above the Ark, framing it perfectly.

Thad was quick on the draw, and in a flash, he was clicking away with his camera while others did the same with their cell phones.

I heard Maria's sweet voice call out, "'I set my bow in the clouds, and it shall be for a sign of a covenant between Me and the earth . . . [and] never again will the water become a flood to destroy all life.' Genesis: 9:13, 15."

CHAPTER ONE HUNDRED SEVENTEEN

LANGUAGE PROBLEM

"**A**wesome!" Spud gasped really getting into the rainbow. "I've seen rainbows before, but this one is . . . is . . . so intense. I mean . . . like the colors of an acid trip." He's now aware everyone is looking at him. "Scratch that last part . . . a . . . rewind."

Jack walked over to him. "Spud, you're a *trip,* man," he said, shaking his head as everyone chuckled.

We continued walking, and I asked Spud, "That can't be your birth name; how did you get christened with Spud?"

Everyone in my group was all ears as Radisson's guys really started to belly laugh. "Go ahead," Jack said, kinda nudging Spud jokingly. "Tell everyone how you got that name." Jack continued laughing.

"Well . . . a . . . when I was a kid, I made a spud launcher."

"What's that?" Claudia asked him.

"It's a length of PVC conduit piping, with a small pin hole near the bottom of one end which is closed off, kinda like a cannon. You squirt a whole bunch of hairspray into the opening, then shove a potato into it, and ignite the small hole with a match or lighter."

"Then what happens?" Claudia asked, trying to picture the contraption in her mind.

"We have . . . well, *had* . . . some really snooty next-door neighbors who had just added a Florida sunroom onto the back of their home. The potato went through both corner windows, broke an expensive lamp, and ripped down a hanging plant—some rare tropical thing."

"Oh, my!" Claudia gasped, covering her mouth with her hand not knowing whether to laugh or just be surprised. "And then?"

"And then, all hell broke loose. A . . . they were sitting in the sunroom at the time. And that's how I got my nick name."

Everyone was in convulsions at that point, picturing in their minds the scene of devastation in the Florida sunroom and the couple up in arms, wanting quick and decisive retribution for the offender—Spud.

As we approached the entrance steps to the Tower of Babel, Jack asked me, while looking at his buddy, Aaron, "If the 'cradle of civilization' thing is bogus, and there is no evolution of humans over millions of years, where did all the races . . . I mean people groups and languages come from then?"

"Ali, you taught them well, congrats man!" I was happy to finally see a smile come to Ali's face.

Ali followed through. "Right from here," he said, pointing to the Tower of Babel in front of us. "Got any other ideas?"

"Man, this Bible thing is giving me an itch I can't scratch," Jack replied. "Okay, let's go inside and see what you got."

Aaron was especially anxious to enter the building, although he was trying to play it cool. The evolution totem pole example really got to him. It is truly amazing how the human condition, more times than not, really wants to know the truth. Whether people submit to it, or act on it, is another matter entirely.

As we entered the structure from the bright sunlight, our pupils needed to adjust to the more subdued lighting in the entrance. The tour began with the evils of the pre-Flood world, and proceeded to the arrogance of the grandchildren and great-grandchildren of

Noah's three sons: Shem, Ham and Japheth. After the Flood, Noah's offspring refused to leave the plain of Shinar in Iraq. Rather, they wanted to keep their families together with a building project in defiance of God.

"What did God want them to do after the flood was over?" Jack asked.

"'Be fruitful and multiply and fill the earth,'" Maria said, quoting Genesis 9:1, "but they defied God and remained in one place."

Cartoon Illustration of One Blood. Image Credit: Answers in Genesis

"How many years passed from the ark landing on Mount Ararat, to Noah and the offspring moving down into Iraq and building the Tower of Babel?" Sonny asked.

"Somewhere around one hundred years," Jim replied. "Even today the word *babel* means confusion, like a baby's incoherent babbling."

"I don't really buy all of this," Jack said. "You guys scored some points with the ark, but the Bible is so full of tall tales and yarns, and this is so far-fetched. There are around seven thousand languages in the world. And you're telling me your God busted up their *one* language into seven thousand? I mean, like really!"

Sonny came to the rescue. "You mean like English, Jack?" Sonny said in a very sardonic fashion.

"Huh?" Jack asked, looking at Sonny.

"You know, I'm majoring in linguistics. Try reading Old English from around AD 1400, like Chaucer's *Canterbury Tales* or *Beowulf*, which is even worse; it's like reading German, from which much of modern English is derived."

"So how many original languages are we talking about, Sonny?"

"Probably about seventy, give or take, what we call root languages."

"Where did these seventy languages come from—Babel?" Jack responded sarcastically to his friend.

"From our secular viewpoint . . . ah . . . we don't really know. But one thing's for sure. As we look back in time and history, we had expected languages to become more basic and primitive. Instead they're *more* complex."

Juan started jumping around doing his monkey sounds and putting his hands under his armpits again. "What, no grunting, growling, or snarling languages?"

Sonny grabbed his chin and rubbed the stubble of his beard, gazing off in contemplation. "You know, it is strange," he said. "We've never discussed it in any class I've taken, but if modern man has been around for sixty to one hundred thousand years—"

"Why do all languages seem to start only around four thousand or so years ago?" Maggie finished Sonny's thought. "According to the liberal mind-set, there is a blank slate for all those *supposed* tens of thousands of years. Then, all of a sudden 'poof,' there were complex civilizations, complex cities, complex structures like pyramids, ziggurats and temples—*and* complex languages."

Sonny, Jack, Aaron, and Spud seemed to be immobilized, listening to Maggie, never having heard anything like that before.

"Sorta like civilization was wiped clean from the earth, due to the flood perhaps," Nate added with some mild sarcasm, "and had to start over again, but with prior knowledge in order to rebuild."

"This just can't be," Jack said, speaking for his comrades. "What about the hunter-gatherers? What about the agrarian societies that led to civilizations?"

"Post-Babel, the large people groups were on the move to different parts of the world. Those are your hunter-gatherers. And why should modern man take sixty to one hundred thousand years to figure out how to construct buildings and develop languages? Or is this speculation, of the highest order, without evidence?" Nate hammered it home.

"Okay, where is *your* evidence for languages and this complex tower," Jack said, retaliating vociferously. "Show me the money!"

CHAPTER ONE HUNDRED EIGHTEEN

THE CURSE OF THE TOWER

"**P**erfect timing!" I exclaimed, as I flipped a coin to Jack. "What's this?" he asked as he proceeded to carefully inspect the gold coin.

Gold Coin with Saddam Hussein. Photo Credit: imgur.com

"What does it look like? You tell me."

"It says Babylon at the bottom, and the dude with the military-style beret looks like that dictator of Iraq . . . ah . . . that nut that Bush hated . . . yeah, Saddam Hussein. But I can't figure out the other guy with the fancy beard," he said, as he passed the coin to his fellow comrades.

"I've got a coin like this," Aaron exclaimed. "My older cousin was a Marine in the Iraq War and brought one of these home for me. The bearded guy is Nebuchadnezzar II, who's credited with the Hanging Gardens of Babylon."

"Nebu who . . . what?" Jack asked, grabbing the coin from Aaron and studying it again.

"Man, you are ignorant! Nebuchadnezzar was the king of Babylon. Hussein fancied himself as a sort of reincarnation of the famous and powerful king of Babylon. Then Daniel—"

"The same Daniel who was in the Lion's Den?" Jack interrupted.

"Yes!" Aaron blurted out a bit frustrated, "Daniel interpreted Nebuchadnezzar's dream with God's help."

"Okay, okay, but what does this Nebu king have to do with the Tower of Babel?"

Aaron looked at me a bit stupefied.

"Ol' Nebu wanted to tear down the Tower of Babel," I chimed in, "which was pretty dilapidated by that time, around 600 BC, and rebuild it. He had a stone carved with the likeness of him next to the new rebuilt tower. There is a replica of the stone just ahead on our tour."

Illustration of Tower of Babel Stele. Photo Credit: biblicallife.wordpress.com

As they reached the exhibit, Thad leaned over to read the inscription. "'Tower of Babel Stele with Nebuchadnezzar'. Could this have been the world's first ancient photo-op?"

"Hey, Tom," Thad called out, pointing to Tom. "You're our historian. What did that Greek father of history, Herodotus, have to say about the Tower of Babel."

"Give me a second, and I'll locate it," Tom said, feverishly punching up the info on his tablet.

In the momentary lull, Jack, who has been closely studying the stele, commented, "I must confess I thought that the Tower of Babel was just a Bible story; I didn't know there were sources from outside the Bible confirming it."

"Ah, here we go," Tom exclaimed. "'On the summit of the topmost tower stands a great temple with a fine large couch on it, richly covered, and a golden table beside it.'"

"What was that for?" Spud blurted out, cutting Tom off.

"Hang on it gets better . . . and juicier," Tom said, chuckling to himself. "'The shrine contains no image, and no one spends the night there except one Babylonian woman, all alone, whoever it may be that the god has chosen. The Chaldeans also say—though I do not believe them—that the god enters the temple in person and takes his rest upon the bed.'" Tom started laughing, which got the others going as well.

"Yeah, that Herodotus guy saw right through them," Jack exclaimed, chuckling away and slapping Spud on his back. "The high priest gets to select the trollop of the tower for the night. Radisson would have fit right in."

"Did Nebuchadnezzar ever rebuild it?" Aaron asked, still very interested.

"No, he never got the opportunity," I explained to the group. "Alexander the Great ended up demolishing it. He had the same goal to rebuild it. Of course, he died at the very young age of thirty-two—in Babylon, of malaria."

"Man, God definitely put a curse on that tower—*permanently!*" Aaron stated emphatically.

CHAPTER ONE HUNDRED NINETEEN

NIMROD'S TYRANNY

"**W**ho was the high priest, anyway?" Jack asked, still interested in the Tower of Babel love nest. "The guy must have been some big honcho."

"He was," I replied to Jack and the group. "He was considered the one to have directed the construction of the Tower and the city of Babylon itself, while controlling a large swath of surrounding country called Babylonia."

"A *very* powerful dude," Sonny remarked.

"Some extrabiblical sources claim he was the high priest for the pagan god Bel or Ba'al, the god of war. Genesis 10:8–10 calls him a 'mighty hunter'."

"Geez, no wonder he was able to pick whichever babe he wanted and have her up in the tower waiting for him," Jack said, sounding impressed. "What was his name, who was he?"

"His name was Nimrod, and he was Noah's great-grandson," Aaron answered with confidence.

"How did you know that?" Sonny and Jack responded in unison, while Spud still seemed a bit lost.

"When I was a kid in Detroit, my grandmother took me to church on Wednesdays and Sundays, and any other time she could, to keep me away from the street gangs. This Nimrod guy was a narcissistic maniac."

"Hey, Matt," I called across the group. "Why not bring up what your ancestor Josephus has to say about Nimrod? And while you're doing that, I'll explain to the group who he was."

"Sure, Doc, I'm on it."

"Josephus was a Jewish military commander and governor of Galilee who fought against Rome. He was captured by the Roman general Titus, who became emperor, and commanded that Josephus write down a historical record of all that had occurred. Out of that, came his book *The Antiquity of the Jews,* which was written in AD 93. We will also—"

"Hey, wasn't Titus," Tom butted in, "the Roman general who sacked Jerusalem and destroyed the Temple in AD 70? He like totally nuked it!"

"That's correct, Tom. You sure you want to go into law?"

"And one important historical figure," Maria added, "correctly foretold the destruction of Jerusalem and the Temple, around forty years earlier: 'Do you not see these great buildings? Not one stone will be left upon another.'"

"My history profs never mentioned a prediction," Tom admitted, turning to Maria. "Wow! Who envisioned that coming?"

"Christ! Check out what Matthew quoted Jesus as saying in 24:1–2, or Mark 13:1–2, or Luke 21:5–6. That's a triple confirmation, Counselor."

"And before we got off on this tangent," I interrupted, a bit vexed and trying to take hold of the conversation again. "Besides Josephus, there will be other extrabiblical sources to confirm the genealogy, or what is called the Table of Nations of Noah's grandsons and great-grandsons, and their families, as they dispersed from Babel."

"And back at the ranch!" Matt announced, tapping his pen loudly on the edge of his tablet to get our attention.

"Oh, Matt, I am so sorry. Yes, what have you found out about what Josephus said about Nimrod?"

Displaying his annoyance, Matt cleared his throat loudly. "'He also gradually changed the government into tyranny, seeing no other way of turning men from the fear of God, but to bring them into a constant dependence on his power.'"

Spud turned and tapped Matt on the shoulder. "Hey man, could you read that again slowly?" he asked.

Matt was happy to oblige if it meant being center stage for the moment. "Josephus said of Nimrod, 'He also gradually changed the government into tyranny, seeing no other way of turning men from the fear of God, but to bring them into a constant dependence on his power.'"

My students absolutely exploded at that quote. "The Matrix, the Matrix!" they kept calling out, leaving Radisson's four guys wondering what all the fuss and commotion was about.

"Hey, what's got your clan all riled up?" Jack questioned me above the melee, "And what's with this Matrix thing?"

CHAPTER ONE HUNDRED TWENTY

EYES OPENED

"It's the name of my course," I answered Jack. "It's called the Matrix Exposed."

Jack was still confused. Pete picked it up and explained, "The Matrix is the government, the powers that be, the globalists, the Deep State, the Illuminati—all of them that really control our lives. It's all about the money which leads to ultimate power and ultimate control over us peons."

"Are you guys some kind of conspiracy nuts? I'm free to think and do whatever I want," Jack replied with invective and annoyance.

By this time, the whole group was circled around Pete and Jack.

"Basically what Josephus wrote about Nimrod, who lived over four thousand years ago, is that the concept of God and his laws must be destroyed so that Nimrod and his government jackals could take over and control the people of Babylon."

"'And bring them into a constant dependence,'" Maria added forcefully. "In our times, dependence through bread and circuses becomes welfare as the bread, and the circuses are the unreal *Housewives of Wherever*, video-gaming twelve hours a day, as well as gladiatorial sporting events on twenty channels. There is *nothing new under the sun*. That's biblical also."

"Man, who's trashing God and saying he's not real?" Aaron inquired.

Pete tried to regain control while the others attentively looked on. "Jack, you said you are free to think and do whatever you want. Really? And, Aaron, nobody *is* trashing God, because you've been brainwashed to believe he doesn't exist anyway, since evolution is taught as fact and is the only game in town!"

"Man, *you* are just talking trash," Aaron rebutted, getting in Pete's face.

"You yourselves said," Pete responded, sweeping his arm in front of him to recognize Radisson's four students, "that you've never heard any of this before. How can you make that statement . . . *unless* you've been brainwashed to believe that the Bible is just a bunch of fairytales? In your defense, we were all indoctrinated by the same education system as you."

With that, Jack and Aaron quietly conversed with each other, as Sonny and Spud listened in.

Jack finally stepped up. "We were just discussing that in all our courses throughout grade school, middle school, high school, and now college, we have never been given a textbook, nor heard a lecture from an opposing point of view. It's always been one sided."

"Yeah, man," Aaron added, "and if anyone in any class attempts to present an opposing or Christian position, he or she is summarily chastised by both students and professors—*especially* by Radisson!"

"I personally witnessed two students over the years sent to the principal's office for . . . a . . . 're-education'," Spud announced.

"And remember guys, that one fellow who was asked by our conservative student organization to speak in Grainger Hall, was not permitted to give his talk. We protested, and practically tarred and feathered him. I'm sorry to say, I was one of those protesters," Sonny admitted.

"My daddy always said it took a big man to admit his shortcomings," Jack said, extending his hand to Pete, who clasped

Jack's hand in his with an overly firm grip; then they started to laugh as each tested the other's strength. Both then locked their arms about the other's shoulders, as they led the way for the rest of us to the next exhibit, still talking and laughing.

CHAPTER ONE HUNDRED TWENTY-ONE

TABLE OF NATIONS

As we were all walking to the next exhibit, Aaron loudly asked me, "I'm confused about something. My cousin, the one who was in Iraq, told me that where the Tigris and Euphrates Rivers are by Bagdad and Babylon, is also nearby where the Garden of Eden was; but they don't know exactly where. Why not?"

"This is a common misconception, Aaron. You seem to know a bit about the Bible, thanks to your grandmother. Do you recall the names of the four rivers that flowed out from the Garden of Eden?"

"Yes, they were the Pishon, the Gihon, the Tigris, and the Euphrates," Aaron said, giving a big, generous smile to all, knowing that he was correct. "Since two of the rivers are right there, it should be easy to find Eden."

"From what I'm told, archeologists have been having a hard time finding any structural remains of the Acropolis in Athens, Georgia, or the Arch of Titus, or the Colosseum in Rome, New York," I said giving him a big smile in return.

"Huh? Oh, yeah." Aaron was a tad slow on the uptake as the group started laughing first. "Italian and Greek immigrants to the states obviously wanted to name places after their homeland, for which they had an emotional connection."

"And after the Flood, when Noah and his descendants moved down into what is now Iraq—"

"Duh!" Aaron interrupted me. "They saw those two rivers, and Noah or his sons, probably did the same as the immigrants to the U.S. That's so obvious to me now. Why do people confuse the issue?"

"If Noah's Flood was really a totally destructive earth-altering event, would anyone know where on the globe the Garden of Eden initially was?"

"Of course not," Aaron responded, "Oh, I see now. Brainwash people into believing that the Flood was a fairytale, and it confuses the issue with Eden, also a fairytale. Man, have we been taken to the cleaners—*mentally!*"

Spud was shaking his head as he looked back at Aaron. "Some people don't need to be brainwashed - a light rinse will do," Spud said, getting some chuckles from the group.

"Speak for yourself, potato head," Aaron said, pushing the smaller Spud, which got another round of guffaws from the group.

"Ah, here we are at the Table of Nations," I proclaimed. "Much of this information, again is from sources outside the Bible, such as Polybius, Tacitus, Plutarch, and Julius Caesar, and yet it confirms the Bible."

"Those are some *very* influential movers and shakers, Dr. Lucci, world class ancient historians and pagans." Claudia was very intrigued as she read the names from the display plaque silently to herself.

"Oh, Claudia," Maria chimed in. "They list our old friends, Herodotus and Josephus who also confirm the Table of Nations."

Philip did a double take. "Sir Isaac Newton's, *Newton's Revised History of Ancient Kingdoms,* is listed here as source material for the Table of Nations," he said, blinking to refocus on what he was reading. "I always considered Newton as only a brilliant scientist," he said, shaking his head in disbelief.

"Wasn't he the apple guy?" Spud asked.

"Apple? Oye, wasn't that Steve Jobs?" Santi commented.

"Apple . . . ah . . . gravity. Newton discovered the Law of Gravity. We're not talking computers, Santi," Juan said, getting exasperated with his cousin.

"Moving on," I said, as I cleared my throat. "The name of a descendant of Noah sometimes became the name of the language or the people. Aaron, give everyone a quick refresher as to who the three sons of Noah were."

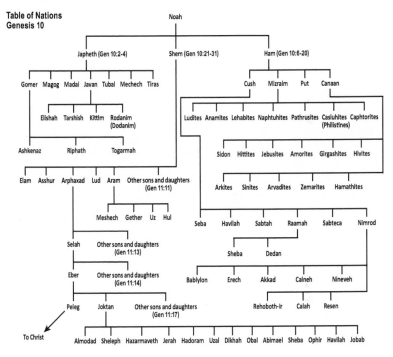

Table of Nations. Image Credit: Answers in Genesis

Again, Aaron rose to the occasion. "Japheth, Ham, and Shem," he said. "And that's Shem, and not Shemp from the Three Stooges." Aaron immediately started with the woo, woo, nyuk, nyuk sounds. Matt and Tom joined him. Passersby looked at our trio of stooges wondering what these antics were all about. I put my hand over my forehead wishing I was not there at that moment. Of course, the rest of the kids were egging them on.

CHAPTER ONE HUNDRED TWENTY-TWO

MODERN EXPERTS

"Matt!" I hollered out, partially to get his attention, and also to break up the Stooges routine. "Tell us, when you were studying for your bar mitzvah and learning the Torah, did you learn the Hebrew name for Egypt?"

I caught Matt off balance, and he had to think for a moment. "Ah . . . it was Mizraim," he said, studying me very curiously. I glanced at Maggie, Maria, and Claudia, and gave them a slight smile.

"Matt, look at the Table of Nations on the plaque in front of us. Find Noah's son Ham, and then find Ham's sons - Noah's grandsons from his son Ham."

Everyone watched Matt as his finger followed the lines of descendants down from Noah. Matt bolted upright. "One of Ham's sons was called Mizraim," he proclaimed, excited and dumbfounded at the same time.

"And Matt, since you are at the display plaque, look up Noah's son Japheth, and his son Gomer." I prayed the kids were too young to remember the TV sitcom *Gomer Pyle, USMC*, as I can't handle another ruckus.

"Got it."

"Great! One of Gomer's sons, who would be one of Noah's great-grandsons, is a name you probably recognize."

His finger scanned across to Japheth, and then down. It stopped, and he leaned close to the display. He mumbled while still bent over with his finger on the name Ashkenaz. Matt got a bit wobbly and dropped to his knees, as he grabbed the rail in front of the display for support. "We can't hear you, Matt," Tom cried out.

Matt tried to get up, but faltered and just stayed sitting on the floor. "My . . . my great-grandparents were Ashkenazi Jews, who were murdered by Hitler in the Holocaust at the Bergen-Belsen concentration camp. That's the same camp where Anne Frank starved to death." He suddenly jumped up. "I've . . . I've just got to call my dad immediately and tell him what I just discovered." He ran off to a corner to have some privacy, and I saw him use the T-chip in his hand to call his father.

With that, almost everyone rushed to the display to check on their lineage in relation to Noah and his sons.

Thad started taking pictures of the Table of Nations, including some close-ups of Japheth's son Javan, while prattling away. "I have some Greek in my heritage. My grandmother told me that her grandfather's name was Javan, and my dad always uses the expression 'by Jove,' having heard it from *his* parents."

"My grandmother, the one who schooled me in the Bible," Aaron said, pointing to the name Cush, one of Ham's sons, "said her lineage was Ethiopian, but her uncle refused to use the modern term Ethiopian, and instead said that they were rightly called Cushites. She didn't know why. Boy, wait until I tell her why!"

"Hey, Doc," Jim called out. "We just finished studying the ecology of the Hindu Kush."

"Where's that place?" Juan asked.

"It's a very rough mountainous region bordering part of Afghanistan and Pakistan, just west of India. Is there any relationship? Could some of those Cushites have also gone eastward toward India from Babel?"

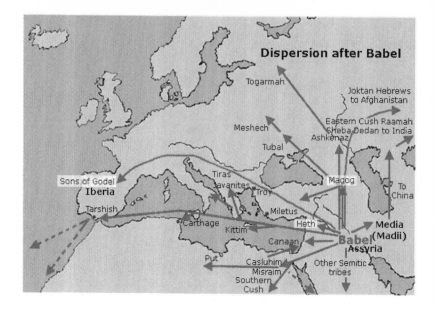

Dispersion after Babel

Dispersion after Babel. Image Credit: Abraham's Legacy

"Very perceptive of you, Jim. In short, yes. In English we, for whatever reason, decided to use a *K* instead of a *C* for the Hindu Kush," I explained.

"Man, this is incredible!" Jack was mesmerized by the whole Table of Nations. "Why have modern researchers belittled the extensive investigations of the likes of Sir Isaac Newton, Julius Caesar, and those other renowned guys? They lived closer to the times of those events than contemporary so-called experts."

"Yeah, Jack's right."

"What gives?"

"Okay, everyone slow down, and let's think in reverse for a moment. Put those thinking caps on. If modern researchers acknowledged the findings of those ancient historians, they would have to admit that the dispersion from the Tower of Babel was true." I stopped to let that sink in. I saw a few of my students wanting to say something. "Let Radisson's guys work through this," I told them.

Sonny, the linguist, was chomping at the bit to answer. "If these so-called modern experts admit to there being a dividing of languages and peoples at Babel, then they have to admit to there having been only one language, which brings us back to Noah's Flood and there being a biblical God."

"And that this occurred only . . . what . . . around four thousand years ago." Aaron was getting agitated as he continued, "Which blows the cork on the whole 'out of Africa/cradle of civilization deal' and the millions of years lie. And I personally don't like the idea of being at the bottom of any totem pole."

My students applauded that comment and slapped some of Radisson's guys on the back, as well.

"I've got something," Spud added with a very serious demeanor. Our group hushed up, awaiting words of wisdom from Spud. "X is an unknown quantity and a spurt is a drip under pressure. So much for our modern *experts*."

A hail of boos and hisses resounded while Jack and Aaron were lovingly smacking Spud, chiding him in the process.

CHAPTER ONE HUNDRED TWENTY-THREE

SPUD'S DECISION

The group needed a breather, including myself. There was only one other section of the Tower of Babel exhibit, which was a short video; then we would take a break.

"There is a café on the premises to grab a bite to eat, and you can explore the gift shop. We'll meet outside on the steps of the Tower of Babel, which hopefully is dry by now."

We walked down to a small open alcove off the hallway. In the alcove was a large video screen with several rows of benches in front of it. The countdown clock read twelve minutes to the next presentation. Perfect!

"Okay, gang we have several minutes before the next presentation. There are restrooms bordering each side of this little theatre area."

Cindy and the three girls immediately bolted for the women's restroom.

"What is it about women?" Tom lamented. "They all seem to need to go to the bathroom at exactly the same time."

"TB!" Matt, who had rejoined us, exclaimed.

"What?"

"TB—tiny bladder," Matt explained for Tom. Some of the guys chuckled.

Spud had been eyeing the girls. "I think I would like to identify as a female today. I need to use the powder room," he said, speaking in a deliberately lilting voice while shifting his bearing toward the women's restroom.

"Okay, if you don't mind getting the crap kicked out of you," Pete commented off the cuff, while making himself comfortable on one of the benches.

"What do you mean?" Spud inquired, suddenly dropping the female persona. "From the Security personnel?"

"No, the girls themselves!" Pete exclaimed forcefully. "They don't cater to all this politically correct LGBTXYZ stuff and will lay you out cold. I know for a fact that Maggie and Cindy have been taking Tai Chi or something."

"In that case, the men's room will be perfectly acceptable," Spud said, making a quick 180 in mid-stride, heading now for the men's lavatory. All of us in the little theatre howled with laughter.

"While we're waiting for *all* the girls to return—including Spud," I said, coaxing a few more laughs from the group. "Aaron or Matt, do one of you recall, from the Table of Nations, one of Ham's sons called Canaan?"

"Sure," Aaron responded immediately. "Guess that's where the Promised Land, given to Abraham, got its name. Canaan was Noah's grandson."

"Excellent! Now, Canaan had several sons, one of whom was named Sineus."

"Yeah," Thad blurted out. "I've got a pic of the Table of Nations and Canaan had eleven sons. Didn't any of these guys have any daughters?"

"Of course, y'all," Cindy said, as the girls returned from the bathroom. "But starting with Adam, men were the head of the household, and the respect that went with it. Only the men were counted in the genealogies."

"Wasn't that sexist, chauvinist, and misogynistic?" Claudia questioned.

"Claudia, argue that point with God. Like any organization, there can be only one head; two or more heads is a monster and only leads to confusion. However, like any organization or household, the leader needs steadfast input from a rational mind like a board of directors or, in the case of a family, a good wife."

"I never looked at it quite like that, Cindy. I always thought we were second-class citizens."

"God designed us to be our husband's *'helpmate'*, not slave. We are the neck that turns the head, girl. But if his final decisions screw things up, it's the head, the leader that takes the blame—and gets the rotten tomatoes thrown at him. Unless of course, bless your little heart, *you* want the responsibility."

Claudia stood there looking at Cindy, very sober, while all of us were silent wondering what Claudia was thinking. Suddenly, Pete stood up to make a statement. He was becoming quite the leader.

"That's why it's called Adam's sin, and not Eve's, even though she tasted of the forbidden fruit *first* and then gave it to her husband, Adam. It was Adam's ultimate decision to eat of it that has caused all this mess for mankind." Pete then promptly sat down.

There was a long, stagnant pause. Everyone, including a few visitors who had joined us, were momentarily paralyzed; Cindy and Pete had given us all something to really chew on. One middle-aged couple was down front. The wife, with tears in her eyes, turned and grabbed her husband's hand; then she leaned her head on his shoulder.

CHAPTER ONE HUNDRED TWENTY-FOUR

PHILIP'S REACTION

"I believe we left off with Sineus, Noah's great-grandson through Canaan and Ham," I awkwardly announced, breaking the tense silence.

"Sineus is the name from which Sinai is derived," Matt explained. He was on it like a frog on a June bug. "Where's Jim? I need a V-8," he said while looking around the small cinema area for Jim. Our group was laughing, while Radisson's team looked confused by the V-8 comment.

"Way to go, Matt," I responded, complementing his quick analysis.

"Now, let's delve into your history expertise, Tom. Ever heard of the Sino-Japanese War or the Sino-Russian conflict on the Mongolian border of China, in the late 1960s?"

"No . . . I mean yes," Tom replied. "Are you saying, Doc, that those offspring of Sineus, the Sinites, went all the way to China from Babel?"

"I'm not saying a thing, Tom. I believe the Babel history speaks for itself, unless you have another theory."

"And the Sinai Peninsula," Matt added, "which would indicate some of Sineus' people also branched off and went south. They probably also had domestic family squabbles back then."

"Like, 'we're outta here'," Tom interjected, "*really* meant something in those days."

The visitors were getting a kick out of the repartee between Matt and Tom. Some of them were chuckling along with us.

"Okay you guys, the video is about to start," I said, as the lights automatically dimmed. "We've got other guests to be cognizant of."

The movie gave an overview of the breakup of language at the Tower of Babel, and then described the different-speaking family groups leaving the Babel area for different parts of the world, taking their unique sets of genes and their memories of the historical accounts of the Flood, and Adam and Eve, and creation with them. They also took their common ship and architectural building skills with them.

Photo of where did all the people groups come from .
Photo Credit: Answers in Genesis

I could hear the aahs coming from the audience as the narrator discussed, and the video showed, photos of the pyramids and ziggurats built around the globe. All as a result of the uniform high-tech knowledge taken by the pilgrims of Babel as they moved from place to place.

I overheard one of the visitors ask her husband why all pyramids around the world were not exactly the same. He replied, "Do you know of any major architect that designs all of his buildings identically?"

Collage of multiple pyramids around the world.
Photo Credit: www.siralio.com

Finally, the narrator spoke of the ancient Chinese people:

"The Chinese claim to have one of the oldest languages on earth. If the Chinese people just somehow evolved around one hundred thousand years ago from the cradle of civilization in Africa and moved eastward toward the land of China as evolutionists claim, they should have no knowledge of a Judeo-Christian God, since He was made up by Jews and Christians only three or four thousand years ago, which is about as far back as written records go for any civilization."

I glanced over at Philip, who was intently focused on the film, perhaps reflecting back on his mother reading him the *Hihking*

Classic, which predates any visit from Christian missionaries to China.

"But if the Babel dispersion is true, the ancient Chinese should have some remembrance of biblical historical events from creation and Adam to the Flood and to Babel, since their ancestors took those stories with them when they left Babel."

"They did!" the narrator proclaimed.

"…and it actually shows up in the ancient language of China. Chinese records also describe Nuah with three sons, Lo Han, Lo Shen and Jahphu, according to the Miautso people of China."

I noticed a bead of sweat form on Philip's forehead; he was leaning forward, his hands firmly locked securely on his knees. Then the first slide came up on the screen "'And the Lord formed man of the dust of the ground…'" the narrator read quoting Genesis 2:7.

ノ	+	土	+	儿	=	先
alive		dust		man		first

Alive, dust, man , first.
Courtesy: Dr.Don Patton dpatton693@aol.com

Then a second slide.

要 = 一 + 儿 + 口 + 女

Necessary	One	Man	Enclosure	Woman

Necessary, one, man, enclosure, woman. Courtesy: Dr. Don Patton

Philip slowly rubbed his hands together. The narrator explained that *enclosure* in Chinese can also mean garden. Philip was ever so slightly nodding his head.

The next slide came up.

©www.Bible.ca

| Ship \| Vessel | Ship | Eight | People |

Ship/vessel, ship, eight, people. Courtesy: Dr. Don Patton

Philip licked his dry lips, trying to moisten them as beads of sweat filled his forehead. Then the next slide.

©www.Bible.ca

Tower | Undertaking | United

Tower, undertaking, united. Courtesy: Dr. Don Patton

Then the next.

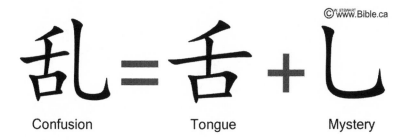

©www.Bible.ca

Confusion | Tongue | Mystery

Confusion, tongue, mystery. Courtesy: Dr. Don Patton

And another.

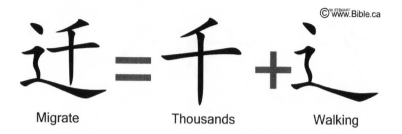

Migrate   Thousands   Walking

Migrate, thousands, walking. Courtesy: Dr. Don Patton

At this point, Philip was visibly upset. He covered his mouth with his hand and rushed headlong from the cinema toward the men's room, which shared a common wall with the theatre.

It was Philip's moment of truth. An atheist's beliefs were crashing head-on with the Bible. This was more than just a gut-check; this was his body's visceral reaction to—the Truth!

His vomiting was so violent and intense that everyone in the theatre could hear him. I was worried and leaned over to Nate next to me, and said, "Better check on Philip." Nate looked concerned. He nodded at me and quickly raced off to the men's room.

CHAPTER ONE HUNDRED TWENTY-FIVE

BEET RED RADISSON

The sun had dried up the water, at least on the white concrete steps leading up to the Tower of Babel exhibit. We were all spread out in groups sitting around, some eating, others talking and laughing, and some having heavy discussions on what they just learned inside.

I took the time to call Emily to see how things were going. She reported no further instances of power failure. Again, I reassured her that it was Dietrich just rattling our chain a bit and not to worry.

As I hung up with Emily, I saw Nate escorting Philip from the building. He wasn't white as a sheet, but his complexion had definitely lightened up and everyone noticed the change. As he reached the edge of the steps he asked, "Anyone have a mint?"

"Here, I've got some Mentos."

"Want spearmint?"

"You can have this pack of Tic Tacs."

Everyone was empathetic, having had that nasty taste in their mouths before.

Pete and Andy stopped by and we talked. I congratulated Pete on the way he handled himself with the discussion on Adam's sin. Andy slapped his brother on the back to show he was proud of him, also. We then just small-talked awhile, sitting on the steps.

Andy was the first to take notice. "Check it out. Look who's coming to the Tower of Babel exhibit."

Sure enough, it was our friends from the Church of Little Green Men. They had decided to take our suggestion and came to the Ark Encounter. X-Box appeared to be leading them, and they didn't have their tin-foil hats on anymore. We gave them a wave and they waved back.

We had some time to kill before heading back to the hotel. It was the last day of our trip, and we were just relaxing, soaking up the remains of the afternoon sun. I was bushed. The past few days had been an intense educational immersion, but everyone seemed to get something out of it.

I was sort of dozing off when Jack, Aaron, Sonny, and Spud came running up. They appeared very jittery and nervous. Pete was the first to ask, "What's up with you guys?"

Spud, who appeared to be the most apprehensive, was almost stuttering, "It's . . . it's Professor Radisson and . . . and his class."

"Yeah," Jack stated, "he looks stomping mad as a pit bull and is headed this way."

I wonder what he wants, I thought. *Lord, is this day going to end on a sour note?*

Sure enough, Radisson climbed the steps quickly and got right in my face. "We're going to have it out right now, winner take all!" His face had that "weaned on a pickle" look that Jude was so famous for.

"I'm going to blow your six thousand-year, stupid theory wide open with some hard facts! Physical evidence, no theoretical nonsense. This will end all debate of this dumb Noah's Flood once and for all, and therefore, your imaginary magical buffoon of a God."

"Oh, for a second you had me worried," I exclaimed. "You wouldn't happen to have any distant relative by the name of Charles

Lyell?" I asked. "He already tried that a while back." My group howled with laughter, making Radisson all the more unhinged.

Radisson's face turned tart red, his eyes were inflamed from sweat, and his blond hair was dripping, the sweat running down his cheeks. "Walter, get out here!" he screamed, as he looked back at his class searching for this Walter, while trying to wipe the burning salt from his eyes.

CHAPTER ONE HUNDRED TWENTY-SIX

POWER OF POLITE

Radisson was huffing and puffing. He must have been running around the park looking for me and my accomplice, Fred, all the while dragging his proselytes with him. And the three hussies looked absolutely ragged and exhausted.

"Walter, where the hell are you? Front and center!"

Pete leaned over to me and whispered, "Demanding little fascist, isn't he?"

"And he smokes too much," I whispered back to both Pete and Andy, who were listening in on the exchange.

Slowly worming his way through the crowd of Radisson's students, Walter finally emerged. He was a short twitchy fellow of slight stature who appeared like he didn't really want the exposure.

Andy commented in my ear, "Geez, the guy looks like Rick Moranis from *Honey I Shrunk the Kids*. He's got the big round glasses and all."

Walter just stood there visibly uncomfortable. Radisson walked over and stood next to him, placing his arm around Walter's shoulder. It was a caricature from the cartoon Mutt and Jeff.

"This is Walter," Radisson said, beaming with expectation. "Walter is a paleo-ecologist with expertise in the Pleistocene period, as well as a climatologist researcher. He's going to demolish this Noah's Flood idiocy once and for all. Oh, and he'll take on all comers who try to refute his cast-iron facts. Won't you, Walter?"

"Y . . . yes," he stuttered, as his eyes nervously darted around our group.

"This poor fellow probably lives in the lab with his computers and test equipment, and writes articles for scientific journals," I said softly to Pete and Andy.

"The guy's a researcher, a geek. Probably very knowledgeable in his field but does not even lecture, let alone debate," Andy commented.

"Not going to send anyone forward to challenge my champion?" Radisson taunted. "Gutless Christian fools."

Pete leaned closer to me and whispered, "Jim and I have been intensely studying about the Pleistocene Ice Age at night, during the breaks, and on the bus. We picked up some great books and magazines from the bookstore at the Creation Museum. No sweat!" And he chuckled to himself.

"Well, we're still waiting," Radisson called out with a malevolent smile on his face.

"Hey, Jim," Pete called across the steps to the opposite side where Jim was sitting. "You want to take this on?"

"You had better do it; I might lose my cool. I'll just stay in the bull pen, in case I'm needed."

Tom then howled out for all to hear, "Yeah, Jim you won't need to warm up; you're already hot to trot." Our students lovingly started to poke fun at Jim, whose Patrick Henry demeanor was already blaringly obvious to all.

I leaned over to Pete, who was going to confront Walter in this lopsided David and Goliath contest, and whispered some words of advice and strategy to him.

"Brilliant, Doc, just brilliant. It'll work like a charm," Pete responded.

"Pete is going to debate Walter," I told Radisson. With that, six-foot-two Pete stood up and, already being elevated on the steps, towered over poor Walter who was almost shaking as he stood on the pavement below.

Pete then walked down the steps, and with a kind smile, extended his hand to Walter, which he accepted. I noted that Walter shook Pete's hand like a dead fish—poor self-confidence. "If you wish to present your facts about the ice age," Pete said in a mild voice, and still smiling politely, "you have the floor."

Walter, who probably has not heard a pleasant word in his direction in a while, was totally stunned by Pete's politeness, and how this gentle giant of a competitor befriended him. Pete then turned around and gave me a wink, and I smiled back. The strategy was working so far.

CHAPTER ONE HUNDRED TWENTY-SEVEN

CLIMATE CHALLENGE

Walter seemed to compose himself somewhat, and began. "Climate scientists are virtually in total agreement that there were approximately thirty separate ice ages over the past 2.5 million years, with the most recent ones lasting forty to one hundred thousand years. That alone, eliminates any even remote possibility for a recent— around forty-five hundred years ago—flood of Noah, as claimed by conservative Christians."

He continued, "I will prove this beyond a shadow of a doubt using multiple cross referencing and testing studies. I will show how the Milankovitch, or astronomical, hypothesis can easily be used to assign ages to seafloor sediment cores, and that ice ages are triggered by decreases in the amount of summer sunlight falling on the high northern latitudes."

Both Radisson's group and mine were like, "What is he talking about?"

Walter rambled on, probably ad-libbing from one of his journal articles. "Both seafloor cores and ice cores, from Greenland GISP2 and Antarctica, tell the story of past climate change. Measurements and calculations of the oxygen isotope ratio $\delta 18O$ confirm this when plotted out on a graph. The 'wiggles'," Walter said laughing inappropriately, "tell us when the ice is at its maximum or minimum. All this is cross-checked using radiocarbon and/or radiometric readings. This also is enhanced using orbital tuning to date the seafloor cores. And we can easily count 110,000 or more annual layers from ice cores at GISP2 using a technique called LLS, or Laser Light Scattering for you lay people. That would be 110,000 plus years, again decimating the concept of a worldwide flood from forty-five hundred years ago."

"Way to go, Walter," Radisson said as he stepped forward and patted Walter on his back. Walter appeared to get nervous again as Radisson approached. "Let's see how your man can counter *those* hard core facts." Radisson glared at me with that last challenge.

Pete and Jim had been totally focused on what Walter had to say.

Pete sat down on the steps and took out a stick of gum, appearing very relaxed. "Walter, I'm just curious about the Milankovitch hypothesis that most of this depends on. It is just a hypothesis, not even a theory, correct?"

"That's right," Walter responded, easily agreeing with Pete.

"Basically, this hypothesis assumes that over the hundreds of millions of years, as the earth revolves around the sun, that the earth's tilt, which is 23.5 degrees, wobbles a bit. That the earth may gain or lose a degree or so, is this not correct?"

"Oh, yeah. That's right."

"Again, this is something that is *assumed;* there is no way to prove it, and even if it did occur, which is a big *if,* it would have been in the unobserved past. There is no way to properly, repeatedly test it according to the scientific method."

"That's true," Walter admitted, again readily agreeing with Pete.

"And you have to admit, plus or minus one degree is a weak hypothesis, at best, for *causing* ice ages. Even your colleague Hecht, in his report 'Long-term ice core records and global environmental changes'—now in the book, *Environmental Record in Glaciers and Ice Sheets,* attests as much."

"Oh, of course, I am aware of that study."

"Again, just curious Walter, if the earth has been revolving around the sun for hundreds of millions of years, why and how would the current ice age only start 2.5 million years ago? Why wouldn't they have been ongoing in a regular, uniform cyclical pattern every 5 or 10 or 50 million years?"

"Yes, we have been working on that aspect of the puzzle."

I noticed Radisson nervously lit up a cigarette.

"Ever been to Australia, the land Down Under, Walter?"

"No."

"I'm sure you, being a climatologist and all, are aware that when it's summer down under it's winter here up north, and vice versa."

"Of course, you're being silly. It's Pete, isn't it?"

Pete nodded, and continued, "And your colleague D. P. Schrag, in his article 'Of Ice and Elephants', in the Journal *Nature*, issue 404—"

"Oh yes, I helped DP. He asked me if I could review this article for him before it went to the publisher, and for peer review. I believe I know the section you wish to refer to," Walter said, quoting it from memory. "'And we don't know why ice ages occur in *both* hemispheres simultaneously when the changes in solar irradiance . . . have opposite effects in the north and south.'"

Radisson seemingly very uptight, exploded at Walter. "Just who the hell's side are you on, anyway?" With that, both groups exploded with laughter.

Walter turned to Radisson, and developed a spine, if only temporarily. Feeling his scientific integrity had been impugned, he exclaimed, "I am an honest scientist; we discuss things openly and forthrightly, wherever the truth may lead us."

This brought on a chorus of cheers and applause from both groups. Radisson completely lost it. He stomped around in circles, puffing away on his cigarette; then he turned to leave. "Who's coming with me?"

No one moved. He looked at his three women. "What about you three?" he asked.

"I want to stay and hear more. This is interesting," one replied.

"Besides, he's cute and easy on the eyes," the most attractive one commented, pointing at Pete, which caused Pete to blush. I don't think I had ever seen Pete get fidgety and turn colors.

"To hell with all of you," Radisson declared, throwing his arms up in disgust and briskly walking off.

Pete extended an olive branch and asked Radisson's people to relax and sit on the warm steps. Both groups moved closer around Pete and Walter, who was now sitting next to Pete.

Walter first peered around as if Matrix spies were looking over his shoulder. He then opened up to us about the shortcomings of the studies regarding the ice age. "If you read the technical journals like I do," he explained, "the challenges are overtly obvious to anyone who can read. Not all scientists are in agreement with these studies, like my friend DP and Hecht, the other researcher. There is much fudging of numbers to make it all fit nice and clean."

"But what about the 110,000 plus annual layers of snowfall in the Greenland ice cores they drilled?" Sonny asked.

"Anyone live near Buffalo, New York?" Walter asked looking around.

One of Radisson's students raised his hand.

"Tell me Price, does your city only get one snowfall a year, or do you have several storms?"

"Man, we measure our snow in feet, not inches."

"Well, then?" Walter asked, giving Price that, "c'mon figure it out" expression.

"You mean to tell us, that the scientists are only assuming *one* snowfall or blizzard or storm or whatever per year? Give me a break! There is absolutely no way to accurately count layers then; it's one big assumption!"

"This was brought to light," explained Walter, "a number of years ago. In 1942, during World War II, six P-38 fighters and two B-17 bombers crash-landed in Greenland. They lay undisturbed for decades and were recovered in 1992 under 268 feet of snow! So Price tell me how many annual layers do you think were counted?"

"Well, based on conventional thinking fifty layers for the fifty years under the ice and snow."

"How about when the shaft was dug to reach one of the planes, they recorded hundreds of layers!"

"What did the scientists say to that?" Price inquired.

The "Lost Squadron" Conundrum

The Lost Squadron. Image Credit: Ark Encounter

"Oh, the scientists said that since the planes were discovered near the east coast of Greenland, that part gets more snow than central Greenland where the GIPS2 core drilling was being done."

"Yeah, but they made that statement after the fact. They never knew how *deep* those planes would be buried until *after* the planes were found," Price exclaimed, getting ticked off. "What did they do with that P-38 fighter, anyway?"

"They rebuilt it and it's flying today. She's called Glacier Girl. I'll bring up a picture for you on my tablet."

Glacier Girl being removed from ice. Photo Credit: Answers in Genesis

Glacier Girl in Flight. Photo Credit: wallpho.com

Walter gave his tablet first to Price, who then gave it to Pete, who passed it around. "Wow! Cool man. I'd love to see that plane.

My dad's a pilot. I wonder if he knows about Glacier Girl?" Price excitedly commented.

After Walter retrieved his tablet back, he lowered the biggest boom of all. "Actually, we really don't know what causes even *one* ice age to start! We haven't got a clue!"

"What?"

"You're kidding, right?"

"Walter's just putting us on, aren't you Walter?"

Walter hung his head and admitted, "I wish I were lying to you."

With that, Pete stoutly spoke up, "Hey Walter, *I'll* explain to you how an ice age is created!"

Walter's head snapped up. "Are you s**ting me?" he asked.

"*Walter*!!" all three of Radisson's women blared out in alarm at his colorful expression. Apparently, they never heard a foul word from him before.

CHAPTER ONE HUNDRED TWENTY-EIGHT

ONE ICE AGE

"A...a...I apologize, it's...it's just I can't believe Pete here seems so confident of how an ice age could occur. I've just got to hear what he has to say."

"Now, Walter," Pete said patronizingly, "a smart guy like you knows what it takes for snow to fall and then turn into ice."

"Of course, everyone knows that. I'll bet that even Heather here, who's been giving Pete googly eyes, knows that. You want to be a weather girl, right Heather?"

"Walter...sometimes...oooh, I wish you wouldn't be so honest and blunt," Heather said through clenched teeth. She didn't seem to need any rouge on her cheeks at the moment. "And we haven't been called weather girls for forty years; we are meteorologists. Sheesh, what a little chauvinist you are, Walter."

"Okay, Miss Meteorologist, what initial factors are needed to cause rain and snow?" Walter asked, definitely coming out of his shell without Radisson present.

"It's called the hydrologic cycle, where evaporation occurs from lakes and oceans and then condenses in the upper atmosphere. If it falls in the upper latitudes and mountains, it generally comes down as snow, and the lower temperate or equatorial latitudes, as rain—so there!"

"Here's an illustration for you, Heather, to show Walter," one of her girlfriends said, as she handed Heather her tablet.

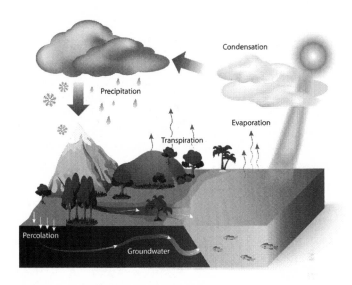

Hydrologic Cycle. Image Credit: Shutterstock

"That's very good," Walter exclaimed, really thinking about her points. "But Pete, the earth would need massive amounts of evaporation, over long periods of time, for snow to keep falling, and then continually turning into ice, *without* any springtime melt. Where would all this heat, to warm the oceans to one hundred-plus degrees Fahrenheit, be generated from?"

Everyone in my class started laughing since they knew the answer already.

"Oye, Walter, ever hear of the fuentes—a 'fountains of the deep'"? Santi called out.

"Nooo, not to my recollection," Walter admitted, still confused as to why all the laughter.

Pete tapped Walter on the knee, "I'm sure you are familiar with the mid-Atlantic ridge and the Pacific volcanic Ring of Fire."

"Of course."

Aaron jumped into the picture without hesitation. "Walter, the Bible talks about all these rupturing on one day which initiated the start of Noah's Flood. That would be a massive amount of *heat* and ash released during the year that the Flood lasted."

"'And God made a wind to pass over the earth,'" Maria added, "It's *after* the Flood that the Bible first speaks of major wind patterns, and therefore a global climate change."

"If what you say actually happened, we are looking at category 7 hurricanes and F-7 tornados. I mean like off-the-charts stuff. Hypercanes and monsoon rains all over the place," Walter exclaimed, getting really hyped-up.

"Wow! What a movie that would make," Matt said loudly, "and it wouldn't be science *fiction* either, like *The Day after Tomorrow.*"

"And I'd be the queen of the evening news," Heather added, bringing both arms and hands palms up, and dipping her head ever so regally.

"Okay," Walter questioned, "but what would prevent the glaciers from melting in the summers and continuing their advance? That is a challenge we also have."

Pete reminded him, "What are most of those volcanoes doing during that time period? Remember even tiny Mount St. Helen's blocked the sunlight midday, which caused local streetlights to turn on. Heck, even Mount Pinatubo in the Philippines, in 1991, erupted violently enough to drop temps 1 degree Fahrenheit globally for almost two years!"

"You're right, Pete. With continuous volcanic action worldwide, the ash would block the sun's rays year round, reflecting most of it back into space, and the glaciers could continue to grow and advance . . . aah," Walter said, smacking himself on the forehead to everyone's amusement. "That explains how *both* north and south poles were affected at the same time, which shatters to smithereens our Milankovitch model."

"And it explains how for a short period of time after the Flood, perhaps a hundred or so years and before the ice age began, that Antarctica had subtropical rainforests complete with palm and macadamia trees. It's been *proven* from the drilling through the Antarctic ice," Pete said, clarifying some points for Walter.

"Walter, how about the Sahara Desert in Africa, which is growing at about thirty miles a year?" Heather mentioned. "It's an area larger than the United States and once was lush and green with crocodiles, hippos, and elephants. I'm betting it started like around forty-three hundred years ago after this Noah's Flood thing when there was a lot of rain at the lower equatorial latitudes, and while the ice age was beginning to form at the higher northern latitudes, as well as down in Antarctica."

"Why Heather, I'm really impressed with your analyzation skills," Walter admitted, truly moved with her thinking.

"I can figure out some things on my own," she stated, putting her hand on her hip and blinking her eyelids once, slowly. "Of course, you scientists blame the growth of the Sahara Desert on global warming—excuse me, climate change. Look at this diagram on my tablet, Walter."

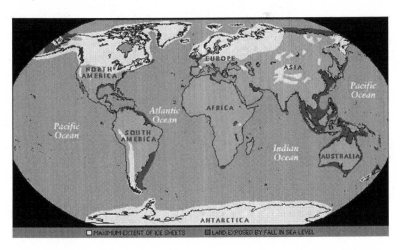

Map of world with ice sheets. Image Credit: wordpress.com

"Yeah, Walter," Aaron busted in. "It's not global warming that's causing the shrinking of today's glaciers and the expansion of the Sahara Desert; we just don't have the same warm oceans from the rupture of the fountains of the deep, and the evaporation and rainfall that existed during the time of Noah's Flood, and shortly thereafter."

"Aaron's right, Walter," Pete said, being supportive of Aaron. "The oceans have cooled off, and the volcanic activity with the resulting ash has subsided dramatically over the past four thousand years; therefore, there was only *one* ice age!"

Heather then pitched in with a whine in her voice, "Yeah Walter, how are we going to have another ice age without all the massive ocean *heat* from those fountain things, and therefore no large-scale evaporation? Tell me that, Walter! Well, huh?"

Walter just sat there with his head in his hands. "Now I know why that co-worker of mine always has his Bible open. One day I walked over to his desk while he had stepped out, and it was turned to Genesis and the Flood. We constantly deride him; and he has been threatened with expulsion from the program."

Sonny and Jack had been brainstorming with each other. Finally Jack spoke up. "From what we can hash out, that post-Flood ice age sucked up a lot of water into those ice sheets and glaciers exposing the land and creating land bridges, especially the one extending across the Bearing Strait connecting Russia with Alaska."

"And I just realized," Spud said, adding his two cents, "that it takes more than just cold weather to create snow."

Jack and the others in the group shot Spud a "how could you be so stupid" look.

Sonny, interrupted the group-stare at Spud offering, "And many of the Babel people groups migrated to the Americas bringing with them their unique languages, partial memories, and accounts of the Flood and Adam and Eve."

With that, Juan and Santi looked at each other and laughed, giving each other high fives. "That old Indio woman and her stories!" Santi exclaimed, clapping his hands.

"And the land bridges," Jim leaned toward Pete and Walter, "also explain how the animals, including dinosaurs, moved to other parts of the world, into different ecological and climatological niches, and with the radical post-Flood climate changes, diversified into more and different species."

"So Walter, what are you going to do with all this new info?" Pete asked.

"I'm going to toe-the-mark in school and the lab, until I get my PhD."

"Then, what are you going to do, Walter?" Heather asked, showing curiosity.

Walter stood up and faced all of us. Adjusting his glasses and rubbing his chin he said, "How do you Christians say it, I'll need to pray on it?"

CHAPTER ONE HUNDRED TWENTY-NINE

BEAVER LICK

We had an excellent dinner that evening with all of Radisson's students - minus Radisson. Pete found out earlier while talking with Heather that they were staying at the same hotel we were and they arranged the dinner. The discussion was very lively, and Walter turned out to be quite the whistleblower revealing the extent of the governmental control over research and academia. Thad enlightened Radisson's group on the breadth and depth of the Matrix's reach into our lives.

"And by the way," Walter interrupted, "I was serious about the fact we haven't a clue about how even one ice age starts. I downloaded this article if anyone wishes to read it. It's from *U.S. News and World Report*, Vol.123, issue 7, page 58. And I quote: ' "We've been chewing on this problem for 30 or 40 years," says Alan Mix, an oceanographer at Oregon State University. "It's a killer," adds Ralph Cicerone, dean of physical sciences at the University of California-Irvine.' It's embarrassing," Walter concluded.

Jim immediately jumped up again railing at the system. "And if they can't figure out how an ice age forms, then they don't know squat about how global warming occurs!" He slammed his chicken drumstick on the table.

While we were dining, the TV news reports gave us updates on the terrorist attacks that had occurred a few days before. The radical jihadists who attacked New York City came from an Islamic terrorist training camp in Hancock, New York, called Islamberg. The attack in Washington originated from their camp in Falls Church, Virginia. Most of Radisson's students were totally unaware of even the presence of these camps, or that a number of these had been in operation and growing, due in large part to Obama's Muslim refugee influx during the past decade or so.

When the conversation again turned to the ice age, Walter informed us that one of the ice lobes had penetrated right into the Ohio Valley. When it retreated, it left a very soggy, salty wetland where many mastodons, giant sloths, and other ice-age creatures hung out for the salt. They ended up becoming trapped and died. The state park was only about a forty-minute drive from our hotel.

"Wow! Way cool," Matt exclaimed. He expressed his desire to go, which was echoed by others in our group.

"Don't look at me guys, ask Brother Francis," I said, passing the buck onto him.

"Okay, but you're going to have to be ready to leave bright and early, by 7:30 AM, as we're going to have a long driving day ahead of us tomorrow if we want to get back to ICC by tomorrow evening."

"What have they found there?" Matt asked Walter.

"This state park," Walter said, wiping his glasses, "is considered the cradle of American paleontology. There are tons of giant bones from these beasts. As a matter of fact, in 1807, President Thomas Jefferson sent General William Clark - of Lewis and Clark fame - to gather wagonloads of these bones and ship them back to the White House."

"Awesome!" Matt exclaimed. He was really jazzed about going. "Hey, what's the name of this state park?"

"Oh, I'm sorry," Walter said. "It's called Big Bone Lick, and it's just west of the town of Beaver Lick," he off-handedly replied.

There was suddenly a total silence around the table. Everyone was completely still. The women looked at each other with gaping mouths, while the guys were utterly speechless, including Tom.

Walter was acutely aware of the sudden silence, "Did I say something?" he asked.

CHAPTER ONE HUNDRED THIRTY

TELEPHONE SHOELACE ENZYME

The next day, we checked out the museum and visitor's center at Big Bone Lick State Park, and then hit the road for home. We headed up 1-71 toward Columbus, Ohio, with Brother Francis in the command seat of the Prevost. Then we went east on I-70 toward Wheeling, West Virginia.

The kids were jabbering with each other for hours it seemed, and texting their friends. They were using their implanted T-chips in a manner reminiscent of the Dick Tracy's wrist radio. We stopped briefly for lunch at a fast food restaurant and were then on the road again.

When we were passing through West Virginia, all the billboards on the road made it clear that we were now in coal country. Of course, most coalminers were out of work. Obama had kept his promise to shutter the industry.

"It's hard to believe that we are literally driving over compressed tree bark remains, now chemically converted to coal," Nate said, reminding us, "All this as a result of the actions of Noah's Flood."

Thad took photos of some visible coal seams where portions of mountain were blasted away to make a thoroughfare for the interstate. Jim pointed out how the coal seams many times were wedged between other sedimentary rock layers. "We have eyes, but we don't see," he said.

Photo of man inspecting coal seams. Photo Credit: imgur.com

Matt, who had been fairly quiet reading some material purchased at one of the Creation museum bookstores, suddenly jumped up. "Hey Doc, you were going to explain to us about how all these guys in Genesis lived to be old geezers."

"Matt, perhaps everyone would like a break." I said. Actually I was the one who was worn out from the trip.

"No, no, we want to hear."

"That would be so cool to live a long time."

"One friend has been texting me," Tom stated, "razing me about the Bible being just a bunch of fairytales, and specifically mentioning the long ages of these guys; I don't know what to tell him."

"See, Doc, we're all in agreement on this," Matt said, pressing his case.

"Alright, alright, you guys win," I conceded, as a number of them hooted and clapped while I stood up and leaned against the pole next to Brother Francis.

"Maybe we're asking the wrong question," I began, scanning our troupe on the bus to get their thinking gears greased up.

"Huh?"

"What do you mean?"

"Well, instead of scoffing at how they could possibly have lived so long, perhaps we should be asking why *we* don't live that long anymore?"

"But our cells just don't live that long," Nate emphatically stated.

"Nate, some of our cells are immortal, and you know it!" I said really trying to get him to think. With that, the bus turned into a buzzing hive as the students exchanged ideas. However, when they settled down, I just got a bunch of blank stares back at me.

"Okay, I'll give you a hint. Anyone ever heard of a lady by the name of Henrietta Lacks?" I asked. Still a dumb silence.

"Let me give you one more hint. Her name was abbreviated to HeLa for her cell line, which is now used by researchers."

Maria catapulted out of her seat. "Cancer cells are immortal! The HeLa cells from that individual are used by today's oncology scientists for study and research."

"Give that girl a V-8!" Jim shouted, hopping out of his seat. "Geez, can't believe I blew that one."

"That's right!" Nate interjected. "Normal cells shut off after a pre-programmed number of replications, but cancer cells' reproduction switch is constantly in the on-mode."

"Yes," Maria said, "we are able to reproduce cells and repair ourselves—bones, skin, etcetera—but eventually the replication and repair processes stop, and we get old and die."

"Man, like where is this genetic switch?" Matt asked, getting revved up. "I could be a multi-gazillionaire, if I could find that switch."

"Matt, we have found the switch; it's an enzyme called telomerase, but I'm getting ahead of myself," I said, while Matt was rapidly writing it down on his tablet.

Maria waved her hand frantically. I think she's in the groove now, so I pointed my finger in her direction. "The capped tips of chromosomes," she added, "have telomeres on them."

"What do they do?" Matt asked, seeing dollar signs as he tried to figure it out.

"Think of these telomeres, which are the capped tips of the chromosomes, kinda the same as the capped tips of shoelaces. They prevent the chromosomes from fraying—"

"Yeah, but what do they do?" Matt asked, interrupting Maria in his hyped-up state.

Maria kept her cool. "Picture the telomere tips as a chain of beads, and each time cells divide and reproduce, one is clipped off, lost and not replaced."

"Well, then, how many times do human cells divide?" Matt asked, still wanting very much to get answers to man's age-old question for immortal youth.

"About eighty times," Maria told him, "assuming some disease doesn't kill you first, or you get run over by a train."

"Or you smoke, drink, or drug yourself to death," Claudia stated, half serious, half humorous.

Matt didn't laugh, but exclaimed, "That's it?! Eighty times, then it's over. Bummer, man!"

Maria looked at me as if to say she had presented all she knew on this.

"I'm putting a little chart up on your Insta-Screens, which I'd like you to study and tell me - based on the information that Maria has already given you, what do you think happened?"

"I'll give you one piece of info to help you," I continued. "How many people got off the ark?"

The kids exchanged ideas, and again Maria put her hand up first. I told her that her companions need to stretch themselves on this one.

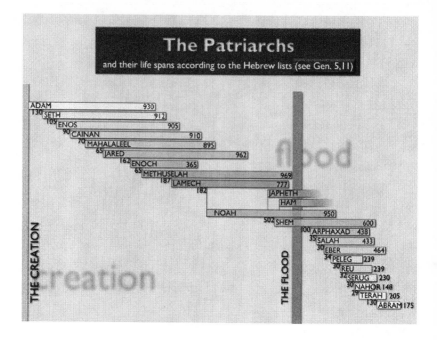

Patriarchs chart of life spans. Image Credit: new2torah.com

Philip nodded his head, and I gave him the floor. "There appears to be a big drop off in longevity with people born after the flood," Philip stated, "which seems to have worsened after Babel."

"Excellent observation, Philip."

"May I add," he said, "that Noah's three sons and their wives presented a major genetic bottleneck. With the other genetic bottleneck revealing itself with the splitting up of people groups at Babel."

"Philip's right," Jim said, giving weight to Philip's position. "Noah himself lived for another 350 years post-Flood, whereas his grandchildren seemed to lack the longevity genes, or a longer telomere length, that apparently were present in Noah and many of his forbearers, like Methuselah."

"That's right, Jim," Nate said, speculating, "probably one, or even all of Noah's sons and daughter-in-laws, were already carrying defective longevity genes or defective telomeres, or its enzyme."

Matt was beside himself, waving both hands in the air. "Hey guys, remember we were discussing the human race 'going zombie' because we're averaging one hundred or so cumulative mutations per generation? That probably has contributed to the decline in ages, especially as Jim just said, if that telephone shoelace enzyme, or whatever it's called, and the other stuff, was negatively affected."

Some chuckling resounded around the bus.

"It's telomerase, Matt," Tom said, correcting him, "which brings us back to a genetically perfect Adam and Eve who screwed things up for us; everything has been downhill since, including our DNA. How did God put it when He threw their butts out of Eden?" Tom asked, looking at Matt.

"Translated from the Hebrew, the curse was 'in dying you will die'; you will get old and die," Matt said, remembering his Hebrew lessons and our prior discussion.

There was a bit of a lull, as the kids reflected on what they had just learned. All I could hear was the whine of the tires of the Prevost on the pavement.

"Doc! Doc!" Thad exclaimed, extremely excited and upset about something. "Turn on the news reports—now!" Thad must have had his tablet set to notify him of any timely news events.

CHAPTER ONE HUNDRED THIRTY-ONE

PERSONAL RIGHTS PROTECTION ACT

I quickly turned on the news so everyone could view it on their personal Insta-Screens.

"And in the aftermath of the attacks on our cities, a group of vigilantes has boldly attacked Islamberg in upstate New York. The blood-crazed posse apparently rammed the main gate with large trucks. There was carnage on both sides, which included innocent women and children who were in the compound at the time."

"The president has asked for Congress to immediately pass stricter gun-control legislation in light of this massacre of peaceful Muslims on their own property. And if Congress fails to act in a timely manner, the White House spokesperson stated, executive orders will be forthcoming, including confiscation of firearms from unauthorized civilian militia groups."

"But they attacked us first."

"And who set us up to be attacked by importing them to begin with?"

"The damn place was a training camp for terrorists; everybody knows that."

Everyone on the bus, except Ali who was playing his video games, was shouting at their Insta-Screens; it was an absolute cacophony. I looked over at Brother Francis who just shook his head. Ecclesiastes

3:8 then flashed across my mind: "A time to love and a time to hate; a time for war and a time for peace."

The newscaster went on for a while giving other details. Most on the bus were not listening through their ongoing rowdy response. I reflected on the spin the leftist lamestream media used to skew people to their way of thinking. Incendiary words—*vigilantes, blood-crazed, massacre,* and of course they must get the bleeding-heart libs pining by including the *innocent* women and children. Are there any *wicked* or *evil* ones? Funny how quickly and deliberately they forgot about the Middle Eastern Christian infants and children who were beheaded by the hundreds in front of their parents by Islamic extremists, not to mention the Muslims in Africa raping infants and toddlers to death.

Thad tried to get everyone's attention and let them know that a new report was coming through. The bus settled down, and we heard the dramatic music prelude the words *Special Report,* which splashed across the screen in bright red.

"An emergency session of Congress has just adjourned; with an overwhelming majority, they passed with bipartisan support, landmark legislation that will affect the entire U.S.," announced the anchor in a deep serious voice.

"Sweeping changes have been made so as not to be offensive to any one particular sect or group. All these are to go into effect Monday, November 28th. There have already been challenges to this new law by radical right-wing religious groups; however, a statement by a Supreme Court spokesperson has indicated that the Court will likely not enjoin any injunction against the legislature at this time."

The anchor proceeded to then give a quick, concise summary of the new law, which created some renewed agitation and confusion among the kids as well.

"Doc, like what does all of this mess mean?" Juan asked with great concern. "It sounds very serious." A number of others echoed their concern, also.

"Let's look at this item by item. Maria, I saw you taking some notes on your tablet of what the newscaster was saying about the new law; can you help us there?"

"I jotted down the high points, Dr. Lucci."

"Okay, give them to us one at a time please, Maria."

"The news anchor first stated that no religious symbols, statues, clothing, or designs are to be visible, so as not to offend anyone," Maria said, clearly becoming upset at this. "Then, the idiot newscaster gave the basis for Congress' law quoting from the First Amendment: 'Congress shall make no law respecting an establishment of religion.'"

"Thanks, Maria. Our legislators clearly see all conflict as being due to religion; therefore, in order to decrease the possibility of conflict and not to offend anyone, any visible religious display of any kind will be seen as a promotion of religion, and therefore shall not be permissible under the Constitution."

Thad, who had his voice recorder out, wanted clarification. "So, no crosses, no stars of David, no nativity scenes, no Christmas trees with lights, no Menorahs, no outside religious statues or Ten Commandment plaques or displays, no wearing of Christian jewelry," he recited, as he looked at Maria who was squeezing her crucifix. "And no religious themed T-shirts. Am I correct?"

"No Christmas music even?" Juan asked, appearing very dismayed.

"If your neighbor hears it," Tom angrily remarked, "he could report you for violating the law and *offending* him!" Tom made a sour face at the word *offended*.

"That's about the size of it, guys. Besides," I continued, my tone getting very snarky and condescending, "all religion, especially the Judeo-Christian form, is just a bunch of nonsense and fairy tales, anyway. It's adhered to by weak-kneed old ladies who need a crutch to get them through life and are afraid to accept the law of the jungle that when you die, that's it; there's no la-la land in the sky, or a hell for that matter."

"Okay, Doc," Nate added, while standing up and scanning his fellow classmates. "We probably all deserved that round-about tongue lashing. I believe I speak for all of us when I say I now more fully understand why you scheduled this class trip to the museums." All heads were humbly nodding in agreement around the bus.

Philip stood up, his demeanor was more modest and servile than usual. He hesitated, possibly unsure of exactly what to say. "I can no longer deny the truth," he said in a firm straightforward way while looking at all his classmates. He then slowly sat back in his seat.

The bus sounded like a beehive again. Some were flabbergasted by the confession of the now former atheist's new conversion. Jim got up and walked to the back where Philip was seated. Everyone's eyes were on Jim and Philip. "Well, man," Jim said addressing Philip. "We'll need to celebrate." He put his hand on Philip's shoulder and asked, "How about we split a V-8 together?" Jim started to chuckle.

Immediately everyone was in uproarious laughter. Philip looked up from his seat at Jim and offered, "How about we make that a beer instead?" to which the bus responded with another round of hoots and hollers.

There was a brief hiatus as the clamor on the bus subsided. Maggie was attempting to stand up, but Maria, next to her, and Claudia, behind her, were tugging on Maggie's sleeve, trying to get her to sit down.

Maggie would not be denied. "And what about the Islamic star and crescent symbols?" she asked, as her temper flared. "I didn't hear the news reporter make any specific mention of *them*," she said, looking directly at Ali, who had been sitting very quietly the entire time just playing his violent video games on his tablet.

Maggie was on a roll, "I'll bet my bottom dollar that the Islamic mosques, especially in Muslim controlled towns and cities, will remain untouched. Anyone want to take me up on that bet; I'll give you 2 to 1 odds."

The students were hesitating, but only for a moment. Nate stood and nervously said, "Maggie is probably right. The crosses and stars of David at Arlington National Cemetery will have to be rubbed out without question. What I'd like to know is how are they going to handle Washington DC's historical buildings and monuments, many of which have Christian words and symbols engraved on them?"

Maria, with her tablet in hand, read from her notes. "The news person said that certain designated historical buildings, monuments, and the like in the United States, which are over one hundred years old, will remain untouched for the time being. However, within the next five years, even they will be subject to this new law, and subsequently Christian references will be removed, dismantled, or sandblasted to eliminate any offensive wording or symbolism."

Tom, speaking loudly to no one in particular, asked, "What's the name of this law that was conjured up from the pit of hell, anyway?"

"Maria?" I asked, as I looked at her. The whole bus waited for her response.

She cleared her throat, and almost stuttering, replied, "The Personal Rights Protection Act."

Claudia was nodding her head. "Classic Orwellian newspeak and doublespeak taken right from the pages of his novel *1984,*" she proclaimed while others were just dumbfounded and amazed at the name of the new law.

CHAPTER ONE HUNDRED THIRTY-TWO

THE LIONESS

We hadn't been back at ICC for more than several days when Thad approached me after a class. "Hey, Doc, I've got great news for you!"

"Really! What about?"

"Early this morning, I was manning the office at the *Veritas Beacon* as Stephen was out of the office on an errand and asked me to take charge for a while," Thad stated with pride in his voice.

"Okay?" I drawled, wondering where Thad was going with this.

"Well, a call comes in asking for the editor-in-chief of our paper. I told her that Stephen was out and asked how I could help."

"Okay?" I coaxed again, leaning my head towards him with raised eyebrows indicating let's get on with it.

"She wanted to speak with the writer of the 'Matrix Exposed' series. I told her that was me," Thad said, as he puffed his chest out a bit. "We talked a while, and she said that she wanted to interview you at her studio and put you on TV. Isn't that awesome, Doc, you on national television!"

"And her name was Kathy Owens, right?"

"How did you know that, Doc? Anyway, I know there has been some bad blood between you two but she wants to put all that in the past."

"And how does she know so much about your 'Matrix Exposed' series? Does she subscribe to our school paper or something?"

"Doc, you're living in ancient times. The *Veritas Beacon* reaches the world—theoretically speaking—on the internet. Anyone can read it. You should see the feedback I'm . . . I mean . . . we're getting. It's good, bad, ugly, and gross. Between what you're teaching and what I'm writing, there is a firestorm brewing—especially over what I've written since we returned from the trip. That's why Owens wants to interview you."

"What's the purpose of it?"

"She said she wanted to offer you a chance to explain to her viewing audience your side of the story."

"Thad, you're majoring in journalism and minoring in astronomy, correct? You better get your head out of the stars and come back to earth."

"What do you mean, Doc?" he asked. I could see he took a bit of offence to my statement.

"The interview will be at her TV studios, correct?"

"Yes."

"She will be interviewing me. It's her show. Therefore, she will be asking the questions, correct?"

"Yeah."

"Owens will be doing the videotape editing afterwards, correct?"

"Okay," Thad said slowly, still not catching on yet.

"Her show, her questions, her editing. So, who's in control here?" I asked, as I crooked my head sideways and raised an eyebrow at him.

"Oh, I didn't look at it that way, Doc."

"Talk about walking into the lion's den. No, thank you, the deck would be stacked against me."

When I arrived home that evening, I told Emily what Kathy Owens had proposed. "You didn't accept the offer, did you?"

"Of course not, Honey. I was born at night, but not last night." We both had a good laugh about it, and Emily served up a wonderful pasta dinner of baked manicotti and meatballs, with a nice red Malbec wine from Chile.

On campus the following day, Father Ed and I were planning on lunch at the Holy Grounds coffee shop. He wanted to hear about the trip, and I wanted to learn how he and Dean Avery handled the media scrutiny of the televised "party bus" incident. Even the bishops' offices in Washington and Richmond were contacted for a response regarding the matter.

Being early November, there was a sharp nip in the air and the leaves had fallen off the trees. The air was crisp and the sky a crystal azure blue, other than several chemtrails making Xs in the sky. Are those pilots trying to tell us something?

Walking along one of the paths at a quick pace, I should have been looking ahead rather than skyward, as I almost slammed into Kathy Owens and her cameraman.

CHAPTER ONE HUNDRED THIRTY-THREE

THE INTERVIEW

I apologized profusely for nearly knocking the reporter to the ground. I had to grab Kathy Owen's arm to keep her from falling. "Geez, who's ambushing whom?" I asked, letting her realize I was well aware of the media tactic of "journalistic ambushing" to catch their prey in an unguarded moment.

As she straightened herself out and fluffed her hair, she said, "Ah . . . well, I thought it might be more convenient for you to meet and talk with me on the campus." I noted her cameraman was starting to film us. She had me cornered, and she knew it.

"Tell you what Kathy, I'll give you your interview; however, it will have to be on my terms, especially since you're on my turf now," I said, looking squarely down into her eyes.

"Okay, what deal do you want?" she asked as her plastic smile morphed into an all-business smirk.

"Just you and me, mano a mano, no camera. We can sit here on this bench; your cameraman, meanwhile, can take a powder."

She gave me a devious look, turned to her cameraman, and said, "Jake, I won't need you for the time being; just relax for now." He walked down the path in the direction of the quadrangle and sat on another bench.

We sat, and she made small talk asking me about my background, about Emily and Father Flanagan, and how I came to teach at ICC.

She was using her people skills to try to set me at ease, giving me soft-ball questions at first, but progressively got more pointed. It was hard for her to remain neutral like Greta Van Susteren, who was an absolute master interviewer. Instead, Kathy's leftist ideology just started oozing through her every pore.

"Don't you think you are being unfair and intolerant with your biased positions on all the topics you are covering with your students?" she asked.

"I agree with you, Kathy. I *am* totally biased, but so are you and everyone else in the entire world. Everyone holds to some biased position or other. There is *no* such thing as an absolutely neutral position."

"All the school systems across the country teach from a neutral viewpoint," Kathy stated. "You bring God into the picture, which is definitely one-sided, and therefore unethical and dogmatic to others who don't believe in God; is that not so?"

"That's a multi-pronged question. Let me break it down. First, our schools do *not* teach from a neutral point of view. They teach naturalism, which in effect is atheism—that the universe, our earth, and life itself developed without any intelligent input. They claim the proof is in, that there is no God, and then proceed to shut down all discussion and debate. All I do is to show in my classes that there is more than enough scientific evidence to the contrary. Now who's being closed minded and biased?"

"But aren't you still being disingenuous and bigoted to those who don't believe there is a God?"

"Wouldn't I be considered discriminatory and bigoted if some people told me that you, Kathy Owens, don't exist, and I shouldn't talk about you because I *offend* them?"

Kathy didn't answer my question but instead moved on with her agenda. "Our education system *encourages* open discussion and debate on *any* topic."

"If so, Kathy," I rebutted. "Show me any science text, from kindergarten through post-graduate studies, that even mentions the word *God,* and presents an opposing viewpoint with evidence. I thought that is what science is supposed to be, a search for the truth, wherever it may lead. Of course, the government position is that we can only evaluate our world using naturalistic explanations, which is a cop out."

She shifted gears entirely. "You oppose reasonable gun control legislation. If we could save just one precious life by eliminating guns, don't you think it's worth it? You do believe life is valuable, don't you?" she asked.

"Absolutely, Kathy. And I see you believe that, also. If we could save just one precious life . . . by eliminating abortion—"

"Doesn't a woman have a right to control her own healthcare?" She interrupted, with a condescending attitude and becoming somewhat boorish.

"Absolutely, Kathy! And who then is assigned to the healthcare of the helpless fetus, if not its own mother? Look, let me make it easy for you. If there is no Judeo-Christian God who has given us the laws of life, then, yeah, do whatever you please. If man makes the laws, man then becomes god."

"Wouldn't that lead to a better world, leaving religionists out of the equation, Dr. Lucci?"

"I believe man playing God, and making his own laws apart from the Bible, has already been tested and failed. Look at the French Revolution's Robespierre, Hitler, Stalin, Mao Zedong, and Pol Pot. All atheists. All evolutionists. Over 200 million tortured, starved to death, and murdered because atheists usurped God's power and authority."

"And what of the religious wars in the name of God?"

"That's a good question. There have been evil men who have done bad things in the name of religion. If we stick with the number of deaths, which is the only reasonable comparison, the results of a study done at Baylor University several years ago showed that throughout all of history there were about 5.5 million deaths, maximum, in the name of Christianity. Oh, and that's including the Inquisition."

"So, atheism, with its underlying belief in evolution, *and* Christianity both have blood on their hands!"

"Please, Kathy, don't play the equivalency game with me. Any person with half a brain would prefer to live under a Christian-based society rather than under a society based on communism, socialism, progressivism, or whatever the current trendy name is today."

"Are you proposing we live under a theocracy?"

"Absolutely not! Some people say we are a Christian nation. We are not - we are a nation of Christians. When the Muslim population exceeds the number of Christians, then the overwhelming vote will be for Sharia law, and you will be forced to wear a hijab and burka. You will not be allowed to travel freely without a male relative to accompany you. You will not be allowed to drive a car; you will be stripped of your civil rights since you're *only* a woman; and if you get raped, you will need four male witnesses to testify on your behalf that you are innocent."

Kathy became flustered with my last barrage of facts.

"There's *no* evidence that we will have Sharia law in the United States!"

"We are bringing Muslims in at the rate of one hundred thousand plus per year. Each man is allowed four wives, each having several children. They are exponentially out-reproducing us. Statistics from the Center for Security Policy survey of American Muslims a few years back, around 2015 I believe, revealed fifty-one percent of them supported having Sharia law. Only about 40 percent felt that they should be subject to American courts, and almost 20 percent of respondents said that the use of violence is justified in order to make Sharia law the law of the land in the United States. And that was only the 20 percent who openly admitted to the survey that they would use violence to enact Sharia law. How many more American Muslims are we really talking about?

Remember that survey was from several years ago. Other studies confirm that almost 70 percent support more government programs. I translate that to welfare—more free stuff!"

Kathy's eyes narrowed as she said, "All this God and sin business is archaic, mystical gibberish from the Dark Ages, created by the church, to control the peasants." I sensed that she wished to terminate the interview having gotten her panties in a twist. Realizing that she has lost her professional demeanor, Kathy did an about face. "Ah . . . Professor Dietrich would like to make a proposal to you," she exclaimed, pasting her plastic smile back on.

"Really, and what may that be?" I asked.

CHAPTER ONE HUNDRED THIRTY-FOUR

KNOW WHEN TO FOLD 'EM

"**P**rofessor Dietrich would like to set up a debate between himself and you, Dr. Lucci," Kathy said, scrutinizing me carefully. "The debate will take place here on the ICC campus with an open forum, taking questions from each other and the audience, as well."

"And where do you fit into this picture, Kathy?" I asked, checking for her response.

"Oh, my local affiliate will be broadcasting it live, linking with other network stations around the country. There has been an immense interest generated nationwide as a result of Thad's articles, as I'm sure you are aware."

"Let's just say that I'll think about it," I replied in a very casual, detached manner, as to imply that I'm just not interested in anything that has to do with Dietrich. Plus, I knew that a highly-rated Nielsen show would put a big feather in Kathy's cap in her quest for an anchor position in the Washington market.

"You may want to give this debate some *serious* thought, Lucci," she said in a threatening tone that implied my refusal would lead to blackmail.

What does she have on me? I thought as I looked at her cynically.

Kathy started adjusting a very elaborate broach pinned to her blouse collar. "Let me be plain with you, Lucci. I've been videotaping our ah . . . interview the entire time. Either you come around or I'll slice and dice this into something your own mother wouldn't even recognize. I'll make you look worse than Pilate condemning that pathetic fool of a Christ. *Now* are you going to play ball?"

I calmly adjusted the clip of my pen in the breast pocket of my sports jacket. "Could you state that again for the record? I'm not sure if I got all that," I said, giving her a big gotcha smile. "You go ahead and do your hatchet editing job; I'll just send my entire unedited videotape to the conservative media like Gretchen Carlson, Sam Sorbo, and Cal Thomas."

Forget the daggers - Kathy's eyes were shooting javelins at me, and her face contorted into one big sneer. Without making a sound, she jumped up from the bench and dashed down the path, her high heels clicking away at 120 words a minute. She blew by Jake, who was playing on his cell phone, and shouted, "Let's get the hell outta here; November 28th is almost here, anyway. They'll see!" He looked up in bewilderment.

By the time I got home, I was floating. I practically danced through the kitchen door. "What's got you so pepped up?" Emily asked, as I grabbed her and planted a big one on her.

I told her about the ambush from Kathy Owens; I explained everything that transpired. Emily looked at me perplexed. "Joe, you don't have one of those fancy videotaping pens," she said, as she reached for the pen in my breast pocket. "This is your dad's old fountain pen, which has an ornamental clip, but—"

"But Kathy didn't know that," I finished Emily's thought. "Besides, she still would have shown the radically edited interview on her show."

"You just bluffed her then?" Emily asked, smiling at me.

"Hey, she was trying to con me," I rationalized, seizing Emily again and dancing her around the kitchen while singing, 'You've got to know when to hold 'em; Know when to fold 'em; Know when to walk away; And know when to run.'"

Emily suddenly stopped, bringing our dancing to a halt. "Did you meet with Father Ed for lunch, Joe?" she asked.

"Oh geez, I totally forgot," I said, stamping my foot on the floor and rubbing my fingers across my forehead.

WHAT WENT BANG?

The very next morning on my drive to ICC, I called Father Ed profusely apologizing and explained why I had forgotten our lunch date.

"That was quick thinking on your feet, laddie boy. No doubt she would have made mincemeat out of you in an edited videotape."

We agreed to reschedule and meet for lunch that day. I also mentioned to him that my sister Carmella wanted to invite him over to her house for Thanksgiving dinner, if he had not already committed himself to any prior engagements.

"Aye, she's a great lass; tell her I would be honored to come. It's been a while since I've seen her."

"Oh, before we hang up, what do you think Owens meant by 'they'll see on November 28th'?"

"I'll tell you over that lunch you owe me."

***

I parked 'the tank', and walked over to the St. Al's science building, crossing through the quadrangle as usual. I hesitated to look up, but did anyway. I always got nauseous seeing the World Ecology flag flying above the Stars and Stripes.

I entered the classroom and sat down in Thad's seat. Some of the kids whispered, wondering what I was doing. Thad entered and went directly up behind the lab table at the front, starting to get his notes and materials together. He then turned and wrote on the white board, 'Yes, I'm teaching this class on Cosmology and Astronomy.' After a few minutes, Tom, being last as usual, rushed in out of breath.

Thad, a bit nervous, picked up his tablet and, with fifteen sets of eyeballs staring back at him, was determined to move on. It was his idea. Thad told me shortly after our return from the bus trip that he was fired up when he watched a series of shows in the planetarium at the Creation Museum with Nate and Philip. He had purchased several books, magazines, and DVDs in the Dragon bookstore and had been gobbling them up ever since. He asked if he could teach one of the classes.

He started to read from his tablet. "'In the beginning there was nothing—no time, space, matter, or energy . . . there is nothing to begin with, in which case there is no quantum vacuum, no pre-geometric dust, no time in which anything can happen, no physical laws that can effect a change from nothingness into somethingness.'"

Thad looked up and saw Jude with his arms folded across his chest; he was quiet with his "weaned on a pickle" expression.

Thad cleared his throat and continued, "'If space-time did not exist, then how could everything appear from nothing?'"

"You don't know what you are talking about, Thad. Physicists have figured this all out already," Jude bellowed out from his rear corner window seat.

"Jude, all those were not *my* words. They are the words of Andrei Linde, a Harald Trap Friis professor of physics at Stanford University. He wrote this in his article "The Self-reproducing Inflationary Universe," which appeared in *Scientific American,* in 1994. Oh, and by the way, he himself is an evolutionist."

"Nineteen ninety-four! That's pre-historic outdated information. All cosmologists agree that the Big Bang began with a quantum fluctuation in the void," Jude retorted.

"Just so I understand you, Jude, are you saying that nothing became unstable and exploded?"

"That's right—absolutely nothing, a 'singularity event' happened! Here I'll transfer this Discover cover story, from April 2002, to your Insta-Screens for all to see."

Discover Magazine WHERE DID EVERYTHING COME FROM
Image Credit: Discover Magazine

"Martin Rees, emeritus professor of astrophysics and cosmology from the University of Cambridge said, 'We still don't know, for instance, what went bang and why,'" countered Thad. "And that's from a more recent article, 'The World's Biggest Ideas: The Big Bang,' published in the *New Scientist*, in 2005. Is that new enough for you? And he's an evolutionist, also."

"Inflation is the answer that makes the big bang work!" Jude snorted, becoming short with Thad. "The universe temporarily went through a period of accelerated expansion."

"Let me bring up on the big Insta-Screen, from my tablet, what Jude is talking about," Thad said, as he fidgeted with his tablet.

Illustration of the Big Bang Theory.
Image Credit: The Kinelisher Young People's Book of Space

"As you can see by looking at the left side of the image, which occurs in a supposed blinding nanosecond from the initial bang of nothing to the inflation period; this blast formed the pre-atomic particles called quarks and then, by one second, hydrogen and helium formed—supposedly. This is not science, Jude. If something happened in the unobserved past, we cannot validate the experiment by repeating it in a lab."

"Neither can you repeat your stupid creation theory - that your God created everything six thousand years ago – you can't test that either!"

CHAPTER ONE HUNDRED THIRTY-SIX

SOMETHING FROM NOTHING

With Jude's comment, a number of the students were up in arms. Even his friend Matt turned around to face him. "Jude, man, like you were not with us on the trip. You could have learned so much about our young earth and universe," Matt commented.

Philip added, "Jude, no one can explain with certainty, what initiated the inflation period; for that matter, neither can they explain what made it slow down and stop—assuming it ever happened at all. I just checked on this, and Paul J. Steinhardt, director of the Princeton Center for Theoretical Science at Princeton University and a member of the National Academy of Sciences, stated as much in *Scientific American*, the April 2011 issue. On page forty-three he stated, 'Others (including me) contended that the problems cut to the core of the theory, and it needs a major fix or be replaced.' And he too, is an evolutionist."

"All of you are just brainwashed fools," Jude said, as he just sat there fuming.

Thad appeared unsettled as he tried to regain control and provide more evidence to Jude. "'The big bang theory can boast of no quantitative predictions that have subsequently been validated by observation,'" Thad quoted. "That's from Eric Lerner, president of Lawrenceville Plasma Physics, in his article, 'Bucking the Big Bang', in *New Scientist*, in 2004. And . . . and—"

"Yeah, I know, he's another evolutionist," Jude interrupted, easing up a bit. "But these are just some rogue scientists who are off the reservation, man."

Thad seemed to have been thrown a curve ball with that last statement by Jude and was not sure what to say. Nate came to the rescue. "I went to the planetarium," Nate chimed in, "along with Philip and Thad, and was deeply impressed. During this debate, I've come up with some interesting findings of my own. There is an open letter to the scientific community written primarily by secular scientists who challenge the big bang."

Tom turned around and called out, "Really! A whole bunch of science guys wrote a letter? That's got my attention. Read it to us—read it!"

Nate addressed the class, "It's in the May 22, 2004, issue of *New Scientist,* for those of you who want to follow along with me." A number of others started to look for it on their tablets. "I'll start with, 'the big bang today' paragraph," Nate instructed, as he waited for his classmates to locate it.

"Okay . . . 'The big bang today relies on a number of hypothetical entities, things we have never observed—inflation, dark matter, dark energy are the most prominent examples. . . . In no other field of physics would this continual recourse to new hypothetical objects be accepted as a way of bridging the gap between theory and observation.'" Nate continued, reading the letter. At the end he said, "This letter has been signed by hundreds of scientists and professors at various institutions."

Claudia spoke up, "I am astounded that no one in the media, or in our education system, has brought this to our attention. Au contraire, we are being force-fed this malevolent belief, as if it was dogma. It's a philosophy, a religion," she exclaimed, as she glared at Jude with some degree of acrimony.

"Yeah, man," Matt said, adding to Claudia's observations, "that dumb TV show of the same name, and most all of our teachers and professors, they are the close-minded ones."

"Could it be," Maggie addressed the class, "that our governmental Matrix which controls education, and the media - who is in bed with them, are singing the same siren song to brainwash us? If the universe made itself, then we are not answerable to anyone but ourselves—and the Matrix who controls us plays God."

Thad was doing his best to keep things on track. "I do have a short YouTube video clip I'm going to bring up on the Insta-Screen. We only need to watch the first two minutes. It's called *Richard Dawkins Knows Nothing About Nothing.*" As many of you are aware, Dawkins is one of the main spokesmen for the atheists."

For the next two minutes the entire class, with the exception of Jude, was roaring in hysterics as Richard Dawkins does his best to explain . . . nothing.

"Oye, Jude, you believe something can come from nothing, sí?" Santi asked turning to face Jude. "Well, what if that something that came from nothing is Dios—God? Would you agree to that, hombre?" he asked, while laughing at his proposition.

Jude didn't answer Santi. He just sat there with his arms crossed and lip poked out.

"Where *did* time, space, and matter come from?" Juan then asked, to no one in particular.

Maria's soft voice replied, "In the beginning (time), God created the heaven (space), and the earth (matter), Genesis 1:1."

Jim started getting wired. "Yeah, Maria, those are the big three, and time itself has three components: past, present, and future," he said. "And space also has three facets: length, width, and height."

Nate then picked up on Jim's statement and added, "They're all threes, like the Trinity—three persons in one God."

"You can't have three separate things in one entity or substance!" Jude snobbishly retorted to Nate.

"I beg to differ with you, Jude," Philip replied. "What about water? It can be a solid, a liquid, or a gas—three for one entity!"

"Ay, caramba, Jude, I think Dios is trying to teach you something, and it's not *nothing!*" Santi said, laughing at himself again, which got the others chuckling along.

CHAPTER ONE HUNDRED THIRTY-SEVEN

IT'S ALL MATTER

"**Y**ou Christians are just a bunch of flat-earthers," Jude retaliated. "C'mon, you have to admit you held science back during your dark ages with your beliefs."

"The Bible," Thad responded to Jude's accusation, "has never claimed the earth is flat. To the contrary, Isaiah 40:22 talks about 'the circle of the earth,' and in Job 26:7, Job states that God 'hangs the earth on nothing.'"

"Sí, like an árbol de Navidad—a Christmas tree ornament," Santi said, still laughing at his own jokes.

"The Bible is not a science textbook," Jude said, trying to gain traction.

"And thank God, it isn't," Pete exclaimed, turning toward Jude. "Science textbooks change all the time." The class clapped and hollered at that one.

As the group calmed down, Pete finished his thought. "However, whenever the Bible does touch on biology, geology, anthropology, physics, chemistry, or now astronomy, it's always correct and accurate," he explained.

"Where has modern cosmology been wrong and the Bible right?" Jude asked, pointing his left index finger at Pete; the sun reflected off that fake emerald stone of the black satanic ring on his fourth finger.

"Excuse me . . . ah . . . may I," Thad interrupted, intruding on the personal conflict between Pete and Jude. "Up until the late 1950s, scientists held to a static picture of the universe called the steady-state hypothesis. However, when scientists discovered cosmic background radiation and red shifts, they realized the universe was expanding and that theory lost favor quickly—"

"And what does that have to do with the Bible?" Jude asked, rudely interrupting Thad's explanation.

"There are seventeen verses that refer to God stretching out the universe. My favorite is again, Isaiah 40:22: '…stretcheth out the heavens as a curtain, and spreadeth them out as a tent to dwell in.'"

"Oye, Jude, Isaiah lived in the eighth century BC. It only took ciencia—science—over twenty-seven hundred years to catch up with what was already correct in la Biblia, hombre," Santi stated, having his own little personal comedy show in the front corner.

Jude looked down the aisle and gave Santi a dirty look; then he addressed Thad. "Look man, do you have any solid evidence for a young universe other than quoting some ancient mumbo-jumbo and cracking jokes?" he asked as he continued to glare menacingly at Santi.

Thad was ready to take it on. "I'm sure we are all familiar with Einstein's theory of relativity and his equation $E=mc^2$, energy equals mass times the speed of light squared," Thad explained. "Experimental physics tells us that whenever matter is created from energy, it also produces antimatter."

"What is antimatter?" Juan asked.

"With antimatter the charges are reversed," Thad continued. "For example, whereas a proton in matter has a positive charge, an antiproton in antimatter has a negative charge. Any reaction where energy is transformed into matter also produces an equal amount of antimatter; there are no known exceptions to this!"

"Why is this important?" Juan asked, still looking for an explanation.

"Because the claim of the supposed big bang, which started only with energy (no matter), should have produced equal amounts of matter and antimatter. However, there's a teensy-weensy little problem."

"And what is that?" Juan queried, really curious now.

"The entire visible universe is composed of virtually all matter, with barely trace amounts of antimatter, which still should be there. This is an absolutely devastating problem for big-bangers."

Juan's eyes lit up as he said, "But for creationists, it's no problem. God created the universe to be essentially matter only."

"And it's a really good thing He did," Philip said, adding his expertise, "because when matter and antimatter come together they violently destroy each other."

"And we are still here, so I guess no gran explosión!" Santi blurted out, unable to stop himself from laughing again.

DUST BUNNIES

"Also, there's a whole bunch of missing stars," Thad said, teasing the class.

"How would you know if any stars are missing?" Tom asked, doubting Thad's assertion. "There's like a gazillion trillion of them out there in space. Have you counted them or something?"

"Not exactly. The big-bangers assert, if you want to refer back to the big bang theory diagram again, that the very first stars which formed would only have hydrogen and helium, and maybe some trace lithium in them."

"Oh, yeah," Tom said, perusing over the diagram on his tablet, "those first stars should have formed around one billion years after the supposed big bang."

"In astronomy," Thad added, "anything heavier than helium is considered a metal. These heavier elements—including carbon and oxygen—were created, they claim, when some of those first stars exploded and formed the next generation of stars, which *now* contain metals. Again, we have a tiny little problem that the big-bangers can't answer." Thad stopped, seeing if anyone had a solution.

"I've got it . . . I've got it," Tom responded. "I bet that those assumed first stars—the ones that are only supposed to have had hydrogen and helium—don't exist. The only stars the bangers find are completed ones with heavy metals in them. Betcha I'm right!" he exclaimed, as he looked around at his classmates.

"Yes, Tom, you're right," Thad complemented him.

"Yee haa," Tom screeched out, with a big fist pump.

Matt leaned forward over to Tom, "Hey man, how did you figure that out?"

"Easy, since the big bang is just bunch of . . . ah . . . Barbra Streisand, why would God create only some half-baked stars out there?" Many in the class nodded their heads in agreement with Tom's correct analysis.

"Can we move on from the big bang?" Jude asked, sounding very annoyed. "Do you have any other evidence? We have stars being born to replace the ones dying out, or exploding and going supernova."

"Speculation is no substitute for observation, Jude," Thad said, giving him a rebuttal. "This business of star nurseries in gas clouds is pure speculation. No one has witnessed the birth of *any* star. Some of these 'clouds' are larger than our entire solar system. When the dust and 'clouds' simply part, voilà a 'new' star is revealed – not created."

Photo of star being revealed from behind gas clouds.
Photo Credit: Shutterstock

"There is another major problem the evolutionists have to overcome regarding star formation," Philip added, "and that is Boyle's Gas Law—I said law, not theory or hypothesis."

"Yeah, Philip," Thad backed him up, "explain that to the class, please."

"May I transfer an illustration from my tablet to the Insta-Screen to explain Boyle's Law?" he asked Thad, who gave him the go ahead.

"As you can see, compressing a gas to half its initial volume doubles the pressure. Ever try inflating a car tire with a bicycle pump—you get my drift."

"How does this relate to evolutionary star formation?" Tom asked.

"That's the point; it doesn't. Gravity in space would need to overcome the obvious force of gas and dust particles trying to escape from being pulled together. Gas always wants to spread out and escape. Ever have the air pump hose pop off the valve stem? Therefore, no star formation is possible."

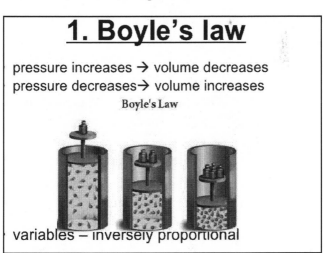

Illustration of Boyle's Law. Illustration Credit: cyberphysics.co.uk

"Yeah, tell me about it," Jim said, mimicking opening a soda can, even making the pssssh sound, which got the entire class howling, remembering his incident with Christmas-tree gal on the patio during lunch at the Creation Museum.

"We do note, however, there are only about two hundred observable dying or supernova star remnants," Thad asserted, "in our Milky Way galaxy; about one every twenty-five years on average, which indicates a young universe. But if our galaxy is 10 billion years old as the evolutionists declare, there should be thousands upon thousands of supernovas visible—but they're not there."

"How do the evolutionists explain star formation, then?" Tom asked, wanting back in on the action.

"Thad?" Philip deferred the question to the stand-in teacher.

"They assert that the explosion of a nearby star going supernova would be sufficient to force the gas and dust particles to compress adequately enough to begin forming a new star, with gravity then completing the process."

"Man, that is soooo dumb," Tom replied, throwing his arms up. "They claim that the first stars didn't even form until about one billion years after the big dud; and then these loonies claim they *need* exploding stars to *begin* with, to create other *new* stars. Buncha idiots—needing stars to make stars!!"

"Mira, I know of one thing that forces dust particles to come together; mi madre told me, its motas de polvo."

"What did Santi just say?" Matt asked, tapping Juan on the shoulder.

"Dust bunnies, man! Dust bunnies."

The class roared with laughter, with Santi's dust bunny gravitational force-field commentary. Thad then waved his hand for silence. "They're going to throw us out of St. Al's if we keep this up," Thad said, wanting some civility and decorum for his first presentation.

Thad noticed Maria wishing to be recognized. He called on her, and then she proceeded to recite from her tablet. "'He made the stars also. . . . He counts the number of the stars and calls them all by their names.' Genesis 4:7 and Psalm 147:4, for those of you who are interested."

Surprisingly, or maybe not so, most of the students brought up those verses on their tablets.

CHAPTER ONE HUNDRED THIRTY-NINE

SUN PARADOX

Thad continued, "Here's a good one about the nearest star, our sun. It's called the 'Faint Sun Paradox,' named by the evolutionary cosmologists themselves. They admit this is a major problem for them, but not for us conservative Christian creationists."

"Okay," he proceeded, "let me give you some basic facts to work from. The sun as we all know, is a thermonuclear furnace which converts hydrogen into helium. This nuclear reaction should be able to proceed for 10 billion years. Now the secular scientists allege that the sun (and our entire solar system for that matter) is around 4.6 billion years old."

"That would mean," Tom jumped in again, "that it's already used up about half its fuel supply, right?"

"That's correct, Tom."

"But that would also mean," Philip said, adding his physics expertise, "due to the complexities of these thermonuclear reactions, the sun would have brightened over the assumed 4.6 billion years by at least 35 to 45 percent, I calculate."

"You're very close, Philip," Thad responded. "The cosmologists calculate around 40 percent over the past 4.6 billion years, and 25 percent over the past 3.8 billion years."

"Yeah," Jim replied, "because that's when they say life began on earth—3.8 billion years ago. So, the sun would have been 25 percent dimmer at the time life purportedly began in Darwin's warm little pond of slime, right? Which would also mean that our planet was much colder 3.8 billion years ago, just when the amoebas were trying to get it on."

"Excellent, Jim! Currently the average earth temperature is 59 degrees Fahrenheit. Anyone want to hazard a guess as to what the earth's temperature was during the alleged 3.8 billion years ago when the sun was 25 percent dimmer?"

Philip's hand went up in a flash. "Anticipating your question," he blurted out, "I've got it worked out. The earth would have been below freezing at about 26 degrees Fahrenheit. Guess the secular cosmologists are going to have to dig up Darwin and have him rewrite his book on *The Origin of Species*."

"Those bacteria," Tom said, cracking up, "would have had to spin their flagella tails at really high RPMs to prevent themselves from freezing to death in that little pond. Oh, excuse me . . . frozen pond; therefore, life would not have been possible."

Jim was really riled up. "Wait until I see my ecology professor who's always yapping about how the early earth was conducive to life due to a greenhouse effect from plants," he said. "Was that supposed to overcome the faint sun paradox of a frozen vegetable earth?"

Thad responded, "Ah . . . well . . . actually that was one of the evolutionists' fallback explanations that the early earth had *more* greenhouse gases than the earth today – which supposedly created a warming effect."

"Yeah, the greenhouse gases came from all those frozen vegetable micro-organisms. They are absolutely pulling at straws."

"But if the sun and the whole universe, for that matter, are only six thousand years old," Nate added, "what were we, Philip, about 0.001 degrees cooler or some such inanity?"

"Mira, maybe that's why they're called theoretical physicists— no facts just teoría," Santi added.

CHAPTER ONE HUNDRED FORTY

BANG-UP JOB

Although Thad was doing an excellent job with his presentation, Jude continued to sit quietly with his arms folded, eyes narrowed, and of course, his lip poked out. I was glad to be able to relax a bit and let someone else do the work; besides, I was picking up some good pointers from the facts he was presenting. Astronomy and cosmology have always been a weak area among conservative Christians; they just don't know how to defend themselves from the onslaughts of the secular community.

Thad appeared to become more comfortable as his presentation went on. "Except for Philip," Thad said, "anyone familiar with the inverse square law of gravitational attraction? Again, this is a law, not some conjecture or inference."

Nate raised his hand and asked, "Doesn't this have to do with two bodies attracted to one another and that the force of the attraction between the two is inversely proportional to the square of the distance between them?"

"Could you translate that into English for me?" Juan asked, sounding totally confused. "And I think Santi, as well."

"Perdóname," Santi said, "I totalmente understand what Nate said. If I half the distance between myself and me novia . . . girlfriend, I take the half and flip it over and square it. The gravitational pull between us is now four times as strong. By the time I'm closer at one-third the distance, I flip it over and square the three, and we are nine times more amoroso with each other, and if we get any closer . . . it's too late," Santi exclaimed sheepishly, as he smiled at the class while blushing a bit.

"Ah . . . well, that will work," Thad said somewhat taken aback himself. "That was actually a really good . . . ah example, Santi." The class melted with laughter into their seats as Juan repeatedly slapped Santi on the back. Even Jude was chuckling.

"Regarding the gravitational attraction of the earth and moon, I've put up on the Insta-Screen exactly what Santi explained between himself and his ah . . . girlfriend."

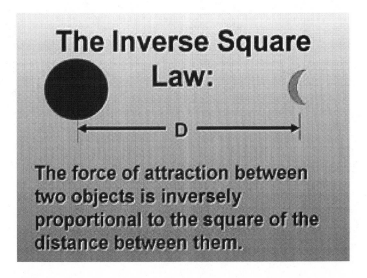

Illustration of Inverse Square Law. Illustration Credit: slideplayer.com

"As the moon orbits the earth 240,000 miles away, its gravity pulls on the earth's oceans creating the two daily tides. This tidal action causes the moon to spin away from us by about 1.5 inches a year."

"Does that mean that last year the moon was an inch and a half closer, and the year before that it was three inches closer to the earth?" Matt asked, wanting clarification.

"Correct, Matt."

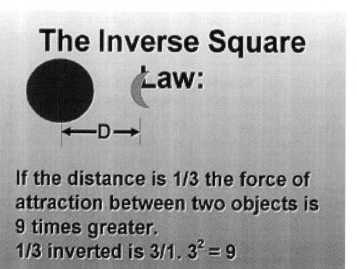

Inverse Square Law 1/3 distance. Illustration Credit: slideplayer.com

"I've got this," Tom shouted, jumping from his seat.

"Well me, too," Matt said, flicking his finger hard on Tom's earlobe. "I just wanted to make sure before I proposed my conclusions, man."

As Matt and Tom were going at it, Thad looked down the aisle at me for a solution. I shrugged my shoulders and gave him a mischievous grin, as if to say, "it's your class now; you figure it out."

"Whoa, fellas," Thad called out. "Let Matt finish his idea; if he screws up, Tom, you can give your solution to this." With that the two settled in their seats, Tom in a bit of a huff.

"Well, reverse extrapolating this thing," Matt said, thinking as he was talking. "It would seem to me that if the solar system and the earth are only about six thousand years old, the moon would be only several hundred feet closer to the earth."

"Less than eight hundred feet, by my calculations," Nate interjected, half speaking, half whispering to Matt as he leaned toward him.

"But if our solar system is 4.6 billion years old," Tom interrupted, trying to get his point across. "The moon would have been in contact with the earth around 1.4 billion years ago. And of course, that never happened."

"And 150 million years ago," Santi chimed in, "during the supposed age of the dinosaurios, the moon's effect on the tides would have been so great, that the dinosaurios would have been drowning twice a day. Last I heard, one can only comfortably drown once a día." Santi laughed at his own joke.

Matt and Tom started arguing with each other. Matt accused Tom of stealing his thunder while the rest of the class laughed at both of them, and Santi as well.

I gave Thad the cut signal, pulling my finger across my neck, as class time was almost up anyway.

"We'll pick this up next time," Thad nervously announced, "as long as it's okay with Dr. Lucci." I gave Thad a positive wave of my hand indicating he could resume his lecture for the next class session.

The class exited still laughing and teasing Tom, Matt, and Santi. I walked up to Thad. "You really did a bang-up job, no pun intended."

CHAPTER ONE HUNDRED FORTY-ONE

AGE OF CONSENT

"How did it go in class today?" Father Ed asked me over lunch at the Holy Grounds Coffee Shop.

"Actually, pretty well; Thad gave an astronomy lecture from a young earth perspective and covered a good amount of material. He's really been pumped ever since our trip to the Creation Museum. As you may remember he's minoring in astronomy."

"How did the students handle it?"

"Quite well, with our one exception; I wish I could reach Jude," I said, as I took a hearty bite out of my BLT on toasted rye bread.

"Anything you wished he had covered, but didn't?" Father Ed asked, as he took a few gulps from his lemonade.

"Thad didn't cover everything. He will do one more class session, and he may cover it there, or perhaps I may suggest he do so."

"What did he leave out?" Father asked, as Cindy brought his overstuffed tuna melt on whole wheat.

Why do his sandwiches always look better than mine? I thought. "About the only other thing I would have added is a quote from John Mather, a senior astrophysicist in the Observational Cosmology Lab at NASA Goddard. The quote appeared in . . . let me double-check that; I had just researched it on my tablet. Yes, it appeared in *New Scientist,* in 1998."

"What was the title of the article, Joe?"

"It was 'Let There Be Light.' What he said was, and I quote, 'We have no direct evidence of how galaxies were formed, how the first stars formed without the help of prior generations of stars, how galaxies evolved. . . . It goes right to the heart of the question of how we got here.' And the guy's still an evolutionist, despite what he said. Unbelievable!"

"Hey, shifting gears Father, what's been going on since that bill was signed into law by our dear leader? What was the name of it? Oh, yeah, the Personal Rights Protection Act."

"The powers that be, Joe, always do a slight of hand, getting the public focused on one thing and then pulling a fast one with the other hand."

"So, Father, what's the low down?"

"A number of things. My Washington connections have been bringing me up to speed on the behind-the-scenes activities. Remember a few years back they stated everyone needed to swap their old bills for new ones. They gave some technical banking explanation that the old bills were no longer legal tender."

"Yeah, I remember," I said, as I choked on a bacon bit, which almost went down the wrong pipe. I grabbed for my iced tea.

"Well, the real purpose was to flush out all the currency that was being stuffed in mattresses and home safes by preppers, small business owners, and just about anyone else who didn't trust the government banking system."

"Now," Father Ed continued, "the ATMs are slowly being converted to recharge your hand-imbedded chip. They will still accept your ID card, which has a chip, but only for a short time." He took a few more swigs of his lemonade.

"That's right, Father, some people refused to accept the 'mark of the beast' but still needed a chip-impregnated credit card for transactions. What's happening to them?"

"Once the card expires or if you lose it, you in effect, must receive that RFID chip. If not, it will be virtually impossible to purchase food, goods, or services of any type. If you receive any government check—federal, state, or local—you will need the chip to get the funds. Without the chip your kids will not be allowed in the government schools and universities, and you and your family will be denied care at hospitals. Since the chip on the card or in your hand has your entire medical history on it, they claim they cannot treat you without it. Something about HIPAA regulations."

"I know, Father, there has been a spike in homeschooling and home births because they are chipping all newborns in the hospital, as well as every old codger who comes into the ED from the nursing homes. We have a gal from the social services department who is assigned specifically to the co-ordination of administering chip injections."

"Joe, it's just a matter of time before these outliers that are trying to avoid the system are caught. And when they are, that individual, and sometimes entire families, will be remanded to a FEMA internment camp. Do you recall those Walmarts that had 'plumbing problems' *all* at the same time? I believe they are possibly being used as processing centers."

"Geez, that's some serious stuff comin' down the pike. I suspect the FEMA camp business is not common knowledge yet, right? And I'm sure the lamestream media has been read the riot act about *not* bringing it up. So, what's the latest on the new law that's about to be enacted on November 28? Even Kathy Owens alluded to it."

"What the news media has *not* been telling the folks is about the riders that were added to the bill at the last moment—deliberately!" Cindy came over and refilled Father's lemonade, as he had been trying to drink the ice melting in his glass.

"Remember a few years back, Joe, the controversy over the LGBT restrooms and how the right-wing conservative Christians didn't want perverts following their little daughters into the bathroom or school shower facilities?"

"Yeah, the conservatives were panned by the media as intolerant bigots." I said, carefully taking another bite of my BLT.

"One of the two provisions had to do with lowering the age of consensual sex to thirteen years old. This way the internet trolls and other deviates could legally get away with pedophilia. Another bennie was for the Muslims to be able to marry young girls without any pushback from conservative legal groups. CAIR - you know the Council on American Islamic Relations, had been lobbying congress anyway, for some time on this."

"Marry?! Marry?! With the onslaught of Muslim 'refugees' into Europe, Sweden has become the rape capital of Europe! Aah, sorry about that outburst, but wasn't one of Muhammad's wives like nine or ten when the marriage was consummated?"

"That's correct, Joe. Her name was Aisha, and according to the Sunni hadiths themselves, he married her at seven years old. Many Muslim males have had this fantasy fetish to marry young girls ever since. A number of Imams still assert its okay for men to do so today, since any action of the Prophet was to be extolled, anyway."

"Curious, Father, why set the legal age at thirteen, and not twelve or eleven?"

"The logic from the ultra-leftist pinko organization that submitted the proposal to its like-minded congressmen, was that a teen-sounding age would be acceptable to the majority of the American public—eighteen and thirteen, kinda sounds the same. The bill's rider was pushed through Congress, and now this warped group is prepared with TV ads, my sources tell me, which will show statistics that the age of girls having sex for the first time has been getting younger and younger, anyway."

"Oh, so that's supposed to justify their actions to tag on this rider. Hells bells, you can't turn on the TV or open a magazine or watch a movie in which they're *not* selling sex. Besides the governmental Matrix is having the schools push it, even in first grade; one wonders why these pubescent teens think it's okay to drop their drawers for either sex!"

There's a screaming voice going on in my head thinking of some of my little nieces, as I took another sip of my iced tea.

"Father, what was the other provision that was added that you were going to tell me about?" I asked.

Father offered a scurrilous laugh, looked straight at me, and with a half dead expression said, "Joe you're going to love this; you're really going to love this one!"

CHAPTER ONE HUNDRED FORTY-TWO

COMMUNION BILL

"From what I understand, Father, by the 28th, no displays of any religious expression will be allowed. Wouldn't that include you wearing your black cassock and collar?"

"Joe, when I was a Marine in Korea, I wore a uniform that said I was a soldier in the service for the United States of America. Today, Joe, I wear another uniform that tells the world that I am in the service of Christ. For me to take my 'uniform' off, places me with the average civilian and does nothing to set me apart from my calling to serve Christ and my fellow man."

"So, since you will continue to wear it, how are you planning on handling the authorities?"

"If I get arrested, so be it. It's in the Lord's hands now." Father Ed seemed at peace with his decision. There was no stress on his face as he looked calmly at me.

"Oh, yeah, Father, what was that second rider that was attached to the bill?"

"Yes, as I was about to say, the second proposition was penned by the devil himself. It states that for health and safety reasons, as per EPA and OSHA regulations, the Catholic Church can no longer serve Communion."

"What the hell?" I practically shouted back at Father Ed, as bacon particles spewed from my mouth onto the table; several patrons looked over at us.

"The pit of hell is exactly where this monstrosity was framed. The Church has, from the time of St. Paul and St. Ignatius of Antioch in AD 110, taken the position that during the Consecration portion of the Mass, the bread and wine is transformed into the literal body and blood of Our Lord. We call this transubstantiation. It of course retains the smell, taste, and appearance of bread and wine."

"How do the EPA and OSHA fit into this travesty, Father?"

"By the idea that human tissue and blood, even though they still retain the appearance of bread and wine, are against health code regulations. Daniel wrote in the Old Testament about twenty-six hundred years ago of a time to come when this would happen."

"Really? I'm not familiar with that passage. The Lion's Den is about where I left off."

"Daniel 12:11 says, 'From the time the daily sacrifice is abolished and the abomination of desolation is set up, there will be 1290 days.' That's three and a half years, Joe."

"That's right, we Catholics properly call it the Daily Sacrifice of the Mass, since Mass is said daily around the world. I have not reflected on that expression for some time." I sat there for a moment squeezing my glass.

"Now to be fair, our Protestant brothers don't interpret Daniel quite the same way. However, they clearly see this as a stepping-stone by the Matrix, as you call them, to dismantle Christianity entirely, by spreading their poisonous tentacles of this abomination of Daniels' to other countries as well. Their plan is to wipe Christianity from the face of the earth—or should I say from Mother Gaia." He half chuckled a bit, referring, I believe, to my ongoing conflict with Professor Dietrich.

"Are you saying, Father, the various Christian denominations are supportive of us?"

"Absolutely! There has been a Facebook and Twitter blitz flooding parishes as well as all Christian denominations throughout the country already. Many of these sects offer Communion as a symbolic gesture; however in support of the Catholics they too will refrain from giving out Communion. Either we all unite or 'we shall all hang separately', to quote Ben Franklin at the signing of the Declaration of Independence."

I put my thinking cap on. "November 28 is less than two weeks away. What's with that particular day?" I took out my tablet and punched up my November calendar schedule. "Figures, it's the Monday right after the Thanksgiving weekend, when we thanked the *Indians*, not God, from the perspective of our new revisionist history," I stated with caustic sarcasm.

"I.O., Joe; I.O."

"Yeah Father, Western civilization as we know it—It's Over!"

CHAPTER ONE HUNDRED FORTY-THREE

LITTLE IO

With the next class session, Thad appeared less apprehensive than he did the first go-round, and Jude appeared ready to rumble for the second round. I sat in Thad's seat and waited for the abbey tower bell to start the action.

"I'm sure all of you are aware of comets," Thad announced at the start of class. "But what are they made of?"

"They're balls of ice and dirt speeding through the solar system and orbiting our sun in elliptical paths," Matt said, jumping the gun before Tom could answer.

"And what happens to them as they orbit the sun?"

Tom responded immediately. "Each time they make a pass around the sun part of their material is blasted away by the solar radiation."

"Can this go on forever? Thad asked.

"Of course not," Matt relied. "The average lifespan of a comet is about forty round trips before it is wasted, unless it crashes into something first like the comet Shoemaker-Levy, which slammed spectacularly into Jupiter in 1994. I've got an impact photo of when it hit Jupiter, and another of a comet itself."

"Okay, Matt, put them up on the Insta-Screen for us, please," Thad directed, as he was excited to see the images too.

Comet impact into Jupiter.
Photo Credit: NASA

Comet flying in space.
Photo Credit: Shutterstock

"Comets seem to be connected with both good and bad omens," Juan remarked, "is that not so?" Santi nodded at Juan's question.

Nate answered him directly. "Halley's Comet," he said, "is famous for this. It has a period or cycle of return every seventy-six years. It was present at the Battle of Hastings in 1066—good for the Normans who conquered Britain; it was present when the Roman General Titus destroyed Jerusalem—bad for the Jews in AD 70. The comet's passing was both a good and bad omen for one Samuel Clemens who was born and died in the years Halley's Comet did its pass-by of Earth."

"Who was Samuel Clemens?" Juan asked.

"Mark Twain," Claudia responded, "was the nom de plume— or pen name—Samuel Clemens gave himself. He was a riverboat pilot on the Mississippi and created his name Mark from the marks used to measure the depth of the river, and Twain - which means two fathoms deep. The *Adventures of Tom Sawyer* and his friend Huckleberry Finn are still popular books today."

The second Claudia finished, Tom wasted no time and blurted out, "Comets will run out of material in a maximum of one hundred thousand years at most."

"Many within ten thousand years," Matt quickly added, as the rivals look at each other.

"So, if our solar system is 4.6 billion years old, as the evolutionary cosmologists maintain, how come there are still comets? Shouldn't the supply of comets have been depleted billions of years ago?" Thad pressed both Tom and Matt.

"Because the Oort Cloud and the Kuiper Belt resupplies our solar system with new comets," Jude called out from the back of the room.

"Been boning up on your astronomy, Jude?" Tom asked.

"Let's just say I'm ready and prepared today," he stated with a smirk.

"Hey, Jude," Tom called, "you do know both the Oort cloud and Kuiper Belt were concocted out of thin air—or should I say thin space, don't you?" Tom asked, laughing at his own joke like Santi.

Matt interjected, "That's because no one has been able to verify *either* of these." He surveyed his classmates to make sure his point stuck. "These secular cosmologists have created a bunch of fabricated yarns to account for the icy lumps kicked into the inner solar system from time to time."

Tom tag-teamed back against Jude. "One of the most favorite late atheist astronomers, Carl Sagan," he added, "whose series *Cosmos,* recently remade for TV, and his book *Contact,* which was made into a movie with Jodie Foster, had this to say about comets in his own book entitled *Comet*: 'Many scientific papers are written each year about the Oort Cloud, its properties, its origin, its evolution. Yet there is not a shred of direct observational evidence for its existence.' Your rebuttal, Jude?" Tom asked, with his best TV lawyer tone.

Jude was obviously frustrated as he sat quietly without responding to Tom. There was a momentary silence in the room.

Thad then clarified his final point on comets. "But if the universe is only six thousand years old, we would expect there to still be comets flying around," he said, as I noted a number of students nodding their heads ever so slightly with understanding.

Without missing a beat, Thad threw another photo up on the Insta-Screen. "This is a picture of a spiral galaxy which are very common. It sorta looks like a pinwheel, the inner portions rotating faster than the outer portions. The spiral galaxy is winding itself up. According to the secular scientists, in less than 1 billion years the arms should have twisted themselves up beyond recognition, but they haven't. And galaxies are supposed to be around 10 billion years old?"

Spiral Galaxy photo. Photo Credit: Shutterstock

"But if the universo is only six thousand years old, there is no problema," Santi exclaimed. "Esa espiral galaxia is hermosa . . . beautiful!"

Juan raised his hand and said, "All the planets in our solar system rotate in a counter-clockwise direction except for Venus and Uranus. And Uranus is tipped on its side ninety degrees. How do the evolutionists explain that?"

"Because they believe," Jude interjected, coming to the defense of the secular cosmologists, "that they were impacted by collisions with large asteroids or other massive space debris, which affected their direction of rotation." He then sat back and smiled.

"Oye, hombre, can they prove that or they just believe that?" Santi asked, as he turned to face Jude.

"Besides," Juan added, "to change their direction of rotation would have required quite a wallop. Do these planets have massive cracks and holes in them?"

Thad immediately answered, "No, no they don't."

"I know why Venus and Uranus don't rotate counter-clockwise like the other planets. It's because God wanted to mess with the evolutionists cabezas again," Santi said. With that the room burst into chuckles. Santi stood and took a bow.

Philip, still leaning back on his rear chair legs, more for comfort now than arrogance, spoke. "In all seriousness," he said, "the nebular hypothesis predicts that as the nebula of gas and dust spiraled inward forming our sun and its planets, allegedly 4.6 billion years ago, the planets should all rotate and orbit in the same direction. Each of the orbits of our planets and their moons, however, are different. Two of Saturn's moons even swap orbits without crashing into each other. The nebular hypothesis is in such disarray that many cosmologists themselves are starting to call it the *nebulous* hypothesis."

"Did Philip just make a funny?" Maggie asked, turning around to Claudia, who also had a somewhat surprised expression on her face.

Thad was focused on completing his lecture on time, and continued, "Now the final few photos I'd like to put up are of little Io, one of Jupiter's many moons. The first photo of Io has just a small portion of massive Jupiter in the background."

Tiny Io with massive Jupiter in background. Photo Credit: NASA

"The second photo of Io is a close up from the Voyager cameras. Notice anything unusual?"

Photo of Io enlarged. Photo Credit: NASA

Juan, being very close to the Insta-Screen, saw it very clearly. "Wow!" he exclaimed, "It looks like the whole thing is on fire."

"Well, it is," Thad, said directing his answer to Juan, "this entire moon is chock-full of active volcanoes. It is the most volcanically active body in the entire solar system. One hundred times more active than earth and it keeps on spewing out the hottest lavas known."

Philip made an astute observation, "Smaller bodies cool down much more quickly than larger ones. And Io is quite tiny on the scale of things in the solar system as a whole."

"I've got it!"

"No, I've got it!"

Matt and Tom were at it again and Thad was getting frustrated. "Doc, please help."

I stood up, giving both Matt and Tom an austere look, and then a gentle smile. "I believe both of them are going to say," I began, "that there is no way that little Io wouldn't have spewed itself out of lava and gone cold, in the range of the minus 300 degrees Fahrenheit of space by now, if the solar system really were billions of years old. Am I correct, guys?" I asked looking at them both. "But it's not a problem for there to be active volcanoes on such a small satellite for six thousand years."

"That's right," Tom said, nodding.

"Yeah, that's what I was about to say, also," Matt confirmed.

Then they both turned and leaned into one another with high fives. Thank God.

With this last example of Thad's, the class seemed fairly well convinced that we live in a young universe, and that evolution was impossible in such a short time span of six thousand years.

Jude then slowly stood up and addressed the entire class in a very harsh and angry voice. "Okay, you Bible thumpers, explain how the light from distant stars and galaxies got to earth during creation week. Your God claims to have made the sun and stars on Day 4, and Adam on Day 6. You yourselves, admit that some stars and galaxies are billions of light-years away from us. Were Adam and Eve unable to see the stars at night? For that matter, Adam would have needed to wait 4.3 years to see even the closest star Alpha Centauri light up. Go ahead, I'd like to see you weasel your way out of this one!" Jude sneered at us and then he sat down, confident with his accusation.

CHAPTER ONE HUNDRED FORTY-FOUR

LAWGIVER

"**D**oc, we're out of time for the class," Thad said, expressing his wish to answer Jude but pointing out the clock had run out.

"I'll stay."

"Me too!"

"I want to hear Thad's explanation," someone else said.

Pete stood up and took charge. "How many are willing to stay overtime to hear this? I know personally that this is one big question that has puzzled me."

All hands excitedly flew into the air, as everyone seemed to have had that same challenging question rattling around in their heads.

Thad looked over at me. "If you're game, Thad," I said, "then go for it!"

Thad organized his thoughts for a moment before he explained some of the ground rules regarding the universe. "One thing we must all understand is that in the beginning, whether by creation or evolution, there was still nothing. There is an element of faith on each side of the argument. One is not pure science and the other mystical drivel - both are religious. Can we at least take that as our starting point everyone?" he asked, as he looked at Jude in particular, who nodded quietly in agreement.

"May I," Philip interrupted, wishing to address the group again. Thad gave him the green light. "It is irrational for secular scientists to rely on the laws of physics to explain the instant of the formation of time, space, and matter since back then there were no laws. Remember there was nothing!"

"Huh? Run that by me again," Matt called out to Philip.

"Nothing means just that—nothing. How can you have laws, which govern the universe, before there *was* a universe? When there was nothing, that means there was no law of gravity. No laws for strong or weak nuclear forces—because there were no atoms. No electromagnetic forces—because there were no gamma rays, nor infrared, nor ultraviolet radiation. There was nothing."

Thad then tried to simplify it a bit for Matt and the class. "The secular community of scientists *assumes*—and we know what that means—that the universe was created by the same process with which it operates today. But how can something—anything—be created to function/to run/to operate, if there are no laws to govern the damn thing!" he said, taking a dollar from his pocket and cramming it into the cussin' jar.

"I get it now," Matt exclaimed, turning to his classmates. "It's kinda like a flashlight."

"The universe is like a flashlight?" Tom asked, with a look of doubt and confusion.

"Yeah man, a flashlight works/operates/runs by converting electricity into light, but the entire physical flashlight was *not* created by this process—by the laws of electricity. Do you guys get it now?" he asked, looking first at Tom and then at the class, all of whom were nodding in agreement.

"So where *did* the laws of nature for the universe come from?" Tom asked, to no one in particular.

Maria interjected, "Every law must have a lawgiver who creates the law or laws. It's common sense to me, which is why I do not have enough *faith* to be an atheist!"

Jude appeared incensed as he said, "You people are avoiding the distant starlight problem. Let's get to it; you're boring me."

"Okay, Jude," Thad said, irked at Jude's attitude, "your secular cosmologists also have a light-travel-time problem; are you aware of that?"

"Whaaa?" Jude announced, totally confused, "No, we don't; you're using delay tactics. You have nothing!" Jude was very heated and indignant.

CHAPTER ONE HUNDRED FORTY-FIVE

LITTLE BIG BANG

Thad looked for some materials on the lab table before saying, "Let's just round off the evolutionary age of the entire universe to be 13 billion years. Is that acceptable with you, Jude?" Jude nodded his head in agreement.

Thad picked up what appeared to be a large deflated balloon; then he took a black marker and put two small dots very close together on the balloon. "Now imagine this is the universe. When we fill it with air, we can see it start to expand after the supposed big bang."

"Would you like me to help you expand your balloon . . . I mean, your universe?" Juan asked, offering to inflate the balloon.

"Sure, thanks, Juan," Thad said, handing the balloon to Juan. "I'll put up on the Insta-Screen a couple of illustrations of what is happening, in different parts of the universe, from the big bang's point of view, and the problem that exists with it."

"Every cosmologist will admit that in any explosion, energy in any form—heat, light, whatever—is not going to be evenly distributed. Think about a grenade going off. The shrapnel and heat released from the initial explosion will not be flying off in exactly equal parts in all directions."

"Yeah, I can vouch for that," Nate said, interrupting, "my great-granddad flew in WWII and explained that an anti-aircraft shell exploding in the air could take you out, while sparing the guy in the plane next to you."

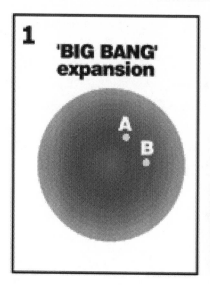
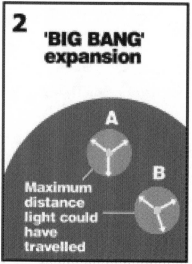

Illustration of Big Bang Expansion 1 & 2. Illustration Credit: creation.com

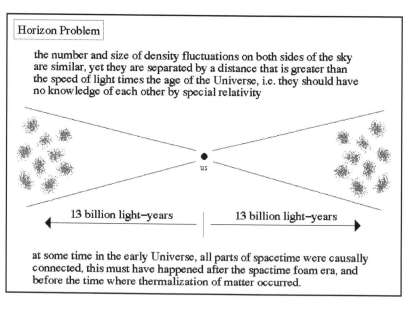

Horizon Problem

the number and size of density fluctuations on both sides of the sky are similar, yet they are separated by a distance that is greater than the speed of light times the age of the Universe, i.e. they should have no knowledge of each other by special relativity

us

13 billion light–years   13 billion light–years

at some time in the early Universe, all parts of spacetime were causally connected, this must have happened after the spactime foam era, and before the time where thermalization of matter occurred.

Horizon Problem Illustration. Illustration Credit: abyss.uoregon.edu

Point A   Big Bang   Point B

"That's actually a good example, Nate," Thad added. "From what we have discovered today, the cosmic microwave background radiation (CMBR), is claimed to be the remnant of the Big Bang. The temperature out in space however, is essentially the *same* in all parts of the universe. Its precision differs to only one part in 100,000, which shouldn't be, but it is!"

"Sí, like the granada . . . grenade explosión, some parts of the universo should be 'hotter' and other parts 'colder'!" Santi exclaimed, waving his hands wildly in the air.

"The CMBR *is* . . . *was* an indicator of the big bang, excuse me!" Jude butted in making a critical pronouncement.

"That's true, Jude," Thad replied, "but the CMBR actually *created* a problem for the big bang theory. According to the big bang theorists, in the *early* universe, the CMBR temps would have been very different in different areas of space, like the exploding grenade."

Juan was scratching his head, and Jim raised his hand. "I see some of you are having a bit of a challenge with this," he said. "Light energy contains heat. Try lying out in the sun's radiation for a while."

Santi said, "Sí, like sticking your cabeza in a microwave oven!" The class chuckled.

Thad pointed to the two illustrations and continued. "The problem is this, even given the big bang's 13 billion year timescale, there has *not* been enough time for light energy/heat to travel between point A and point B," he said, indicating the opposite ends of the universe."

"I've got it!" Tom shouted, overpowering Matt and holding his hand down. Both were jumping out of their seats.

"Okay Tom, you first, then Matt," Thad said, becoming exasperated with the two of them.

"However, different regions of space, *do* have equal uniform temps according to the current CMBR in those regions, despite the fact that these regions in space—A and B—have not had enough time to communicate light, and therefore heat with each other; that's the light-time-travel problem the evolutionists face, *Jude*," Tom said, turning to the back of the room to face Jude.

Matt now piled on, as he stood up to face Jude. "Yeah, while the big bang timeframe of billions of years gives light enough time to travel from most distant galaxies to earth," Matt explained, "it does *not* provide enough time for light to travel from one side of the visible universe to the other! Yet the CMBR temperature is equally the same in every direction we look. You've got a big problem there, buddy."

"And please don't fall back on the inflation model as an explanation," Philip chimed in while still leaning against the back wall. "We've just been through that, and it doesn't hold water—unless you can give us a detailed explanation of what started, and what stopped, the so-called inflation period."

Nate gave the final blow when he said, "Jude, think! The only reason the inflation concept was developed to begin with was to save the big bang's lack of explanation of the CMBR's uniform/equal temps throughout space. Now some other theory is needed to save the inflation theory."

"Thanks, Nate," Thad said, picking up the ball again. "Riccardo Scarpa, another frustrated evolutionist, of the European Southern Observatory in Santiago, Chile, said essentially the same thing, and I quote: 'Every time the big bang model has failed to predict what we see, the solution has been to bolt on something new—inflation, dark matter and dark energy.'"

Jude looked like he was ready to explode. The class got quiet as they soaked up Scarpa's quote; and Jude just sat fuming in the back.

When suddenly—BOOOM!!! The entire class jumped from their seats.

"Sorry," Juan said apologetically. "I was just so mesmerized watching as those two little black dots move away from one another and the balloon kept on expanding . . . and . . . ah, we did have a big bang, didn't we? Heh, heh."

The entire group looked at Juan like he was a buffon, and their expressions indicated the joke also went over like a lead balloon.

CHAPTER ONE HUNDRED FORTY-SIX

CENTER OF THE UNIVERSE

"Enough of this charade," Jude bellowed from the rear corner. "You Christians need to explain the dilemma of distant starlight coming to earth from *your* six thousand-year timeframe. These distant galaxies *must* mean that the universe is billions of years old."

"Before I proceed further," Thad interjected. "I would like to thank Dr. Jason Lisle, whose materials I have drawn from heavily."

"Who is Dr. Jason Lisle?" Juan asked as he tossed the popped balloon into the trash can.

"He holds a PhD in astrophysics from the University of Colorado at Boulder, which is not a Christian university by any stretch. He was a writer, speaker, and researcher with Answers in Genesis and now with the Institute for Creation Research (ICR). Nate, Philip, and I watched his planetarium expositions at the Creation Museum regarding a young universe. I then went to the Dragon Bookstore and bought up everything I could by him on astronomy. I hope I do him justice."

"Okay, okay, just get on with it," Jude said impatiently.

"Again, as a reminder, any attempt to scientifically estimate the age of something will necessarily involve a number of assumptions, whether from an evolutionary or a biblical point of view."

"Currently, it takes light (in a vacuum) about one year to travel 6 trillion miles. Also, many people assume that time flows at the same rate - this assumption is false. Einstein discovered that the passage of time is affected by motion *and* gravity."

"Like, man, you're losing me already," Matt said shaking his head. "Do you have some simple example you could give me . . . ah . . . us?"

"Okay, Matt, the faster an object moves toward the speed of light, the slower time goes. So, if you were able to travel at speeds near the speed of light, the watch on your wrist would slow down. Reach the speed of light, and your watch would stop. This is called time dilation."

"So, Thad, are you saying time actually slows down?"

"That's right, Matt. Gravity also slows the passage of time. A clock at sea level ticks more slowly than one on the top of Mount Everest, since the clock at sea level is closer to the source of gravity. This time dilation effect has been confirmed using atomic clocks."

"So, if I get this correctly," Matt said, straining to understand the concept, "if I'm on the top of Everest and Tom is down at the seashore, whatever event is happening on top of Everest is happening more quickly, in a shorter span of time, than an event down at the seashore?"

"Yes, of course, but not by much, because the difference in gravitational pull is relatively small; however, in the vast reaches of space, the differences are very big; and this principle can be applied to distant starlight."

Tom jumped up waving his hand, followed a nanosecond later by Matt hollering that he had it first. Poor Thad just shook his head. "Okay, Tom you were out of your seat first."

"Yeah, but I was hollering first," Matt argued, claiming the win.

"Matt, if you don't chill out, I'm going to send you to the dean for a paddling," Thad exclaimed, running out of options between the two of them.

The class was in an uproar laughing at the thought of Matt getting a spanking at his age. Matt quickly sat down and the class mellowed out.

"So that means," Tom said, finally getting to explain, "light, even from the most distant reaches of the universe, that would take billions of years to reach earth, could do so in only thousands of years."

Nate wished to add something, and Thad recognized him. "Thad, are you familiar with the Sloan Digital Galaxy Survey, which shows that galaxies seem to be clustered in concentric rings about *our own* Milky Way galaxy? I have it on my tablet already. If you wish, I could put it up on the Insta-Screen?"

"Yes, please do—this is incredible everyone, thanks Nate!"

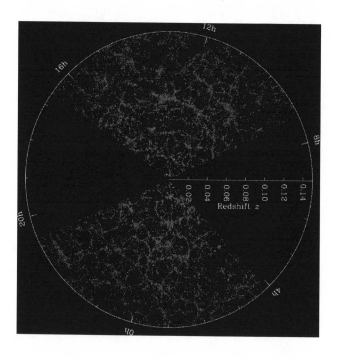

Sloan Digital Galaxy Survey. Image Credit: astrobites.org

"Our Milky Way is in the center of this map of known galaxies," Nate explained this to the class. "The atheist astronomer, the late Carl Sagan, looked upon humanity as irrelevant in the grand scheme of life and the universe. He made this statement in his 1980 book *Cosmos*, 'We find we live on an insignificant planet of a humdrum star lost in a galaxy tucked away in some forgotten corner of a universe in which there are far more galaxies than people.' If he were alive today, I wonder if he would humbly retract his statement?"

From my position in the back, my eyes darted across the room to where Jude sat. He was now upright in his seat and leaning forward, studying the Sloan Digital Galaxy Survey map on the giant Insta-screen very intently with wide eyes and nervously biting his lip. He must have been reflecting that we *are* at the center of the universe.

CHAPTER ONE HUNDRED FORTY-SEVEN

NOT ALL EINSTEINS

Philip put his hand up and said, "If this Digital Survey of the galaxies is accurate, and I have no reason to believe otherwise, that would put our solar system and, of course, our earth at the very center of an immeasurable giant gravitational well."

"What Philip is saying," Thad said, nodding to Philip to thank him, "is that this is the mountain and the seashore on an unimaginable scale. Time would flow more slowly on earth than anywhere else in the universe."

"Everyone agrees," Philip said, wishing to expand on his point, "that the universe is expanding, and physics demands that such gravitational effects would have been stronger when the universe was smaller and younger, and clocks on earth would have ticked much more slowly than clocks in deep space."

Matt didn't wait to be recognized and immediately added, "Thus light from even the most *distant* galaxies would arrive on earth in only a few thousand years, as measured by clocks on earth."

"Carumba!" said Santi seeing the light. "Adam therefore, would have been able to see the stars in our *local* Milky Way Galaxia when he was created on día seis . . . six!"

"Finally," Thad said, looking exhausted, "there is the topic of synchronization: how clocks are set so that they read the same time at the same time." Thad tried his best to clarify this difficult subject as he continued, "Einstein's relativity has shown that synchronization is *not* an absolute. There is no way that two clocks, separated by great distances, can be synchronized in an absolute sense. *We choose what constitutes synchronized clocks.*"

"Okay, there you go again," Matt said, "you must have some example you can give us; we're not all Einsteins here."

"Alright, Matt," Thad explained, "say you get on a plane in Kentucky at 4:00 PM, and two hours later you land in Colorado at 4:00 PM." He let Matt mull that over in his head.

"Well," Matt said, "that's because the *local* time in Colorado says 4:00 P.M. when I land, even though I got hemorrhoids after sitting for two hours in the air." A few people chuckled.

"So, Matt, the trip takes two hours as measured by *universal* time; however, as long as the plane is traveling west fast enough, it will arrive in Colorado in *local* time because of arbitrary time zones that we, as humanity, have all agreed on."

"Ah, as you said, Thad, '*we choose* what constitutes synchronized clocks.' Got it!"

Thad perceived a new conflict about to brew, and Tom and Matt both put their hands up. "Now Tom had his hand up first, Matt; I'm tired of fighting with you two guys."

Matt conceded, and with a contrived pout, put his hand down. Tom said, "I'll bet there is a cosmic equivalent to *local* and *universal* time, and that astronomers use cosmic *universal* time—it takes light one hundred years to travel one hundred light-years kind of thing."

"Yeah, and historically," Matt countered, "cosmic *local* time has been the standard. God created the stars on Day 4, and their light would also reach the earth on Day 4 cosmic *local* time, right?"

"The rule is," Jude belligerently added, "nature is all that there is, and all phenomena must be explained *only* in terms of natural law."

"And who made that rule, Jude?" Tom asked, with a sassy tone. "Are only the atheists and evolutionists allowed to make the rules? Is that how you're going to play the game?"

Nate turned toward Jude and said, "God is not bound by natural laws. After all they are *His* laws, as we have discussed already, and God can use the laws of nature He created to accomplish His will, if He so chooses."

"Besides," Maggie added, joining the fray, "distant starlight may have arrived on earth by supernatural processes, and all that *supernatural* means is that God can choose if He wants to bend or break His own natural laws. Of course, we call that a miracle."

"That's irrational!" Jude screamed from the back of the room.

"Listen, bud," Maggie said, not taking any of his guff. "Just because something cannot be explained by natural processes observed today does not make it irrational."

"Like instantly changing water to wine?" Jude rudely shot back.

"Actually, the polar compound water—H_2O—being converted to ethyl alcohol—C_2H_2OH—*without* the fermentation of grape sugars is a very good example of an inexplicable chemical change, *Jude*." Maggie replied with a snippy demeanor.

Philip laughed at Jude while rocking his chair back and forth against the rear wall.

"What do you find so funny?" Jude asked, turning toward him with a disparaging attitude.

"The fact that you are accusing Christians of believing in miracles—water to wine—when you evolutionary atheists believe in miracles yourselves—actually the biggest miracle of all."

"You're off your rocker," Jude said, with a snide laugh while pointing at Philip's chair.

Philip planted his chair squarely on the floor, and calmly but firmly said, "You people deny the existence of the first *law* of thermodynamics - that all matter can neither be created nor destroyed!" His eyes burrowed straight into Jude.

"You're nuts; what's your point, man?"

"My *point* is - that you *deny* this law, because you believe the entire known universe and all that it contains popped into existence from *nothing*. In my book, that's a miracle!" Philip said to Jude's consternation.

Thad looked at the time on his cell phone he had propped up on the lab table and motioned for everyone to simmer down. "I'm sorry, I wish I could have presented a better lecture on all of this."

Maria stood to act as a spokesman for the group. "Thad, you were awesome. I believe all of us, and I mean *all* of us," she said, zeroing in on Jude, "really appreciate all your research. I don't think any of us believes that the young earth creationists have all the answers, but I also believe that we have come to the conclusion and realization that the evolutionists and atheists *definitely* don't. The problem lies in the fact that the Matrix, which controls us, refuses any open debate and discussion because it's always about the money which leads to power and control, like Dr. Lucci always says."

Claudia's hand was up. When Maria sat down, Claudia stood up and addressed the class. "St. Paul traveled with a young man whom he mentored by the name of Timothy. This was Paul's advice to him: 'Timothy, guard what has been entrusted to your care. Turn away from godless chatter and the opposing ideas of what is falsely called science, which some have professed and in doing so have departed from the faith,' from 1 Timothy 6:20–21." She then graciously and elegantly took her seat.

There was stunned silence for a moment, then the class blurted out, "Claudia?" in unison, as they were shocked at Claudia's recitation from the Bible, of all things.

UNHOLY RENOVATION

Emily, Father Ed, and I arrived at my sister Carmella's in my car, 'the tank'. Since it gave Father Ed more room for his long legs, Emily had been kind enough to sit in the back, which was still very roomy. Besides, she needed to protect the three bottles of wine from breaking.

While the women were putting the final touches on the turkey and bounty of tasty side dishes Carmella had prepared, Father and I played with my nieces and nephews.

When we were called for dinner, Father gave the blessing over the food and we all heartily dug in. Carmella had a habit of cooking and baking enough for a small army. She must have been a mess sergeant in a former life, albeit a highly trained one.

Afterwards, we were all vegging out on the couches and sofa watching the game, waiting for the food to digest before diving into the panoply of desserts Carmella was now arranging on the dining room table. Father approached me asking if I would take a walk with him since he wanted to stretch his legs.

"Sure, let's go, Father; I need to burn off some of this turkey and stuffing and . . . everything else before dessert and coffee, anyway. You know the area well, which direction do you want to go?"

"I'd like to go to the campus, Joe; it should be very peaceful and quiet there today, and the weather is absolutely perfect."

"Don't you think that's a bit far to attempt to hike, Father?"

He gave me one of his hearty laughs. "No, me lad, I meant for us to drive there and then stroll around the ICC grounds."

The weather *was* perfect. The past week the temps had been in the mid-thirties during the day and at night dipped to below freezing. That day however, turned out to be magnificent. It had been a bit chilly in the morning with temps hovering around forty; I had worn a bulky winter sweater over a collared shirt to Carmella's, which I needed to remove. By the time we went on our walk it was a bright, balmy afternoon in the low sixties, with nary a breeze.

As we drove up to the ICC campus in 'the tank', Father's face seemed to enliven, almost glow with the aspect of being where he loved most. Immaculate Conception College was the crowning achievement of his life. It was his baby with all the birth pangs he had endured in making it come to life.

We walked silently, barely speaking a word along the paths at ICC. The trees were barren and stripped of their leaves, sensing winter was around the corner. We passed by the chapel and failed to notice that the cross on the steeple was now no longer part of the elegant design reaching skyward to the heavens. One arm of the cross bar was completely severed and the other arm was just a stump.

Approaching the quadrangle, Father was about to light one of his Camacho Ecuadors when we heard heavy loud hammering, and a voice barking orders. Once we were in the open of the quadrangle, we could easily see what was transpiring. Erik was the one giving commands to three laborers from maintenance. Two of Erik's Blueshirts were there, as was another gentleman dressed in a ritzy black suit standing off to the side, observing and noting the goings on in some official capacity.

The workmen were over by the statue of Mary, and had already ripped up the naked rose bushes on each side of the statue, and were using sledge hammers on the concrete trellis behind Mary.

I was stunned and overwhelmed at the sight. I couldn't move. Father however, rushed forward to confront Erik and stood a few feet, directly in front of Mary, his back to the statue, planning on protecting her.

"Stop!" His voice boomed like the Almighty Himself; he stood firm and rigid his hands on his hips. A puff of wind rustled Father's cassock, otherwise, for a moment, the entire scene was a freeze-frame.

CHAPTER ONE HUNDRED FORTY-NINE

TASED

"**W**e have our orders, *priest*!" Erik said, standing his ground and pointing his nightstick at Father. "Today is the twenty-fourth and the law goes fully into effect on Monday, or haven't you read your directives from the administration?"

"You sniveling little asswipe, I ought a—" the Marine in Father definitely emerging.

"You ought a what? You're in no position to do anything, you old sot!" Erik paced back and forth about fifteen feet in front of him. The two Blueshirts were chuckling off to the side making fun of Father Ed, while the guy in the black suit was just standing like a statue himself, expressionless behind his dark sunglasses.

Erik stopped pacing for a moment and pointed his nightstick at the three laborers who had stopped their work when Father approached. "You three get back to work," he yelled, "and level that Jew whore excuse for a virgin."

I recognized one of the workers from maintenance. His name was Vasily, a Russian Orthodox from the Ukraine, and a strong devotee of Mary. I had spotted him praying the rosary in the ICC chapel by her small statue in a small alcove of the church. He always lit a candle afterwards.

Vasily stepped forward, taking off his twenties-style newsboy cap, and in a servile posture begged Erik to absolve him of the assignment. His eyes were full of tears, and he was falling apart under the pressure.

"Enough! This is an outrage and a sacrilege," Father shouted in a thundering voice again.

Erik's blue eyes suddenly darkened, and he quickly moved behind Father, as if summoned by a demon. He took his cudgel and forcibly struck the back of Father's legs. Father didn't flinch. Again, Erik assailed him, and Father just turned his head and stared him down, his stone face set as flint.

For the first time, I noted a strange fear in Erik's eyes, and he backed away, ordering his two Blueshirts in between himself and Father Ed.

"Let him have it!" Erik practically screamed.

One of the Blueshirts turned and asked, "Both of us?"

"Did I give you an order, or didn't I?" Erik screaming, his face red as a beet.

The Blueshirts removed their taser guns from their webbed belts and looked at each other, never having had to blast two tasers at once into a person. They pointed their weapons at Father and fired. Four darts hit him, square body mass. A moment later, Father was on the ground as the tonic contractions incapacitated his neuromuscular senses. Several seconds later, Father barely started to come around.

"Again!" Erik screamed, tapping his baton on the shoulder of the Blueshirt on his left. Father's body resumed its spasms.

"Now you," Erik said tapping the shoulder of the Blueshirt on his right. Father's body had no time to recuperate as Erik moved his billy club back and forth like a diabolic metronome between the shoulders of his two men.

Vasily was on his knees, cap in both hands, openly crying and pleading with Erik to stop. His two coworkers were leaning on their sledgehammers nonchalantly observing the fun and games; the black suit was still standing off to the side stationary and emotionless.

Erik was going to kill Father unless I did something. I started to walk swiftly toward the torture scene, but as I passed the suit on my right, I felt something hard slap my back, and I turned quickly. I was looking down the barrel of a .50 caliber Desert Eagle and instinctively backed up a few steps. The thing was a cannon. He must have pulled it from a shoulder holster.

Suddenly, it all came together. The black Giorgio Napoli suit, the Geoffrey Beene poplin button-down white shirt, the K. Alexander solid black necktie with a brushed silver executive tie clip, and the Kenneth Cole Oxford dress shoes in black. The guy was a carbon copy of Agent Smith from the *Matrix* trilogy, right down to the dark shades, and of course, the matte black Desert Eagle. What threw me was his curly red hair and ruddy complexion. Otherwise this suit from FEMA or wherever, had duplicated his hero to a T. He didn't say a word - he let the Desert Eagle do the talking.

My mind was racing. I've got to do something and quickly. I formulated a plan and said a quick prayer for success.

I threw my arms up in the air, and in a frustrated tone, exclaimed just loud enough for "Agent Smith" to hear me, "To hell with all of this." I started to walk past him back toward my original spot. He kept his Desert Eagle, now on my left, trained on me. As I was about to pass him, I pulled my arms down, dropped to one knee, and with blinding speed, grabbed the long barrel of the semi-automatic with my left hand and pointed it away in a safe direction. Simultaneously, I thrust my right ridge hand, with all its centrifugal force, into his groin. I felt and heard the symphysis pubis (the connection of the two halves of the pelvis) crack as the force lifted him off his heels. His Matrix sunshades flew off and his eyes rolled up. He dropped unconscious as I lowered him to the paving stones of the quadrangle and tucked the weapon in my belt.

Since Erik and company were busy attacking Father, they didn't see what I did. Their backs, and those of the maintenance workers, were turned. Vasily was the only one who could see both myself and Father Ed, and he wasn't about to say anything.

I cried out, "This man has collapsed; I think he may have hit his head."

Erik momentarily stopped to look over to see me on the ground supporting Agent Smith. He shrugged his shoulders and resumed the chronometric torture of Father Ed, tapping his Blueshirts rhythmically. Father looked, at that point, like a writhing mass of chaotic protoplasm.

ORCHESTRATED ASSAULT

I jumped up, and hastily took a few steps forward toward Erik and his storm troopers, withdrawing the Desert Eagle at the same time, "You *will* stop. Now!" I projected as loudly and forcefully as I could.

The entire group turned toward me. "Drop 'em!" I demanded pointing the weapon toward the two Blueshirts who complied immediately. Erik faced me straight on, raising his nightstick.

"Go ahead, fool," I commanded. "You are aware that the government uses the new exploding tips for their ammo now; this .50 caliber round will make a beautiful hole right through you. So - drop it!" I took another step toward Erik. He looked straight down the cavernous opening of the Eagle and decided he would rather live. He dropped his wooden baton.

"You with the mustache, call 9-1-1," I directed, as I pointed the heavy weapon at one of the Blueshirts.

"Mu . . . mu . . . me?" asked the mustached Blueshirt, quaking as he fumbled for his cell phone.

"Tell the dispatcher that a man is down and suffering from prolonged electrical shock, and possible hypothermia." I knew Father Ed had been on the cold ground for a while. "Tell them to drive directly to the quadrangle on the ICC campus. Got all that?" I asked, as I shoved the weapon in his direction. "Oh, and let the dispatcher know that Dr. Lucci needs them pronto."

"What about the FEMA agent?" Erik asked, suddenly all concerned about his state of health.

"I'll have EMS deal with him in due time," I said, before turning to the maintenance workers. "You two go home and have a nice turkey dinner with your families," I instructed, as they absentmindedly gawked at each other. "That's *today!*" I added with a forceful bitter sarcasm in my voice. They took off at once.

"Okay, you three, turn around and get on your knees, and put your hands behind your heads," I commanded after the mustached Blueshirt had completed the call to the EMS.

I looked around for Vasily, and he'd already knelt beside Father having taken his heavy work coat and placed it over him. He cradled Father in his arms, still crying.

Within minutes, the EMS truck pulled into the quadrangle. I had never seen such a quick response. Laura, Jackson, and Smiley hopped out, rushed over to Father, and strapped him carefully onto the stretcher, as I explained the situation to Laura.

"Who's covering the ED today?" I asked her.

"Dr. Melone is on duty."

"Good, tell Mike what happened, and when the other unit arrives for 'Mr. Smith' over there, have them tell Dr. Melone that he has pelvic trauma and some ah . . . testicular problems, as well. I'll be there shortly."

"Pelvic trauma and ruptured testicles?" Laura asked, echoing my statement. "What *happened* to him?" she pressed, as she pointed to Agent Smith.

"It's . . . it's complicated. I'll explain later."

"What's with the piece of heavy artillery and those three kneeling over there? Should I call the police?" Laura queried, still confounded with the entire situation.

"It's a university policy matter. It's all under control. Right, Erik?" I inquired, as I raised my voice in his direction.

"Ah . . . yeah, it's all under control." He knew he was going to catch hell from Dietrich for bungling this up.

"As a matter of fact, you boys can go home now, but leave your toys behind."

Erik made an attempt to reach for his security blanket club. "I said to leave the toys - *all* of them!" I stated firmly. He stood and jogged to catch up to his men who were already beating a path to the parking lot.

The second unit arrived shortly, and began to load up Agent Smith, who was by then, repeatedly moaning with a low visceral cadence. I slammed the rear door on Laura's unit, and then went to comfort Vasily, who was overwrought with grief.

"Father is going to be all right, I promise, Mother Mary protected him." He gave me a big Russian bear hug, and was about to turn and leave. Still wiping the tears from his face, he asked in his heavy Russian accent, "Is there anything I can do?"

"Yes, Vasily. Do me a favor and take the tasers and the nightstick, and drop them off at Dean Avery's office on Monday, if you don't mind."

"Sure, I do that for you," he said, and then picked up the articles of torture and slowly walked off.

The quadrangle was finally calm and tranquil. I put the Desert Eagle in my belt and sat down on the small wall at the flagpole, mentally exhausted. I don't know what possessed me, but I gazed down the walkway toward the social sciences building and looked up. There in front of the large palladium windows in his second-floor office was Dietrich; both his hands were pressed flat against the window as he leaned against the glass. He had orchestrated and witnessed the entire onslaught.

I can't even remember standing up. But there I was, and my Italian blood was boiling.

TO BE CONTINUED....

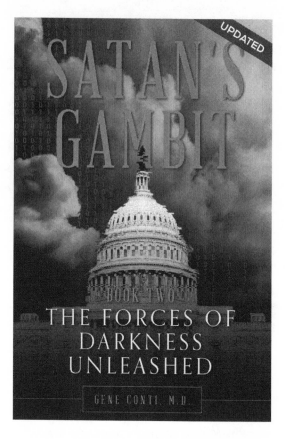

To contact the author, Gene Conti, M.D., for interviews or presentations, use the information below:

www.satansgambit.com

To order more copies of the novel, you may order through the above website or directly from Amazon.com.

Also Available:
Satan's Gambit – Book One: Battle Lines Are Drawn
Satan's Gambit – Book Three: Rise of the Beast